LUCKY CHARM

A SWEET, FAKE RELATIONSHIP ROMANCE

ANNE-MARIE MEYER

To Travis Kelce and Taylor Swift
Thank you for the inspiration

STONE

Senior Year

My face stung as the cool evening air whipped around me. I made a sharp left and sped down Jordan Lane on my way to Cayden's house. The only place in this town that I actually felt safe. I flicked my gaze toward the review mirror and took in the handiwork my dad just left on my face.

He was in a rage tonight. I was used to my dad being drunk, but tonight he was destructive. Half the kitchen dishes lay shattered on the ground when I finally approached him to get him to stop. That was the wrong move. He threw me against the wall, and I collapsed on the ground. Before I could get up, he pinned me down and punched me in the face until I almost blacked out.

I managed to get him off me long enough to grab my

keys and hurry out the back door. He didn't follow after me, and as I pulled out of the driveway, I could make out his shadow as he stalked into the living room. I didn't have to be there to know he was seconds away from passing out face-first on the couch like he did every time he drank.

I shook my head, wincing as my head pounded, and turned my attention to the road. Dad was an asshole, and I was finished with him. Cayden's mom always told me that if I needed it, I could live with them. I used to just smile and nod at her offer, but tonight I was done. I was on my way to the Kings' house to take them up on the offer.

Cayden and I had been friends since middle school. We played ball together. We even started a podcast last year for fun. He was like my brother. He was there for me when my mom died and helped me plan for my future outside of this small town.

All I needed was to get an offer to play ball at college—any college—and I would be on the first flight out of this godforsaken town. I would never look back. Not even if I got drafted to the NFL and the man I had to call "dad" came crawling back. I was done.

The Kings' familiar blue house came into view. I pulled up along the sidewalk and turned off the engine before pulling the key out of the ignition. I grabbed the packed duffle bag I kept in the back of my car for an occasion like this and opened the driver's door.

I pulled the strap further up onto my shoulder as I made my way up their driveway and over to their front door. I knocked a few times and waited. Finally, the door opened and Emerson, Cayden's younger sister, stood there. Her smile slowly faded, and her eyes widened.

She looked so beautiful while I was sure I looked like a monster. Her blonde hair was shoulder-length, and it fell in waves around her face. Her glasses were perched on her nose, hiding her green eyes that I got lost in every time I allowed myself to linger.

Without knowing it, my gaze drifted down her yellow sundress to her legs and then her white slippers. If Cayden didn't have the ridiculous rule that none of his football buddies could date his little sister, I would have already made a move on Emerson.

She was perfect.

"Stone," she whispered as she took a step closer to me, drawing my focus back to why I was here. I turned my face, not wanting her to see what my dad had done. But she caught my chin with her hand and tipped my face so she could get a better look. "What happened?" she asked.

The smell of her perfume and the feel of her fingertips against my skin had my heart pounding. I wanted to step back. I needed to stop allowing myself to have feelings for my best friend's little sister. Cayden was clear that he'd pummel any of his friends if they even looked at her wrong. I needed to stop these thoughts. Right. Now.

"Cayden home?" I asked as I pulled back and glanced behind her so I could see into the house.

Emerson turned to follow my gaze before she glanced

back at me and shook her head. "He left with my parents to go talk to a scout."

Jealousy churned in my gut. Cayden was a football scholarship shoo-in. Two universities were showing interest in him. I was not so lucky. It felt like everything was three times harder for me than it was for anyone else.

"Wanna come in?" Emerson asked. Her voice was soft as she stepped away from the door. She pushed her black glasses up a bit further on her nose, and her gaze was soft as she stared at me. "I can help you clean that up." Her gaze lifted to my eyebrow, and she nodded toward it.

I reached up and gingerly touched my brow. A sharp pain radiated through my head. And even though I knew I should tell her that I was fine, I just nodded. "Okay."

I stepped into the house as Emerson shut the door behind me. I set my duffel bag down on the ground and kicked off my shoes.

"Come with me." Emerson walked past me, leaving me in a cloud of her scent as she motioned for me to follow her up the stairs.

All rational thoughts left my mind as she led me up the stairs, down the hall, and to her room. I paused, standing in the doorway, not sure if I should go in. She was halfway through her room when she turned and looked surprised that I hadn't followed her. Her gaze met mine before she smiled.

"The first-aid stuff is in my bathroom," she said,

motioning to the door on the far wall. "I promise I won't bite."

I flicked my gaze toward the door and then glanced back down the hallway, wondering what Cayden would do if he found me not only in his sister's bedroom, but tucked away in her bathroom.

"They won't be home for a while."

I turned my attention back to Emerson. She must have read my mind. Her smile was soft and understanding. In that moment, I threw caution out the window and walked into her room. My gaze landed on her bed. Her guitar had been hastily perched against it, and papers were strewn all over her comforter. I didn't know a lot about music, but it looked like she'd been writing notes with a pencil.

"How's that going?" I asked, nodding toward her guitar as I walked around her bed and followed her into the bathroom.

She motioned for me to sit on the toilet. I obeyed. "It's going fine," she said as she stepped closer to me. She grasped my chin between her thumb and forefinger before bending down so she could inspect my face.

I tried not to, but I couldn't help but stare at her. With her this close, I could see the different shades of green in her eyes. Her eyelashes were dark and long. She had a splash of freckles across her nose. She chewed her bottom lip, drawing my attention to her mouth. Her cupid's bow was perfectly formed and kissable...

I cleared my throat as I straightened, breaking the

connection between us. Emerson seemed unaffected as she turned to the bathroom cabinet and pulled out a red case with a white plus sign on the top. She flipped open the lid and started rifling around inside.

She grabbed some gauze and turned toward the sink, resting her hand on the faucet while her fingers dangled in the water, and she waited for the water to heat up. She looked over at me and met my gaze before she moved her attention to my face.

"Are you nervous for Friday's game?" she asked as she wiped her hand on a towel and dipped the gauze underneath the warm water.

I shrugged. "Kind of. I mean, I want to get an offer, but I don't think I will." I sighed as I stretched my legs out in front of me. "Some people just have all the luck." I knew I sounded bitter, and my meaning wasn't lost on her. I loved my best friend, but sometimes I wished I had just a little sliver of the luck that he seemed to have in spades.

"I'm sorry," I said as I dropped my gaze to my hand that was resting on my lap. I didn't want to drag Emerson into my disappointing life.

"It's okay. I get it." She turned off the faucet and focused on me. She leaned closer as she grasped my chin once more and tipped my face up. Then she began to dab my eyebrow with the gauze.

I sucked in my breath, causing her gaze to drop to mine, but I just smiled with the hopes that she would keep going.

"I'm sorry," she whispered.

"It's okay. I'll be fine."

She nodded, but I could feel her hesitation as her hand lingered next to my face without actually touching it. I reached up and engulfed her hand with mine before bringing the gauze to my skin.

Her body seemed to be frozen. I knew I should let go of her hand, but I didn't want to. The closer she got to me, the more I wanted...

I wanted everything.

But Cayden and his threats rolled through my mind. If I didn't have the Kings, I would have nothing in this small town. I needed to focus on moving on, or I would end up like my dad. A drunken loser.

Distracting myself with girls wasn't in my plan.

I dropped my hand back down onto my lap, pulled my gaze from hers, and focused on the yellow tile at my feet. That seemed to be what Emerson needed as well, because in no time, she had my skin cleaned up and a butterfly bandage affixed to my brow where my skin had split.

I helped her clean up the bathroom, all the while forcing myself not to think about how close she was to me. I waited in her room as she turned off her bathroom light and shut the door. I was staring at her when she turned to face me. Her gaze lingered with mine. She folded her arms and leaned against her dresser. Her smile was soft, and I wondered if she wanted me to stay as much as I didn't want to leave.

"Thanks," I said, my voice lower than I'd intended.

Crap. My resolve to keep my distance was dissolving. I needed to get out of here before I did something stupid.

Her lips tipped up into a smile. "Of course."

I hesitated and then forced myself to start walking out of the room.

"Stone?"

I paused and glanced back at her. "Yeah?"

Her expression was hard to read. She glanced around her room before her gaze landed on her nightstand.

She crossed the space in a few strides and pulled open the drawer. After rifling around, she emerged with something gold grasped in her hand. She walked over and extended her hand as if she wanted to give it to me.

"What is this?" I asked as I opened my hand.

"This is for luck," she whispered.

Her hand looked tiny against mine as she dropped the cold metal item onto my palm. When she pulled back, I saw that she'd given me a gold four-leaf clover keychain.

"What is this?" I asked as I brought it closer to inspect. There was an inscription in a language that I couldn't read.

"It's the keychain my grandfather bought the day he met my grandmother in Ireland. They were married for sixty years before they passed away in each other's arms. He told me that it would bring luck to anyone who had it." She smiled up at me. "I figured you could use a bit of luck."

My fingers curled around it as I brought my gaze up to hers. "Thanks, Emerson."

She shrugged before folding her arms. "Of course." She

chewed her bottom lip. "You deserve good things, Stone Walker."

I clenched my jaw in an effort to stop myself from saying what I wanted to say. After what felt like an eternity, I met her gaze. "You do, too."

She smiled before nodding. "Thanks."

I wasn't sure how long we stood there, staring at each other, but I realized that if I didn't leave right then, I wasn't sure I was ever going to. I slipped the keychain into my pocket and made my way out of her bedroom. Just as I stepped out into the hallway, I glanced back at her. She hadn't moved. Instead, she stood there, watching me walk away.

One Week Later

"I DON'T KNOW what's wrong with Cayden King tonight but thank goodness for Stone Walker. If he wasn't on the receiving end of those throws, the Panthers would have lost tonight." The announcer wasn't shy in his assessment as his voice boomed through the stadium.

I glanced over at Cayden as I squeezed the water bottle, spraying a stream of water through my face mask and into my mouth. Cayden's shoulders were tight as he stood there, listening to coach shout at him. Something was up with him tonight. This wasn't the same quarterback that had carried our team to the semi-finals.

I handed the water bottle back to the water girl and made my way toward Cayden, lingering as I waited for coach to finish yelling. Cayden nodded, and Coach turned and focused on another player, so I took that break to walk up to Cayden.

"Hey, man," I said as I laid my hand on his shoulder. "Everything okay?"

"I'm fine," Cayden said as he shrugged off my hand and walked away.

I watched him retreat, wondering if I should follow him, but then I shook my head. Cayden needed to get his head in the game, and me talking to him wasn't going to help. He'd turn it around. He always did.

Cayden only got worse as the game progressed. I nearly threw out my shoulder trying to leap to the side to catch his throw. My body was sore by the time the final horn sounded and a cheer erupted in the stands. The Panthers won 21 to 14. Coach clapped me on the back as I made my way to the sidelines. Through my helmet, I heard his words of praise, and the team surrounded me to lift me up on their shoulders.

I could see Cayden standing in the distance. His helmet covered his face, but his body language told me that he was pissed. I just hoped he wasn't pissed at me.

After Coach talked to the team, we ran off the field and into the locker room. The chatter was loud as we changed out of our football gear and into street clothes. There was a party tonight, and invites were being thrown around. I nodded when Spencer asked me if I was going. He then turned his attention to Cayden, who hadn't said a word as he changed.

When Cayden didn't answer, I shot Spencer an apologetic smile. Spencer just shrugged and wandered off to talk to someone else. The silence between Cayden and I was deafening even though the noise around me made my ears ring.

"Everything, okay?" I asked as I sat down to pull on my tennis shoes.

"I don't want to talk about it," Cayden said as he straightened and slammed his locker shut.

"Dude, we all have off nights. It's not that big of a deal."

His gaze whipped to mine. There was a fire in his eyes that I'd never seen. "This was the game I was supposed to dominate. All the scouts were here tonight." He mumbled under his breath, "Not a big deal..."

"They can't judge your ability from one off night."

He scoffed as he shoved his feet into his shoes. "Yeah, right."

"Stone!" Coach's voice cut through the noise. I turned to see him standing in the doorway of his office next to a man in a Polo shirt. I'd seen this man before. He was the scout from the University of Texas.

I glanced at Cayden, whose jaw clenched when he glanced in Coach's direction.

"Cayden..." I started, but I didn't know what to say.

He grabbed his backpack and slipped his arm through one strap. "Go, Stone. I'm not surprised he wants to talk to you. You played amazing tonight." He turned and walked away from me.

I thought about calling after him, but there was no point. He was mad, and there was nothing I could do to change that. I raised my hand to Coach to let him know I heard and quickly finished tying my shoes. Then I stood and hurried over to join him and the scout from Texas—Cayden's number-one school pick.

I left the locker room that night with an offer to play for Texas. It came with a full-ride scholarship and a living stipend.

I drove to the Kings' in a daze. Never had I thought I would get noticed, much less scouted. I pressed my foot down on the gas, my excitement getting the best of me as I drove. I couldn't wait to share this news with the only people on the planet who seemed to care about me.

I pulled into the spot that Mr. King had told me I could park in and climbed out of the car. I stuffed my keys into my front pocket as I crossed the yard and jogged up the front steps. I moved to open the door just as Mrs. King pulled it open. I startled and stepped back, confused as to why she was greeting me at the door.

"Stone, come on in," she said, her voice monotone.

"Um, thanks," I said. I studied her as I stepped into the foyer and kicked off my shoes.

Mrs. King closed the front door and then turned to face me. "We should talk in the kitchen."

My stomach was doing flips. All I could do was nod as I followed her. Mr. King was leaning against the countertop with his arms crossed and a stern look on his face.

This wasn't good.

"Hey, Mr. King," I said, my voice coming out hesitant and unsure.

"Stone," he said. He nodded to me and watched as I sat down on the barstool Mrs. King motioned for me to sit on.

"Everything okay?" I asked.

He looked at Mrs. King before turning his attention to me. "Well, Stone. You should probably know that none of the scouts have any interest in Cayden."

My face fell. I frowned. "What?"

"All of the scouts. They're done with Cayden."

"Oh my gosh."

Mr. King picked up the coffee mug next to him and took a sip. "Trent from Texas told me that he gave Cayden's spot to...you." The way his voice lingered on the last word and the way he was staring at me made my skin crawl.

There was an expectation in his voice that I didn't like. "So..." I didn't want to accuse Mr. King of asking me to give up my spot for his son. I worked my ass off tonight. I deserved this chance.

"You know how hard Cayden has worked to play for Texas. That's his dream team. One night shouldn't define his future."

"Mr. King, are you asking me to turn down the offer?" I was done dancing around this topic. He needed to fess up to what he was asking.

His eyes widened before he shrugged. "I just think you should remember what this family has done for you. Where your loyalties lie. If you are a true friend to Cayden, you would do what is right."

My blood began to boil. He wanted me to walk away from my future because Cayden was more deserving of the offer. His words felt like a sucker punch to the stomach. I expected my dad to beat me because that was who he was. I never expected Mr. King to do the same.

"I worked hard for that spot, Mr. King. If Texas saw something in me that they didn't see in Cayden, that's on them." I pushed my hand through my hair as my anger boiled hotter and hotter. "I'm not giving up my future. If Texas wants me to play for them, then that's where I'm going."

Mr. King's face had turned a deep red. He looked as if he were about to explode. No longer wanting to stand here and listen to his words, I headed down the hall to their guest room.

"Get out!" Mr. King's voice reverberated off the walls.

I stuffed my clothes into my duffle bag and then shoved the strap up onto my shoulder, not caring that I couldn't zip the bag closed. "Way ahead of you," I mumbled as I walked past him to the front door. I grabbed my shoes on the way out.

I didn't stop until I was in my car. I slammed the car into reverse and spun my wheels in the gravel as I backed up. I drove until I could no longer see our small town. Then I pulled over and punched the steering wheel as Mr. King's words kept playing through my mind.

I rested my forehead on the steering wheel and closed my eyes. Adults sucked. People sucked. Family sucked. Everyone eventually left me.

I leaned back in my seat and closed my eyes before I sighed and put my car into drive and made a U-turn. I had my ticket out of this town, I just needed to focus on keeping it.

Fifteen minutes later, I pulled into my dad's driveway and turned off my car. I grabbed my bag and got out. Dad wasn't home when I scouted out the house, which I took as a blessing. I showered and climbed into bed.

One thing was for certain, I'd rather be here with my dad's fists than at the King's house with their passive-aggressive manipulation. I flipped to my side and grabbed my phone off my nightstand. The screen lit up as I swiped it on. I found Emerson's name in my contacts, and my thumbs hovered over the keyboard as I contemplated what I would say to her.

And then I shook my head. I wasn't going to say anything to her. The truth was, I was messed up in more ways than one. It would be best if I just disappeared from her life like the Kings wanted me to.

I turned my phone off and set it back down on the night-stand. I needed to forget about them—about her.

It was the only way I was going to be able to walk away come graduation. It was the only way I was going to be able to move on.

1

EMERSON

"Tell me I'm a genius," my best friend, Tilly, sang out as soon as I answered her call and sandwiched my phone between my shoulder and my ear.

I was currently sitting on my bed with my guitar in my lap, eating licorice and avoiding the massive pile of half-full boxes that littered my room. To say that I was avoiding this move would be an understatement. I hated that my landlord had rented my apartment out from under me. And even though I knew I was going to have to leave, I was currently the president of the island called Denial.

If only Tilly would join me, we could rule it together.

I slipped my guitar pick between my lips before I leaned over my guitar to draw a B-flat on my sheet music. I mumbled out an incoherent, "Why are you a genius?"

"What?"

I straightened and took the pick out of my mouth before

strumming the chords I'd just jotted down. "Why are you a genius?"

"Why aren't you packing?"

I winced. "I'm packing."

"Then why did I hear your guitar?"

"I'm taking a break, and then I'm going right back to packing." I sighed. She couldn't expect me to work the entire time she was gone.

"Emerson Marie King. You need to pack. You promised me that you would pack." Her tone became more and more staccato with each word. "You have to be out of that place by Sunday."

The panic in her voice was making my heart pound.

"And I am doing that," I said, instantly feeling guilty for lying to my best friend. "As soon as I get down this verse, I'll get back to packing."

"I don't believe you."

Changing the subject felt like the right move. "Why are you a genius?"

"Oh, right," she said, her voice changing to a giggle. "Hang on. I just pulled up to your building. I'll be up in a second."

She hung up before I could respond. Not wanting to get a second lecture from her when she arrived, I unfolded my legs out from under me, slipped my guitar back into its case, and closed the lid. I leaned it against the wall before gathering the sheet music that littered my bed and stuffed it into my backpack. Then I turned to focus on taping the bottom of a box.

Three sharp knocks sounded from my front door. I set the tape dispenser down and headed out to the hallway that led to the front door. After I unlocked the dead bolt, I pulled open the door. Tilly smiled when she saw me. She lifted her hand up so I could take the drink holder she had in one hand. She'd pulled her blue hair up into a high ponytail, and she was currently blowing the wisps of hair that framed her face away from her cheeks.

"Thank you," I said as I brought the drink holder up and inhaled the steam coming from the small opening of one of the coffee cups. The nutty scent mixed with vanilla filled my nose, and a smile emerged on my lips. "I needed this," I said as I pushed my glasses up.

"We need to get to work," she said as she pushed past me.

I kicked the door shut and turned to follow after her. "Yes, ma'am," I mumbled.

She shot me a look from over her shoulder but didn't respond. She let out a giant sigh when she stopped in my bedroom's doorway and stared inside. Her hands were planted firmly on her hips, and I could just feel her disappointment seeping from her stance.

"It's not that bad," I offered, hoping it would distract from how much we needed to get done.

"It's bad, Emerson."

I grabbed my cup of coffee and took a sip, ignoring the

fact that I practically burned my mouth in the process. Tilly turned to face me before reaching over to remove her drink from the tray and take a sip as well.

We stared at each other from over our cups before we lowered them in unison.

"We need to get moving—"

"You said you were a genius—"

We both started and stopped talking at the same time. Tilly pursed her lips as she narrowed her eyes. I could tell that she was weighing her desire to scold me for not packing against her desire to tell me whatever grandiose plan she had for fixing my life.

I loved my best friend. She agreed to be my manager when no one wanted to take me on. She believed in me and my music more than I did at times. If I ever made it in this industry, it was going to be because of the sheer grit of my best friend. I was broken, and she wasn't going to rest until she fixed me.

The smile that emerged told me that she was going with the news that made her a self-proclaimed genius. She grabbed my hand, pulled me into my room, and motioned for me to sit on my bed before she started pacing in front of me.

"So, you know Cadence?" she asked before taking a sip of her coffee.

"Cadence. As in your older sister Cadence?"

She stopped to stare at me before she returned to pacing. "The only Cadence I know."

"Yes, I know her," I replied as I leaned back on one arm and proceeded to take small sips of my coffee. "What about her?"

"Her boyfriend's sister, Poppy, is looking for someone to sublet her apartment while she's on a six-month work trip in Europe to take pictures of..." She paused and tipped her head to the side as she stared off into the distance. Then she shook her head. "Birds, maybe? I don't really remember."

Her words had me sitting a little straighter on the bed. Six months would be amazing for me. Six months might be exactly what I needed to get my life back on track. "How much?" I asked, wincing as I thought back to the meager amount currently sitting in my bank account. The life of an aspiring musician who worked as a barista at a coffee shop didn't come with big bucks.

Tilly sucked air through her teeth which told me I wasn't going to like what she was about to say. "It's a little more than what you were paying here." She smiled a little too enthusiastically.

"A little more." I narrowed my eyes. "*How* much more?"

She pursed her lips before whispering, "Five hundred."

My jaw dropped. "Tilly! Five hundred? As in, dollars?" I flopped onto my bed and stared up at the ceiling. Fate was mean, always dangling what I wanted in front of me before ripping it away.

The mattress shifted as I felt Tilly sit on the bed and then flop down next to me. Her arm rested against mine, and from the corner of my eye, I could see that she was staring at the ceiling as well.

"I told her you were going to take it."

Her words lingered in the air around me. I frowned as I tipped my head to the side so I could look at her. Did I hear her wrong? Did she say she already agreed to have me sublet the apartment?

I sat up. "What? Why did you do that?"

I felt Tilly's gaze land on me as she moved to sit as well. "You have to stop living like you aren't going to make it." Her gaze intensified. "I know you're going to go all the way to the top. You need to start living like you are the star I know you are."

I appreciated her confidence, but there was no way I could afford another five hundred dollars to my rent. "I can't afford that, Tilly," I said, my voice cracking from emotions. I wanted to be the big star she seemed to think I was, but I felt like I was trying to walk up a muddy mountain in the rain. I just kept slipping down no matter what I did.

"I know." Her smile turned mischievous. "I have a plan."

I frowned. I didn't like the way her smile looked or the tone in her voice. "You do?" I asked.

She nodded. "Yep." She climbed off the bed. "Let's go look at the apartment."

"And feel tortured by what I can't have?" I reached forward and grabbed my pillow. I hugged it to my chest and rested my chin on its fluff.

"Maybe seeing what you *can* have will help your mind-set. If you believe you can only afford to live in a subpar apartment where you landlord is a dick and rents your apartment out from under you, that's what you'll get."

I raised my eyebrows. Tilly was all, "Visualize what you want, and you'll get it." I loved my best friend, but sometimes, you just needed to stop fighting reality. I wanted to believe that I could be a star, but I was getting to the point where I just needed to accept how far I was going to be able to go. And that was this crummy apartment in the outskirts of Nashville. Always on the outside looking in.

But she looked so hopeful, so I forced a smile. "Okay. I guess we can go check it out," I said.

Tilly squealed as she moved to get off the bed. "Let's go! We can grab some lunch while we're downtown."

I groaned, but she just stuck her finger up in the air in front of my lips to silence me. "I'll pay. After all, I need you indebted to me so when you're the big shot singer you'll feel too guilty to ignore your lowly commoner friend."

I pulled her into a hug. "I would never forget you," I said.

She laughed and pulled back. "You better not." She searched my room before she found my cowboy boots and tossed them to me. "Get your boots on. Thankfully, you already look adorable," she said as she waggled her finger in my direction.

I was wearing a pair of cutoff shorts and a Van Halen t-shirt that I'd distressed with bleach. I'd cut the neckline so it would slip off my shoulder and expose the lacey bralette I had on underneath. I'd pulled my long, blonde hair up into a messy bun this morning, and I contemplated convincing Tilly to let me freshen up, but then pushed that thought from my mind.

Relationships and men were the last thing I needed. Especially after my latest breakup. The relationship only lasted a few months before I put a stop to it. I could never seem to get past the first few months. Maybe it was because I always compared every new relationship to my grandparents'. Their romance was one for the books.

My grandfather met my grandmother when she owned a trinket store in Ireland. He was on a self-exploration trip and went into the store on a whim. He bought a four-leaf clover key chain with the words *a chuisle, a chroí* etched into it from my grandmother.

Later that night, he found her at the local pub and asked her to dance. They spent the evening drinking and eating, and in the morning, he flew home convinced he would never see her again.

Two years later, he found that key chain in a box and put it on his key ring. When he got to work later that day, she walked into his law firm in Brooklyn. He swore that day he would never let her go again. He married her two months later, claiming the key chain he'd bought that day was his lucky charm.

Any relationship seemed ridiculous when compared with theirs. It's probably why Cayden and I were still single in our twenties.

"Let's go," I sang out as I slipped my purse strap up onto my shoulder. The bottom tassels that hung from the bag tickled my leg, but I ignored the sensation as I grabbed my key and waited for Tilly to join me in the hallway before I locked up.

My eyes widened as Tilly drove me from my run-down apartment to downtown Nashville. I could feel the wealth the further we went, and my purse began to feel like a weight on my lap. There was no way I could afford to live here.

Sure, it would be great for my singing. There were so many bars and stages for me to try to get on to, but this was so far out of my tax bracket that I wanted to cry.

Tilly's hand appeared in front of me as she patted my thigh. "Let's just see it," she said as if she could read my mind.

"I don't think they will even let me into the building," I whispered.

She pulled up to the parking garage for the Elysian Heights Apartments. It was a white brick building that looked older but refurbished. The car engine idled as Tilly rolled her window down and punched in a code she'd pulled up on her phone. The garage door opened with a creak and a groan.

That was a good sign. Even though this place was in downtown Nashville, maybe there was a chance that I could belong here. From what I could make out of the building, there were stairs that went up to each apartment. There was no doorman or lobby. It seemed simple enough, so the location had to be what was driving up the rent.

Tilly pulled into the parking space with a white 25 sprayed on the concrete. I glanced over at her, and she gave me a hopeful smile before she pulled on the car door release. I did the same and then walked around the hood to join her as we made our way to the elevator at the end of the parking garage.

"So, when does she need someone to take the apartment over?" I asked as the elevator car took us up to the fourth floor.

"Today," Tilly said as she shot me a smile. "Which is why this place is perfect!"

"A thousand dollars a month sublet is far from perfect," I muttered.

Tilly slipped her arm through mine and pulled me to her side. "We'll figure something out, but you can't beat this location. You'll be so close to so many mics that someone is bound to discover you. You just have to believe."

I smiled at her. "Sure, Tilly. We'll go with that."

I used to believe that anything was possible, but when my life started to crumble around me, it had been hard to be optimistic. During my junior year, Cayden lost all of his scholarship opportunities and spiraled. Dad and Mom divorced. The day I graduated high school, Cayden got arrested, so he missed seeing me walk. My parents got in a fight and they both ended up leaving before the ceremony was over. I was stuck on the sidewalk in my cap and gown, waiting for someone to come back to get me.

I spent three years at college, only to have my dad go bankrupt, and I lost all financial aid. I never graduated. Instead, I decided to focus on my music, which brought me here...evicted from my apartment and with no place to live.

So, while Tilly wanted me to believe, I was going to be realistic. Some things weren't meant to happen.

The elevator chimed, and the doors slid open. We stepped out onto the landing and looked around. The stairs were directly in front of us. One set went up and another went down. There was a door to our left and one to our right. I waited for Tilly to move first since she had the key and the address.

"It looks like it's..." She scrolled on her phone. "This one," she declared, pointing toward the apartment door that had 4B affixed under the peephole.

I waited as she slipped the key into the lock and followed her into the apartment, shutting the door behind me. One look around and I knew this had been a mistake. I loved everything about this place. It was older, but the ceilings were high, and the doorways were arched. The long wall in the living room was a continuation of the exterior brick that had been white washed. Every room had a window. Even the kitchen had a window above the sink. Sure, it looked out to the landing, but the natural light had my soul singing.

"She said she's leaving the furniture."

"That's perfect," I breathed out as I glanced around. Whoever this woman was, she and I had the same taste in just about everything. Her color palette was neutral with pops of green, purple, and blue. This place felt like home.

"So..." Tilly's voice sounded next to me.

I startled and glanced over to see her standing inches away from me with a grin spread across her lips.

"This isn't fair," I said as I sat down on the couch and nearly disappeared in the pillowy cushions. I groaned as I sat back. "I'm dreaming...this is a dream, right?" I asked as I lifted my arm and pinched it a few times.

Tilly sat down next to me. "All you have to do is say yes," she said, using her shoulder to bump me.

I glared at her. "That's all? And what, a genie will suddenly appear and grant me all my wishes?"

Tilly shrugged. "Something like that."

I hated that she was being so cryptic. I wished she'd just tell me the truth. "What aren't you telling me?" I folded my arms and gave her a stare that told her I wasn't interested in half truths. I needed to know what she was talking about before I agreed to any of this.

She pinched her lips together. "Let's just say that you have a fan who's willing to help you reach your dreams."

I frowned. "A fan?" Recognition dawned on me. "Not the guy that sent me his hair." My gag reflex activated, and I had to swallow a few times just to settle my stomach.

"Creeper? No." Tilly swatted my shoulder. "I wouldn't take anything from him."

I studied her. I couldn't think of anyone who liked me enough to want to help my career take off. "Who is it?" I asked, leaning forward and staring her down.

She brought her phone close to her chest and shook her head. "I can't tell you."

"Tilly!" I lunged for her phone. But she must have anticipated that I would try to get it from her because suddenly, she was on the other side of the room, tucking her phone into her bra.

"Emerson," she said, raising her hands as I stalked toward her. "Emerson!" Her voice got louder as I approached. "I really don't know," she wailed when I was inches from her.

I stopped to stare at her. "You don't know?"

She shook her head. "I don't. But I promise you that this is legit. They just said they don't want their identity to be known."

"Then how do you know this is legit?" I folded my arms.

She sighed, blowing the hair that had fallen out of her ponytail away from her face. Then she took a step back and narrowed her eyes. "I'll show you if you promise not to yank my phone from my hand."

I narrowed my eyes but then nodded. "I swear."

She sized me up for a moment before she slipped her hand into her bra and removed her phone. She swiped at the screen and typed something in. Then she turned the phone around. "They already deposited the money into your account. The six-month sublease has been paid."

At first, I didn't know what I was looking at. I wasn't used to seeing that many digits in my business account before. My jaw dropped as I leaned forward. "They what?" I glanced at her over her phone.

"I told them that you needed some help, and they offered to pay your rent."

My mind was reeling from Tilly's words. Who would have done this? My parents? No. They were constantly hitting me up for money. Cayden? Naw. Last time I saw him he was sharing an apartment with three other guys. I was so confused; I didn't know what to say.

"So?" Tilly's question broke through my thoughts.

"So..." I blinked as I glanced around the living room. This seemed like a once-in-a-lifetime opportunity. I'd be stupid to turn this down. Even though I wasn't sure what this person's angle was, I couldn't turn down their help. If I did, I would have to move back to my hometown, and there was no way I would get discovered there.

I sucked in my breath, prayed that I wasn't going to regret this, and nodded. "Yes."

Tilly's eyebrows rose. "Yes?"

Excitement brewed in my stomach. "Yes."

Suddenly, Tilly closed the space between us. She wrapped her arms around me, and I let my enthusiasm take over as we both started jumping in a circle.

"You live here!" she exclaimed.

"I live here!"

Just then, I realized that we were on the fourth floor and

someone most likely lived beneath us, so I stopped jumping and stepped away from Tilly.

"I'm going to call Poppy to tell her."

"Awesome," I said as I moved to look at the trinkets on the shelf by the TV.

I half-listened to Tilly as I began to daydream about where I was going to create a music corner. The sound of snapping fingers drew my attention over, and I turned to see Tilly standing by the door, waving her hand to get my attention.

"Your neighbor," she mouthed as she pointed at the peephole.

I nodded and moved to join her. Butterflies erupted in my stomach as I squinted and peeked through the hole. I hoped they were nice and that we would get along.

It was a guy. He had brown hair and was built like a tower. He was wearing a leather jacket. A motorcycle helmet was tucked under his arm while a few white grocery bags hung from his hand. I ran my gaze over his back as he turned the key and pushed open his door. Disappointment flooded through me as I watched him walk into his apartment. I wasn't going to see who I was living across from.

But just as he moved to kick his door closed behind him, he stopped and slowly turned. He brought his gaze up to my door, and I got a good look at who was standing there.

My entire body froze as I stared at his familiar blue eyes and brown tousled hair. I gasped and turned away from the peephole, like he could see me. I clutched my pounding heart as Tilly stepped up to me with a frown on her face.

"Who is it?" she whispered as she moved around me so she could look through the peephole.

I took in a few deep breaths before I said, "Stone Walker."

2

STONE

I sucked in my breath as I positioned my shoulders under the bar. The metal dug into my skin as I straightened my legs and lifted the weights off the hooks. I mentally counted as I squatted in rhythmic fashion until I completed the set and racked the bar.

My muscles throbbed as I left the power cage to grab my water bottle and a towel to wipe the sweat from my face.

"Nice," Theo, the team's trainer, said as he clapped me on the back. I was trying to max out today, so he made it a point to hang close to me.

"Yeah," I said as I tipped my water bottle and squeezed water into my mouth.

"Facing those demons?" he asked, fiddling with the clipboard he was holding.

I clenched my jaw as memories involuntarily flooded my mind. But as quickly as they came, I pushed them away. Not wanting him to know that his question got to me, I shrugged and set my water bottle down. "Something like that."

"Well, you're a beast. If you keep this up, I think another Super Bowl is in the bag," Theo announced, and the entire gym erupted in cheers.

"That was never a question. We will kick ass," I said as George and Jayden came up to me and offered me their fists. The Tennessee Tigers were coming off a Super Bowl win, and I couldn't wait to see what we did this year.

"Check it out," Jayden said as he waved toward the TV, which showed Priscilla George interviewing me.

The guys whooped and hollered before they glanced over at me and wiggled their eyebrows.

"Man, Priscilla is looking fine," Jayden said as he gripped my shoulder before sucking his breath in between his teeth. "Please tell me you've finally locked that down."

My body tensed at his words. I stepped to the side, not wanting to address what he was asking. Sure, it was no secret that Priscilla was interested in me. The way she smiled at me. The way she leaned in close when she was interviewing me. And the way she texted me late at night asking to come over. I wasn't an idiot; I knew what she wanted. But I wasn't interested in Priscilla.

At least, not in the way she was interested in me.

"I'm turning up the volume," George said as he approached the TV.

The gym grew quiet as Priscilla's voice filled the air.

"Everyone wants to know the plan for the Tigers this

year," she asked. Her perfect white teeth glinted in the sunshine.

"We're going to dominate," I said, glancing at the camera and smiling. Hayden, my assistant, had dressed me in a black suit with a grey button-down shirt and white tie that day, and I looked good. I would be lost without her.

The gym erupted into cheers. A smile crept over my lips as I nodded, feeling the energy that came from being around my team.

"So many people credit your success to luck. You just happened to be at the right place at the right time. What do you have to say to those people?" Priscilla tipped the microphone back to me.

My face fell just like it did on screen. I swallowed against the lump that had formed in my throat. Thankfully, I managed to pull it together in the interview and say something poetic about how luck is a mixture of tenacity and grit before changing the subject.

But standing here in the gym, my entire body felt numb as my thoughts slipped back to high school, standing in the Kings' house while Mr. King glared down at me. Something happened that night. A shift in fate. And suddenly, I was the one with all the lucky breaks.

I went to the University of Texas. I played my heart out and got drafted after college to the Tennessee Tigers, the best team in the league. Two years in and the team won the Super Bowl, and I got the coveted title of MVP.

Sure, I lost my best friend the night I got the scholarship.

After I moved back with Dad, I avoided Cayden. I didn't want to tell him that his dad was a dick and let him know what his dad had asked me to do. I told myself I didn't want Cayden to have to pick between me and his father, when what I really feared was to hear the same words from my best friend.

Cayden didn't seem to have an issue with casting me aside. We stopped talking and hanging out, and we even retired the podcast we'd started. It was like we went from best friends to strangers overnight.

Emerson tried to talk to me once or twice, but I just walked away from her. She didn't deserve to get caught up in the mess that was my life, and the best thing I could do for her was encourage her to move on. I focused on my grades and football and that was it. I was going to go to Texas if it was the last thing I did.

Anger boiled in my gut, so I turned my back on the TV and focused on lifting weights until my arms felt like they were going to fall off. I worked hard to keep my past locked in a box in the back of my mind. That's where I kept the memories of people who I'd thought had my back only to find out how easy it was for them to walk away from me.

The only person that mattered in my life was my grand-mother, who was currently on a cruise around the world. She came back into my life after graduation and stayed. She never asked me to do anything for her. She loved me uncon-ditionally. Other people were a distraction that I didn't need.

Especially the guy who'd sworn he was my best friend, but when I got what he wanted, he'd dropped me like we didn't have years of friendship behind us.

"He still gets under your skin, huh?" George asked as I returned the dumbbells to their rack and pushed my hand through my hair.

"Who?"

He shot me a look that said, *you know who.* "Cayden."

I inwardly groaned. I'd gotten drunk one night and told George everything about my past. I hated that I'd been weak that night and that now he knew my deepest, darkest secrets. I shrugged and picked up my water bottle and towel. "I really don't think about him. He used to be my friend and that's it." I clapped George on the back. "You just focus on throwing the ball to me, and I'll focus on getting it to the end zone."

I could tell that George wanted to say more, but I really wasn't in the mood. I shot him a quick smile before I nodded toward the locker room. "I'm gonna shower," I called over my shoulder as I walked toward the door.

I made my way to my locker. I set my water bottle on the top shelf and grabbed my shampoo and soap before heading to a shower. I let the hot water beat across my back as my thoughts returned to Cayden.

It had hurt more than I cared to admit when my best friend—basically my brother—decided to turn his back on me. I didn't know what his dad told him, but I heard through friends that he thought I'd cheated him out of the Texas scholarship. Even though we'd spent so many years together, one look of pure betrayal from him and I'd known our friendship was over.

And with the dissolution of our friendship, my relationship with Emerson was gone in a puff as well. She'd looked confused when I walked away from her when she'd tried to talk to me. That girl haunted my thoughts in more ways than one, but when Mr. King told me to leave and never come back, I complied.

I walked away from the King family. I walked away from the family that had been my sanctuary from my drunk dad and his angry fists. It hurt more than when my parents walked away from me. I'd expected my mom and dad to leave. I'd never expected the Kings to do the same.

I pounded my fist on the tile next to me as I cursed under my breath. I grabbed my shampoo and aggressively washed my hair. I spent too much energy keeping my mind on the game, and at the mere mention of Cayden, I spiraled.

Why wasn't I stronger?

By the time I was coming out of the shower with a towel wrapped around my waist, the other guys had filtered into the locker room. They were all in a different state of undress. I kept my focus on my locker as I dressed. Just as I was pulling my black t-shirt over my head, my phone buzzed.

"Who's that?" Ezekiel asked. His locker was next to mine.

I grabbed my phone. Poppy's name flashed on the screen

along with the text message icon. I groaned as I set the phone down. "My neighbor."

"Ooo!" Ezekiel said as he punched me in the shoulder. Isaac, a lineman, inquired what had happened, and Ezekiel was more than happy to tell him that I was sleeping with my neighbor.

I shot him an annoyed look. "It's not that. She's interested, but I'm not." Ezekiel pursed his lips and lowered his eyelids. A look that told me, *sure*. I shook my head as I turned my attention over to Isaac. "She wants more, but I'm not interested."

Isaac didn't look like he believed me either, and I realized that this was an effort in futility, so I grabbed my phone and swiped it on. As soon as I located her text message, I started reading out loud. "Hey, Stone. Just wanted to let you know that I'm subletting my apartment. I have a chance to go to Europe to photograph the migration of birds, so I won't be around. Hope you keep an eye on my apartment and that we can connect when I get back." I sent a quick thumbs-up emoji before I closed the text and glanced up at Ezekiel and Isaac. "See."

"Ooo, she wants to *connect* when she gets back," Ezekiel said before he started simulating humping. I tossed my sweaty shirt at him, which landed squarely on his head. He yelped and tossed it to the side. "Come on, man. You're the only one of us not in a relationship. When are you going to find someone?" Ezekiel sighed. "I'm tired of my girl always talking about how you should date one of her friends."

"He's just tired of hearing his girl call your name at night," George said as he walked up to us and dropped his arm around Ezekiel's shoulders.

Ezekiel tossed George's arm off his shoulder and turned to land both palms squarely on George's chest and shoved him. "Say that again," Ezekiel said as he followed after George, who had to stumble back to catch his balance.

George simulated punching Ezekiel, but instead of landing a blow, he wrapped his arm around Ezekiel's neck and pulled him over, so he was bent at the waist. We all stepped back so they could finish their tussle. It ended with both of them laughing and high fiving before turning their attention back to me.

"I'm good, guys," I said as I slipped on my leather jacket and grabbed my wallet from the small tray on the top shelf and stuffed it into my back pocket. "Girls are a complication that I don't need in my life." I grabbed my motorcycle helmet from the bench in front of my locker and tucked it under my arm. "I'll leave the heartbreak to you guys."

I shot them a grin and then made my way through the locker room. When I got out to the parking lot, the sticky summer evening air hit me like a wall of water. I could feel my skin prick under my leather jacket, but I swore to Gran that I would wear it no matter the weather. She hated that I rode a motorcycle, and agreeing to wear the jacket was the only way I could calm her nerves, so I did it.

Once the wind hit me as I sped down the road, wearing

a leather jacket wasn't too bad. Plus, the sun was beginning to set.

I made a quick stop at the grocery store and picked up some protein bars and milk. Then I rode home and parked my motorcycle in the garage before heading toward the elevator with my plastic grocery bags in hand.

The doors opened on the fourth floor, and I stepped out. My keys dangled from my fingers as I unlocked the door and walked in. Just as I moved to shut the door, my thoughts returned to Poppy's text. I glanced at her door as I shut mine, wondering when she was leaving and if the person subletting her apartment had already moved in.

I liked my anonymity, and I didn't want someone to let the public know that I was living here. I'd agreed to stay in Gran's apartment until she got back, so she didn't lose her lease. I didn't want to have to leave because reporters or football fans wouldn't stop showing up.

Maybe I should just offer to sublet it from her. It might be nice having this space all to myself. I shut the door and turned to bring the groceries to the kitchen. Once the milk was put away and the protein bars were stuffed in the cupboard, I headed over to the couch and plopped down.

I slipped my phone from my pocket and checked my email. A smile spread across my lips as I saw the unread email from Gran. She sent me one every day. I clicked on it. It opened up, and I read all about her day yesterday. What she ate, the games she played, the puzzle that she and her best friend, Rose, were putting together. She was tired of being at sea and couldn't wait to get to the next port.

I was happy that she was happy. I wanted the best things for her.

Just as I closed the email and set my phone down, I got another notification. I picked my phone back up to see that Poppy had texted me again. I rolled my eyes and contemplated not reading it but then felt bad.

Poppy wasn't terrible. She was a good neighbor. We watched each other's apartments just like she'd done with my grandmother. She even gave me access to her doorbell camera to keep an eye on things when she would leave for long photography excursions. I just got the impression that she wanted something more than I was willing to give her.

Or any woman.

I swiped my screen on and read her message.

Poppy: I found someone to sublet! She's a sweet girl, and I hope the two of you will get along. Just keep an eye on her so that she doesn't burn my place down. Thanks, Stone.

I nodded as I typed back.

Me: Will do. Have fun in Europe.

She texted me a heart-eyed emoji. I set my phone back down and glanced around the room. My gran's cat, Oscar, was curled up on the edge of the loveseat next to the window that overlooked the street. The sun was low enough to cast its rays through the drapes and spill across Oscar's orange fur.

I leaned back on the couch, letting my legs relax in front

of me. My eyes began to close when my phone chimed once more. I sighed, sat up, and grabbed my phone, anticipating another text from Poppy. But it wasn't. It was Hayden, my assistant.

Hayden: Anything you need tonight, Boss?

Me: I'm good. Have a great night.

I tipped my head against the back of the couch once more as I closed my eyes. No need to have her come here when I didn't need her.

I wasn't sure if any of the guys were going out tonight, and I contemplated texting them but decided against it. They always drew attention when we went out. If I went out by myself, I could slip into a bar and avoid being recognized. Right now, a cold beer and some stale peanuts sounded divine.

I glanced at my watch. After I took a quick nap, I'd head out. It'd be dark by then, and that was when Nashville came alive.

3

EMERSON

"This is not good. Not good," I repeated over and over as I paced the length of the living room.

Tilly was following me, desperate to figure out what I was talking about. She kept asking who Stone was, but I couldn't gather my thoughts long enough to explain the history between Stone and my family. She was left in the dark, trying to piece together a puzzle with a lot of missing pieces.

Finally, I stopped pacing, and Tilly almost ran straight into me. Her hands wrapped around my upper arms to keep herself upright. She took this moment to stare into my eyes. "Emerson. *Who* is Stone?" she asked.

I blinked a few times, realizing that this was real life—I wasn't in a nightmare. Reality came crashing down around me as I whispered, "I can't stay here if my neighbor is Stone Walker."

"That doesn't explain anything," Tilly said. I could hear her frustration as she pulled out her phone and typed Stone's name into her search bar. "Stone Walker is the Tennessee Tiger's Super-Bowl-winning receiver." She glanced up at me. "You know him?"

I plopped down on the couch to my left and buried my face in my hands. "Stone was best friends with Cayden until Stone stole Cayden's scholarship to play at the University of Texas. Cayden wanted to play for them ever since he could throw a ball." I glanced over at Tilly so she could see my panic. "Cayden would kill me if he knew who was living next door."

Tilly frowned. "What? Why?"

Frustration boiled up inside of me. "Cayden *hates* Stone. They're, like, Capulet-and-Montague-level rivals."

"But Cayden can't play football after his ATV accident."

I shook my head. "It doesn't matter. To Cayden, Stone stole everything from him. Stone stole his future. And if my parents found out?" I sucked in my breath. "They would march me out of this apartment so fast." I winced at the drama that would ensue. It would epically explode the already fragile threads that held our family together.

"Even if you're just living next door?"

I nodded. "That won't matter to Cayden. This"—I waved my hands to encompass the walls around us—"is over before it even began."

"But I already told Poppy that you would take the apartment. I can't just pull back now. Plus, we got the money. I can't just give it back."

I stared at her, frustrated that Tilly didn't understand how dire this situation was. There was no way I could live here anymore. It had been hard enough when I told my parents that I was going to live in the same state as Stone. For them to learn that I was living next door to him would be the final nail driven into the family coffin.

My family was why I was so driven to be discovered. Cayden had lost his chance, but I still had mine. If I could only get luck back on my side, then maybe I could heal the mess.

"Tilly, I just...can't."

She pulled back and started to pace. She pinched the bridge of her nose as she closed her eyes and tipped her face toward the ceiling. The silence in the room was deafening, but it was finally interrupted with the sound of her phone chiming.

She stopped moving and pulled her phone from her back pocket and swiped it on. I watched as her eyes scanned the screen before she looked up at me. She held my gaze for a moment and then slipped her phone into her back pocket and clapped her hands.

"Here's what I think we should do. Let's just put a pin in this for now and get ready for a gig tonight."

All thoughts of Stone and Cayden faded into the back of my mind as I focused on her last words. "Gig?"

Her smile widened, and her eyes were sparkling now.

"Yes. Someone had to cancel, and we got their slot at Night Spirits."

My heart started pounding as I held her gaze. "You're lying." I couldn't hold in the squeal that emerged despite my best efforts. "Please tell me you aren't lying." This was what I needed to help soothe the wound of having to give this place up.

"I'm not lying," she said as she crossed the space between us and held onto my hands. "And the best part?"

I stilled so I could take in what she had to say. "What's the best part?"

"If you lived here, you could just walk to the bar."

I narrowed my eyes at her but inwardly cursed my best friend. She always seemed to know what to say that would cause me to throw my resolutions out the window.

"Don't start," I said as she pulled open the front door. Even if I agreed to live here, my things were still at my old apartment, which now felt like a suffocating shoebox. I was never going to be happy with what I could afford after knowing that I could have lived here.

I tried to hurry Tilly along as I stood on the landing, waiting for her to lock the door. The last thing I needed was for Stone to come out of his apartment and discover me standing a few feet from his door. I was certain that Stone felt the same for the Kings as the Kings felt for Stone. We were all better when we were nowhere near each other.

I hooked my arm through Tilly's as we waited for the elevator to take us down to the parking lot. Tilly was going on and on about all the famous people who had played at Night Spirits and how, depending on which scouts were there tonight, this could be my big break.

My stomach was twisted into knots as I climbed into her car. I finally had to beg her to talk about the weather as she drove me back to my apartment. Once we got inside, I hurried into the bathroom and turned on the shower.

I walked out to grab a towel to find Tilly ripping open already packed boxes of clothes to find the right outfit. I gave her a pointed look, but she just waved me off stating that she would spend the night repacking them if it meant me getting a talent scout interested in my songs.

I smiled as I disappeared into the bathroom to shower. Once I was finished, I dried off and then slipped on my satin robe before sitting at my vanity with my hair wrapped up in a towel. I busied myself with putting on my makeup while Tilly settled on a pair of distressed overalls with a strapless lace tank. She found my jewelry box and laid out some chunky bracelets with blue stones and varying lengths of necklaces for me to wear.

With my makeup finished, I worked on curling my hair, so it lay in soft waves around my face and spilled down my shoulders.

It was 7:15 when we finished, and my stomach was grumbling, but I was too nervous to eat. I slipped on my cowboy boots, and she slipped on her tennis shoes. We grabbed our purses and headed out the door. My time slot was 10:30, and we still needed to drive back downtown with bumper-to-bumper traffic.

Thankfully, we got to Night Spirits by 9:30. We had to park a few streets away, and I could feel Tilly's gaze on me as we met up on the sidewalk. I knew what she was thinking. If I lived in Poppy's apartment, we would be there already.

I just gave her a big smile as I shifted my guitar case to my other hand, so I could link arms with her as we made our way down the sidewalk. I was shivering with excitement by the time we got to the front doors of Night Spirits. A bouncer was standing outside, and he raised his eyebrows as he studied us.

Tilly told him that I had a time slot and showed him the email on her phone. He didn't speak; he just nodded and stepped to the side so we could enter.

The place was packed as we slipped through the doors. There were so many bodies that we had to keep to the walls to get through. I kept my guitar close to my body, so it wouldn't hit anyone. I followed Tilly over to the DJ booth sitting on the far wall. The music and crowd were so loud that I couldn't hear what they were saying, but when the DJ flicked his gaze in my direction, I knew they were talking about me.

Tilly turned toward me and extended her hand. "Give me your guitar," she yelled as she leaned in.

I frowned, but she just wiggled her fingers. "Troy said he'd keep it back here until it's time for your set."

I hated giving my guitar away. It was like giving up a limb. But there was no way I could hold onto it in this crowd, so I reluctantly handed it over. Troy lifted it over the table and tucked it against the wall behind him.

Guitar-less, I followed Tilly as she pushed through the crowd to the bar. She ordered a basket of fries and two beers. Once she had the items in hand, we squeezed our way through the crowd until we got to the tables set in front of the stage. Thankfully, just as we approached a table, a group of drunk women got up, so we dropped down onto the seats before anyone else could.

We ate and bobbed our heads to the music, unable to talk over the bass blaring from the speakers and the conversations going on around us. The fries disappeared, and all that was left was the beer. I sipped it, not really liking the taste but needing it to calm my nerves.

Tilly tapped me with her foot. I drew my attention up to her, and she smiled. "You okay?" she mouthed.

I forced a smile and nodded. "Just nervous," I mouthed back.

"You'll do great." She gave me a big smile.

It was moments like this that I was grateful I had Tilly in my corner. She had this level of optimism that I could never seem to conjure up for myself. It was silly, but with my family's bad luck, I went into every situation with a pessimistic attitude. Tilly always managed to help me see the sunlight through the clouds.

We enjoyed the next few sets, but when Tilly moved to

stand and I followed after her, everything around me began to fade away. All I could think about was what I was going to sing. I took slow breaths as we picked up my guitar from Troy and followed his directions to get backstage.

I stood offstage, watching the band currently performing finish their song and gather their things. Tilly was talking to me, but I was so nervous that I couldn't make out what she was saying. All I could hear was the pounding of my heart in my ears.

The MC grabbed the mic and introduced me before extending his hand to invite me onstage.

"Smile!" Tilly hissed into my ear before she pushed me to get moving.

My feet carried me across the stage. I managed to thank the MC and wave to the audience before I grabbed the stool that was brought out for me. I strummed a few chords on my guitar to tune it. In the familiarity of those actions, I could feel my nerves slowly melt away. It was just me and my music.

That was all I needed.

I closed my eyes and tipped my face up to the microphone. My fingers fell into place on the strings. I sucked in my breath before I parted my lips and strummed.

Just breathe.

4

STONE

The bar was crowded tonight. One nod at Billy, the bouncer at Night Spirits, and he stepped to the side to let me in. He clapped me on the back as I walked by.

The employees at Night Spirits knew me, but they also knew that I liked my anonymity. They did little to draw attention to me, which I appreciated.

When I got inside, I made my way to the bar. Collin was bartending tonight. I settled on my normal stool near the wall, and Collin nodded in my direction to acknowledge that he saw me and that he'd be right with me to take my order. I pulled my cap down lower and studied the bar in front of me.

"Regular?" Collin asked as he set down a napkin.

"Yep," I said.

A moment later, a Moscow mule appeared in front of me. I settled back on the barstool as I took a sip. The familiarity of the ginger, lime, and vodka washed over my taste-buds, and I felt my body relax. The band that was currently playing was pretty good. Troy could pick some bad bands, but this one had me feeling the music. I turned to rest one arm on the bar, so I could watch them play.

When they finished, the crowd erupted in cheers. I set my drink down and started clapping with them.

"They must be good if you're clapping for them." Collin's voice drew my attention over. He was standing there with a big grin on his face.

"Troy's getting better at who he's picking," I said as I picked up my drink and took another sip.

"He's really trying to get the scouts to come out here. I think he said one would be in the crowd today."

I nodded. Even though the music world was drastically different from sports, I knew what it was like to have someone in the crowd who could change your entire life. The nerves that came from that knowledge were like nothing I'd ever experienced since.

"I hope someone gets discovered," I said as I shot him a smile.

"Ladies and gentlemen, we have a newbie on our stage tonight," Henry shouted into the microphone. He was Troy's new MC and was doing a good job keeping the crowd pumped for the next set. "Let's give Emerson King a huge Night Spirits' welcome." He held the microphone with his thumb as he clapped and waved for her to approach.

My entire body went numb as her name reverberated in

my mind. I glanced around, wondering if I was the only one who heard the name he just called. But I seemed to be the only one affected. Everyone around me was staring at the stage, clapping and smiling, like the girl they'd fallen for in high school wasn't moments away from walking on to the stage.

The entire world seemed to slow as Emerson walked toward Henry. She was holding a guitar, wearing a pair of overalls and a small tank underneath. Her hair was longer now. It fell in curls around her shoulders, and when she smiled at Henry, she tucked it behind her ear.

I knew I should pull my gaze away. I knew I shouldn't be watching her, but I couldn't help it. She was a ghost from my past, and yet she was standing in front of me, alive and breathing.

She pulled the stool closer to the microphone and settled on it. Her lips tipped up into a smile as she glanced around at the crowd. "Thank you so much for such a sweet welcome," she said.

I closed my eyes for a moment as the familiarity of her voice caused my heart to pound. I'd spent so many years trying to forget her, yet one glance and all the memories came crashing into my mind like waves against the beach during a hurricane.

I wasn't sure how long I watched her sing, and it didn't matter. I was mesmerized by the way her lips moved as she sang. Her fingers effortlessly danced on the guitar strings as she closed her eyes. I'd heard her play back in high school, but this...this was something completely different.

Emerson was born to play.

A group of guys moved to stand in front of me. Normally, I'd just turn back to the bar, but this time, anger rose up inside of me. I didn't want to stare at the back of their heads. I wanted to see Emerson. This might be the only chance I got to see her. I wasn't going to waste it.

I grabbed my drink and slid off the barstool. Collin said something, but I was too busy listening to Emerson to care what he said. I moved around the group of guys and made my way closer to the stage. I kept to the shadows, not wanting her or anyone else to see me. I found an empty space on the far wall and leaned against it. I was about twenty feet away from her.

Far enough where she wouldn't recognize me but close enough to make out the freckles that still dusted her nose. I sipped my drink and listened to the words that she was singing. Something about a broken heart and a broken family. I wondered if her lyrics reflected her life, but then I shook my head. One thing was for certain, she wasn't singing about me, so the meaning didn't really matter.

Her gaze drifted toward where I was standing, and I pulled my ball cap further down to shade my face. My entire body tensed as I waited for the familiar feeling of her gaze drifting over me. I studied my drink, praying that she didn't recognize me. I didn't want to bring up the past for her if she'd moved on—unlike me.

When I finally glanced back up, I saw that she'd turned her attention back to those sitting in front of her, so I let my gaze linger on her face. Her song ended, and everyone cheered. I set my empty mug down on the floor, so I could join in on their applause. She asked if they wanted an encore, and everyone cheered in agreement.

A smile spread across her lips, and my heart pounded in my chest from the sight. She looked so happy. I'd always wondered what happened to her. Where she went after graduation. The fact that she was up on stage told me that she'd chased her dream, which made me happy for her.

She deserved the world.

"Isn't she amazing?" The guy I was standing next to had leaned closer to speak to me.

I glanced over at him and saw how happy he looked. He was smiling and clapping like he knew her. Did he?

"She's great," I mumbled.

"I never miss it when she plays," the guy said. He glanced over at me and smiled. "I'm Emerson's number one fan."

The urge to punch him rushed through my muscles. I hated that he knew where she was going to be. I hated that he knew her name. I hated that he seemed to have an uncomplicated history with her—unlike me.

I stared at him, wondering if this was some kind of cruel joke. Not only did I have to stare at the girl I couldn't seem to get out of my mind, but I had to stand next to the guy she seemed to have some sort of relationship with? Was she actually dating this tool?

Fate was a cruel mistress.

I turned my focus back to Emerson. And then guilt formed in my chest as our history came floating back into my mind. She wasn't some stranger. We had a past, and I had been instrumental in ending our friendship. Suddenly, I felt selfish, standing here, taking her in like she was just another singer on a stage. This was her moment, and I felt like I was stealing it.

I shook my head, grabbed my mug, and pushed through the crowd over to Collin. I set the mug down on the bar before pulling a twenty out of my wallet. He nodded at me as he picked the mug and money up. He parted his lips to ask me a question, but I just shook my head.

"Keep the change," I said before turning to leave. I couldn't stand here and watch Emerson sing. I needed to leave.

I was halfway to the door when I felt a hand on my forearm. Her nails dug into my skin as my cap was pulled from my head. Alcohol-drenched breath washed over me as the woman shouted, "Stone Walker?"

Everyone around us turned, and I could feel their gazes on me as I moved to take my cap back.

"It is! It's Stone Walker." The woman had no interest in letting me go. "Babe, take a picture. My dad's never going to believe this." She shifted her body—all the while still clinging to my arm—until she was standing next to me.

Flashes went off around me, and all I could see were black spots. The music stopped as a crowd began to form around me. I turned to see if Emerson had noticed what was going on, but with the people and the residual blindness from the cameras, I couldn't make anything out.

"Step back," Billy's voice boomed out. The woman's hand was pulled away as Billy stood between me and her. He leaned toward me and said, "Follow me."

I nodded and kept close to him as he pushed through the crowd to the door that led to the back room. People had their phones out and were snapping pictures, but I'd rescued my cap from the woman, so I pulled it down over my face as I kept my head bowed.

As soon as we were through the door, Billy shut it on the crowd. My ears were ringing in the absence of the chatter. I leaned against the cool brick wall and took in some deep breaths.

"Sorry about that, man," Billy said.

I shook my head. "It's no big deal. I should have stayed by the bar where it was safe."

He nodded. "Still, you should be able to move around without someone grabbing onto you." He pushed his hand through his black hair and then glanced to the side. "There's a back door if you follow this hallway down and then take a right." He lifted his arm and used his forefinger to emphasize the directions.

"Perfect. Thanks."

"Let me know if you need assistance."

I raised my hands and shook my head. "I should be good. Seems simple enough. I'll wait until the crowd dies down a bit, and I'll slip out."

He studied me for a moment before he clapped me on the back and then slipped out the door. Now alone, I leaned my head back, tipping my face up and blowing out my breath. My stomach was in knots.

It had to be from seeing Emerson and then wondering if she saw me. After all, I was used to people stopping me to take pictures. That was an everyday occurrence. But with Emerson in the room? Did she see me? Did she know that I was there?

Did she care?

I cleared my throat and straightened. She probably had no idea that I was there, and if she did, I doubted that she cared. I was just a blip on her radar, that was all.

I saw some movement to my left, and I glanced over to see two girls peeking around the corner. They were giggling. I turned and nodded in their direction. "Ladies," I said as I walked past them.

"Go Tigers," one of the girls called out.

I glanced over my shoulder and smiled. But just as I did, I ran into someone. She let out a soft, "umph," and without thinking, I reached out and grabbed onto her.

"I'm so sorry," I stammered as I pulled the woman to my chest to keep us both upright.

It took me a second to steady myself. When I was certain that she was going to be okay, I glanced down. My entire body froze when I saw who I was holding on to. Her blonde hair and creamy skin were unmistakable. She didn't have to look up at me for me to know who it was.

"You can let me go, now," Emerson said.

I dropped my arms and jumped back like I'd just touched fire. My entire body heated, and the only thing I could think to do with my hands was to push one through my hair as I stared at her.

She took a moment to compose herself before she turned to face me. Her familiar green eyes studied me before she parted her lips and said, "Stone."

5

EMERSON

My brain was going a million miles a second as I watched Stone glance at me before he dropped his gaze to the ground. I still couldn't believe that he was here. What were the chances that he'd decide to come to the same bar I was playing at.

And then he made a scene while I was singing. It didn't seem like something he would do. But then again, I never imagined that he would steal Cayden's scholarship and leave town, never to look back.

I guess people always have a way of surprising you. Mom always said Stone was just showing who he really was, and I tried to believe her.

Not wanting to stand in silence, I steeled my nerves and nodded in his direction. "Stone," was all I could manage.

His gaze snapped up to mine. His blue eyes were dark and stormy as he studied me. "Emerson," he said.

Shivers rushed across my skin at the sound of my name on his lips. It wasn't like before. His voice was deeper now. He looked similar to what I remembered, just older. Hotter.

My skin prickled at that thought, and I forced my mind to focus on what I was going to say, not how Stone made me feel. "It's good to see you," I said.

He frowned like my words had caught him off guard. "Really?" he asked before he cleared his throat and said, "You too." He shoved his hands into his front pockets and nodded toward my guitar. I'd forgotten I was still holding it. "So, you made it."

I glanced down as I chewed on my response. What was I supposed to say to that? I didn't want him to know that I was struggling to get gigs, but I also didn't want to lie. I just shrugged. "I'm getting by."

His half smile that I had seared into my memory flashed in front of me. He nodded as he looked approvingly at me. "I'm glad. From what I heard out there, you must be doing amazing for yourself."

My skin flushed from his compliment. I didn't want to tell him that I'd lost my apartment and that I still hadn't landed a recording contract, so I just smiled. "Thanks." I waved toward him. "You, too. You got everything you wanted."

Just as the words left my lips, I realized what I'd said. I pinched my lips together, and silence fell around us. Stone glanced to the side and then slowly brought his gaze up to meet mine.

"Yeah," he mumbled.

I wanted to backtrack. I wanted him to forget that I'd said anything. But it was too late. The words were out in the ether. "Listen, I—"

"I should go," Stone said as he nodded toward the hallway behind me. "I've got practice in the morning."

Suddenly feeling like I was trapping him here, I nodded and stepped to the side. "For sure."

"You did amazing!" Tilly's singsong voice grew louder as I heard her approach me from behind. She wrapped her arms around me and squeezed before her whole body stilled. I could only assume she had just noticed Stone standing in front of me.

"Who are you?" she asked as she came to stand next to me. She extended her hand. "Are you a scout? You know, I'm her manager. You can't negotiate without me present."

Stone parted his lips, but Tilly wasn't taking a breath, so he just shook her hand. "Stone."

It took a moment for his name to register in Tilly's mind. Her jaw dropped open as she turned to face me. "Stone? As in *the* Stone?"

My face felt like it was on fire now. I leaned over to shush her before turning to see Stone studying me with a curious expression on his face. He'd heard her, and the meaning wasn't lost on him.

The last thing I needed was for him to think that I was just randomly talking about him to my friend. Sure, I thought about him on a regular basis, but I didn't need him to know that. I forced a laugh as I waved my hand as if to wave away her comment.

"It's funny because I just rented the place across from you. It's why we were talking about you." There. That seemed plausible enough.

Stone's smile faded as he stared at me.

Tilly looked shocked before she squealed as she gripped onto my arm. "That's right. My sister knows Poppy, so we were scoping out the place this afternoon, and Emerson saw you through the peephole."

If I could will a sink hole to open up and swallow Tilly whole, I would. I wanted to shush her. But Stone would notice, and I didn't want him to think that I was in any way uncomfortable with him standing in front of me.

"You're moving into Poppy's apartment?" he asked.

I nodded. "Just for the time she's gone. My lease was up on my apartment, so I needed something fast and close to the bars around here." I glanced over at Tilly, who was beaming over at me. "It is the perfect place."

"Perfect," she said as she smiled at me.

"Wow." Stone looked shocked as he glanced around. "Well, I'm happy for you, neighbor."

"It's not like we'll see each other a lot. You have practice during the days, and I have work and gigs at night." I laughed, hating that I sounded so discombobulated. "I'll barely be there."

When I glanced over at Stone, he was studying me. He nodded when he met my gaze. "Okay."

I forced a smile. "Okay." Then I turned to Tilly. "Should we go?"

She frowned. "Should we?"

I nodded. "We're going to go. You were on your way out. We won't hold you here any longer." I turned, taking Tilly with me, as we walked back down the hallway that Tilly had just come through. We took another left, and when I was certain we were out of Stone's earshot, I blew out my breath and collapsed against the wall.

Tilly was peeking around the corner to see if Stone had followed us. Thankfully, he hadn't, and as the seconds ticked by, I could feel my anxiety lessen.

"So *that* was Stone," Tilly said as she moved to lean against the wall across from me.

I was pitched forward with my hands on my knees, taking deep breaths. "What the heck, Tilly?" I finally managed out.

She frowned. "What?"

"*The* Stone?"

Her cheeks flushed as she grinned. "What? It's not like he even noticed."

I shot her a *yeah, right* look. "I'm pretty sure he picked up on that."

"What does it matter? You said your families used to be friends. It was only normal that we would have talked about him. I am your best friend."

I straightened and raked my fingers through my hair. "It matters."

She waved away my words with her hands. "The family feud. I know, I know."

If Tilly really understood, she wouldn't be this flippant about it. My family would disown me if they found out that I'd entertained a conversation with Stone. They'd practically made a blood pact that the Kings would hate Stone Walker forever.

Tilly's expression morphed into a smile as she studied me. "So, we're moving in?" she asked.

My stomach churned as the memory of what I'd said slammed into my mind. Now that I'd confessed I was staying across from him, how would it look if I suddenly backed out?

"Oh, no." Tilly's words drew my attention.

"What?" I asked.

"I know that expression," she said as she motioned to my face. "You want to back out."

I feigned shock. "What? I do not."

She narrowed her eyes. "Mm-hmm."

"I want to live there."

"Wanting and actually doing are two different things." She sighed as she pulled out her phone. "I guess I'll keep looking for a place that's the exact opposite of Poppy's apartment." She scrolled on her phone, her focus completely consumed by her screen.

The tug-of-war inside of me became too much. I was torn between my family and this fabulous place to live. I reached out and grabbed Tilly's phone from her. "Stop," I said as I clicked on the side button and the screen went black. "No more looking."

She stared at me, her expression unreadable.

I sighed as I handed her phone back to her. "I'll stay in Poppy's apartment."

"Are you sure?"

I nodded.

A huge smile broke out on her lips as she lunged toward me, wrapping her arms around my neck and pulling me close. "Yay!" she yelled before a guy appeared from the stage and shushed her.

She let go of me and stepped back, nodding an apology before she turned back to me and let out a silent scream.

"Just for the six months," I said.

"We won't even need the six months. You'll have a contract before then." She reached out and grabbed my guitar. "Let's go celebrate," she sang as she turned and headed toward the back door.

I followed after her as my decision rolled around in my mind. There was a part of me that wanted me to change my mind. Living next to Stone was a huge mistake. But the other part of me was louder, the part that knew that down-town—where I could have experiences like this every night—was where I needed to be.

I knew that living with my family's anger in the fore-front of my mind put me on the fast track to stagnation. If I wanted to have a future, I needed to put myself first. That meant living where I had the most opportunities.

Besides, I could survive living next to Stone. From our earlier conversation, it was clear I was the last thing on his mind. He was focused on football, and I was focused on music. I doubted we would ever see each other, and if we did, well, our interaction tonight told me that we could be cordial to each other. And that was all I needed to know.

He'd live his life, and I'd live mine.

We didn't need to talk to each other. It wasn't like living at Poppy's required me to hang out with him. We were just neighbors, that was all.

And Tilly was right. Once I was discovered and signed a contract, then I would move. I doubted Stone would even notice or care when that happened. The tabloids had stories about him with different women on his arm every other week. I was fairly certain the geeky little sister to his ex-best friend wasn't even on the map.

Living in Poppy's apartment was what I needed to do for my future. And I was ready to start living.

I was ready to start living for me.

6

STONE

"Tilly! Tilly! Stop! It's slipping!"

I paused my chewing and tipped my head toward my front door. The sound of Emerson's voice cut through to where I was standing in my kitchen. I set my bowl of cereal down and walked around the peninsula. I pulled open the door and peered out only to be greeted by a queen-size mattress that was flopped haphazardly on the landing between Emerson's apartment and mine.

I glanced up to see Emerson's bright red face as she stared at me. Her hair was pulled up into a messy bun on the top of her head, and I was trying hard to ignore the way her long legs looked in her cutoff shorts. She fanned her neck, which drew my attention to her orange tank top.

"It's not funny, Tilly," Emerson said as she shot her friend an annoyed look. Tilly was doubled over and laughing so hard that no noise was coming out.

Tilly straightened and worked to relax her face. "It was hilarious."

I leaned against my doorframe and folded my arms. I glanced between the two of them and then raised an eyebrow. "Do you need some help?"

"Yes."

"No."

I glanced between them and widened my eyes.

"I think we've got this," Emerson hurried to say, shooting her friend a look before giving me a quick smile.

I took my time glancing down at the mattress before meeting her gaze once more. "Uh huh."

"She's being modest. We definitely need your help," Tilly said as she tapped the mattress with the toe of her tennis shoe. "We got it stuck, and we can't lift it high enough to unstick it." She blew out her breath. "Why are mattresses so unwieldy?"

I glanced over at Emerson, who seemed to be content looking everywhere but in my direction. I took a moment to study her and could tell by the way she was twitching she didn't want me here. I didn't blame her, but I also thought it was a tad ridiculous that she was this uncomfortable taking help from me. After all, we were neighbors now.

My phone vibrated, so I shifted my weight and pulled it from my back pocket. It was a text from George.

George: A group of us are coming to get you. Get your shoes on and don't ask any questions.

I frowned and contemplated texting back that I wasn't

interested but decided against it. George wasn't known for listening, and if he kept to his MO, he was most likely only a few minutes away.

"Well, good news. Some of my football buddies are on their way. We can help you unload the rest of your stuff."

"That's great," Tilly exclaimed as she shot Emerson an over-exaggerated smile. "Isn't that awesome?"

They traded a series of facial expressions before Emerson forced her frown flat and glanced in my direction. "That's great. We appreciate the help."

I nodded and then I grabbed a hold of the door before swinging it shut. I had every intention of helping them, but the guys weren't here yet, and I wasn't going to torture myself by standing out on the landing while we waited.

I finished my bowl of cereal and was rinsing it out in the sink when I heard the guys' voices immediately followed by three solid knocks on the door. I wiped my hands on the dish towel that Gran had embroidered and moved to open the door.

George, Isaac, Jayden, and Colt were all standing in different spots on the landing to avoid the mattress in the center. George was nearest to the door, and he shot me a confused look.

"What's going on out here?" he asked.

I sighed. "New neighbor. I told her that we'd help."

George's eyebrows instantly went up. "Her?"

I glared at him. "Don't get any ideas."

He held up his hands. "I didn't say anything." But then he leaned in. "Is she young?"

I punched his shoulder, and he winced before bringing his hand up to massage his shoulder. "I'll take that as a yes."

"Knock on her door," I said, motioning to Jayden. He obeyed, and we waited for a few seconds before the door was pulled open.

Emerson was standing there. She moved her gaze to everyone else but me. Me, she skipped right over.

George let out a low whistle, and I punched him in the shoulder once more. "Guys, this is Emerson. Emerson, meet some of the guys from the team."

I could feel George's gaze on me. There was a familiarity in my tone that he seemed to pick up on. His expression asked me how I knew this girl, but that wasn't a question I wanted to answer. Instead, I moved toward the mattress and instructed Jayden, Isaac, and Colt to each pick up a corner.

I kept hidden behind the mattress as Emerson instructed Jayden where she wanted it to go. I'd been in Poppy's apartment before. She'd invited me over a few times for drinks until I realized what she wanted from me and I put an end to that. We were friends, but nothing more.

After we set the mattress down on the box spring, we moved out of Emerson's bedroom and into the living room, where Tilly was waiting for us. She instructed us to follow her downstairs to unload the rest of Emerson's things.

I snuck a look at Emerson, but she was focused on Tilly.

Feeling like an idiot, I dropped my gaze and focused on Tilly as well. We followed behind her as she jogged down the stairs to the moving truck that was parked in the loading zone.

As everything does between us guys, the number of boxes we could carry became a competition, and we were loading each other up with an insane number of boxes. I carried the most at ten boxes, and by the time I got to Emerson's apartment, my body felt as if it were on fire. Thankfully, Tilly and Emerson were there to unload me as quickly as they could.

Emerson's hand brushed mine, and electricity shot up my arm. I almost dropped the remaining boxes, but I caught myself before I made a giant fool of myself.

It only took about a half hour before we had their truck unloaded, and her apartment was bursting at the seams. Emerson was moving boxes to different rooms while we lingered in the living room.

Colt asked her if we could help, but she was quick to brush him off, telling him that she had it under control. Tilly was watching her and glancing over at us like she wanted to say something but wasn't sure how Emerson would take it. She had to know the history between me and Emerson. At least, that was implied last night at Night Spirits.

Not wanting to overstay our welcome, I started to usher my friends to the front door. "Well, we'll get out of your hair," I called over my shoulder while I silently prayed that they wouldn't say anything before we got out to the landing.

"Wha—what are you doing?" George asked as I wrapped my arm around his shoulder and led him out the door.

"We're letting my new neighbor unpack," I said.

Just as we stepped out onto the landing, Tilly's voice stopped us. "Wait."

We turned to see her following after us. She glanced hastily back into the apartment before turning her attention to us. "Do you guys have plans for the day? We'd like to take you to lunch for helping us move."

"We would?" Emerson asked as she suddenly appeared next to Tilly.

"Free food and cute girls?" Isaac asked as he clapped Colt on the shoulder. "I could never say no to that."

I shot Isaac a death stare before glancing over at Emerson, who looked like she was struggling with what to say. Tilly, on the other hand, was loving it, nodding and smiling at Isaac.

"I think we're okay. After all, George had something planned," I said, offering Emerson an out if she wanted one. "I mean, you've got things to do."

She glanced up at me before she looked at the guys and then over at Tilly, who was staring at her a bit too hard.

Emerson pulled back just a bit before she sighed and glanced back at us. "We'd be happy to take you out for some lunch."

The guys whooped and high-fived like we'd just won another Super Bowl. I studied Emerson, who looked uneasy as she smiled at us. Why was she doing this if she didn't want to? Or maybe she *did* want to...

I felt so confused.

"Let me get changed out of my scrubby clothes. Meet on the landing in 15?" Emerson began to step back into her apartment.

The guys all mumbled in agreement before they turned to head into my apartment. I followed after them, but just before I cleared the door, I paused and glanced over toward Emerson's apartment. I hated that I felt excited that we were going to spend the day together. I hated that I wanted her to be excited about it, not pressured into it by Isaac and Tilly. Would she ever be excited to spend the day with me? I doubted it.

I sighed as I shut my door and glanced at the guys, who had circled around me, each with a huge grin on his face. I glared at them as I folded my arms. "What?"

"Dude!" George said as he leaned back and clapped his hands, lifting his face toward the sky and howling. "Thank God, finally!"

I grabbed onto him, praying that Emerson couldn't hear what he was saying. "Will you knock it off?" I asked.

He grinned at me, the excitement in his gaze telling me he had no intention of stopping.

"She's hot," Isaac said. I could feel my hands curl into fists. He stepped back and raised his hands in surrender.

"She is," George said. He knew me well enough to know

I wasn't going to fight him. Instead, he punched me on the shoulder and wiggled his eyebrows.

"She's off limits."

Colt shrugged. "We're thinking for you."

His words were like a knife to my gut. I glared at them as I stalked over to the fridge to grab a soda. My body was hot, and I needed something to cool it down. All the guys followed me, gathering around the opening to my kitchen to watch me down the can.

When it was empty, I tossed it into the recycling and glanced over at them.

George looked hopeful as he waved toward my front door. "Dude, you have to do something about that. She's into you. We could tell by the way she looked at you. You can't pass this up."

I was clenching my jaw muscles so hard that they hurt. I shook my head before scrubbing my face and pushing my hand through my hair. "She's off limits," I said again.

George looked frustrated. "We know. She's off limits to us, but we aren't thinking about us. We all think you should make a move."

Frustration boiled up in my gut as I moved to walk away. I needed a moment to cool down, or I was going to fight someone. Just as I stepped in front of my friends, I paused to look over at George. He looked so hopeful that he'd finally found the perfect girl for his perpetually single friend.

I sighed as I shrugged. "I wasn't saying she's off limits to you guys." I blew out my breath. "She's off limits to me."

7

EMERSON

"**W**hy did you have to do that?" I asked after I'd shut the apartment door and collapsed against the nearby wall. I leaned forward, resting my hands on my knees as I took a few deep breaths. This afternoon did not go the way I thought it would, and my mind was racing a mile a minute.

I needed a second to catch my breath.

"I don't know what you're talking about," Tilly sang out. Her words were followed by the sound of ripping tape.

I glanced up to see her elbow deep in one of my boxes. "What are you doing?" I asked as I straightened and moved to see what she was digging out. When I saw the colorful patterns that made up my wardrobe, I narrowed my eyes. "What are you doing?" I asked again, slower this time, so she knew just how serious I was.

"I can't have you going out with half of Tennessee's

NFL team looking like a hobo," she said, her gaze never leaving the jumper she'd just pulled out and stretched out in front of her. She wrinkled her nose as she shook her head and tossed it onto the couch before she started digging around once more.

Tilly was being purposely obtuse. "I meant, why did you offer to take those guys out?" I hated that she'd done it. But I especially hated how quick Stone had been to dismiss the offer. Like they were too good to have us take them to lunch. It was a strange sensation to simultaneously not want to be around him and be offended that he was attempting to stay away.

She shrugged. "It's the hospitable thing to do. Especially since they brought all the boxes up here." She turned her attention back to the clothes. "Ooo," she said as she pulled out a denim romper. She held it up toward me, squinted one eye and tilted her head. "Yep, I can see it." She shook it out and moved around the box to make her way toward me.

"I think it would be smarter if we hung out here. You know, I need to unpack...work on a song." I raised my eyebrows to encourage her to listen to me as she continued to hold up the outfit.

"Going out with the Tigers is work," she said as she bunched the outfit together and handed it to me. "Go get dressed."

I stared at her, hoping that she would see my reluctance. But if she did, she didn't care. It became a stare-off until I sighed, took the romper, and headed to my new bedroom. "You're insane, you know that?" I called over my shoulder.

"But that's why you love me," she called back.

I shut my door and stood in front of the full-length mirror that Poppy had affixed to her wall. I stared at my reflection, suddenly self-conscious that a group of extremely attractive men had seen me in my scrubby tank and shorts. The desire to show them what I really looked like rushed through me. I headed into the bathroom to get ready.

Tilly was a genius. The romper that she picked out for me was designed to be off the shoulder. It had shorts, but when I stood, it looked like I was wearing a denim mini dress. I found the box with my jewelry and dressed the outfit up with some chunky necklaces. I picked my large, gold dangly earrings.

I used a curling iron to create waves in my hair, and after studying my reflection, I pulled my hair into a half updo. I freshened up my makeup, gave myself a once over, and headed out into the living room, where Tilly was waiting for me.

She held up a pair of white sneakers and a pair of wedges. I picked the wedges and slipped them on as she studied me. I glanced up at her, and my stomach sank. "What?" I asked, drawing out the word.

"Don't hate me," she whispered.

I sighed, straightened, and folded my arms as I stared at her. "What did you do?"

"I can't go with you."

"Tilly!" She was the reason I'd forced myself to get dressed. There was no way I wanted to go by myself to hang out with a bunch of guys I didn't really know. Sure, Stone would be there, but he really wasn't high on my list of people I wanted to talk to.

She held up her hands. "I know, I know. But Cadence needs me to watch Trinity. She has to take Beth to the doctor. Plus, I need to drop the moving truck off, so we don't get charged for longer than we have to." She clasped her hands together, pleading. "Please, just go. Have fun. Make connections." Her lips tipped up into a smile. "And don't hate me."

I sighed as I stared at her. All I wanted to do was slip back into my sweats and turn on *Friends* while I unpacked. But she looked so hopeful. And hanging out with a group of Tennessee Tigers wouldn't hurt me. Plus, I was curious about what they had planned for the day, and I'd been taught to never turn down an invitation, especially when you were the one doing the inviting.

There were three knocks on the door, and Tilly clapped her hands together, her eyes twinkling. "They're here," she sang out as she headed toward the door.

Before I could stop her, she pulled the door open in one flourishing movement. She stepped to the side, and the guys came in.

Stone was the last one to enter. He had on a black t-shirt and a pair of dark jeans. His hands were shoved into his front pockets. His elbows were tucked in like he was scared to touch anything.

Realizing that I was staring, I pulled my gaze from him and smiled at his teammates, who were listening to Tilly. She was explaining how she couldn't go, but I was still going to treat them.

They took turns glancing over at me. They all nodded and offered to take a raincheck, which sounded like a great idea to me. I stepped forward to take them up on that, but Tilly was quick to wave away the offer. I snapped my gaze to her, but she just ignored me.

Instead, she moved to stand behind me and started ushering me toward the door. She was saying something about how we should have fun. I was too focused on not tripping to resist being shoved out of my own apartment. The guys followed after me, and Tilly pressed the down arrow for the elevator before she bid us farewell, disappeared into my apartment, and shut the door.

An awkward silence fell around us, and I instantly felt Tilly's absence. She was the social lubricant that I depended on. Without her here, my thoughts gummed up, and I couldn't form coherent sentences.

"She's interesting," the tall blond said as he smiled over at me.

"She is," I said, blowing out my breath and reminding myself to smile. "That's why I keep her around. She pushes me to get out of my comfort zone."

He smiled. "Name's Isaac." He extended his hand. "We

haven't been formally introduced."

I slipped my hand into his. "Emerson."

"Isaac." Stone's voice had us both turning to look at him.

His gaze was frozen on Isaac, and I could tell that he was trying to send a message, but I couldn't understand what he was trying to say. And I really didn't want to put in the effort to figure it out.

Isaac seemed to decipher it and dropped my hand just as the elevator doors opened. I glared at Stone as I waited for the guys to go first, but they all seemed prepared to wait for me. I got into the elevator, and the guys followed.

I was standing next to the buttons, which meant I was standing right next to Stone when he got on. He'd waited for his friends to file in, and I could sense his entire body stiffen when he realized that he was going to be standing next to me.

I kept my gaze forward, trying hard not to be offended by his reaction. I was trying really hard not to care at all, though I seemed to be failing epically.

Two of the guys, who introduced themselves to me as George and Jayden, were talking to each other. That filled the silence as the elevator brought us down to the ground floor. We all got off, except for Stone. He moved to stand by the buttons.

"Where are you going?" he asked. His arm was extended, and he was pressing the "door open" button.

Confused, I glanced to the other guys. Was Stone bailing?

Isaac looked at me before he glanced over at the other guys. "Um, how about Tony's Pizza?"

"On Pennsylvania?"

Isaac nodded. "Unless you know of one closer."

Stone shook his head. "Nope. I'll meet you guys there. I'm going to ride my bike." He pulled his hand away, and the doors began to slide closed.

My brain hadn't caught up with my ears until Stone was gone and I was left standing with four of his friends. Great. First Tilly, now Stone. It seemed like everyone was content with abandoning me. I didn't really care one way or the other what Stone did, but he was the only one I knew in this group.

"We'll get you there safely," Issac said.

I gave him a grateful smile as he nodded for me to follow him and led us over to the parking lot. They let me sit up front in Isaac's Ford F-150. I had to hoist myself up to get into it. The other three guys stuffed themselves into the back, and it was comical to see them sitting shoulder to shoulder.

We kept the conversation light as Isaac pulled out onto the street and took a right. They were actually really nice guys. They told me where they were from, their girlfriends' names, and even showed me some pictures. They asked me where I was from and what I did. When I told them I sang, they all said they wanted to come to one of my performances.

It didn't take long before Isaac pulled into the parking

lot and found a spot right next to Stone's motorcycle. He was pulling off his helmet and setting it on his seat when Isaac turned off his engine and pulled out the keys.

"Crap," Isaac announced.

Everyone in the truck turned to look at him.

"You know what, we forgot that we have that thing," he said as he glanced at George in the back seat.

"Er...yeah! That thing Coach wanted us to do."

I glanced between them. "Um, okay." I wasn't sure what was happening; this felt a little forced. But who was I to call them out? Maybe they really did forget. "It's okay, we can do lunch some other time." I just wished they had come to this realization before they drove me all the way to the restaurant. I could've been in my sweats eating chocolate right now.

"You know what? Coach only needs us. Why don't you treat Stone to some food, and we'll call it even." Isaac's smile was wide as he studied me.

"Treat Stone?" I repeated.

"For sure. No need to pay for all of us. Just get him some lunch, and we'll be square." Isaac extended his hand.

I didn't know what to do, so I just let instinct take over. I shook his hand and then pulled back. "That's all you require as payment?" I asked, my brain trying to catch up with what was happening.

"That's all," George said.

I glanced at each of them before I turned and pulled on the door release. "I'll buy him lunch, and we'll be good," I said as I swung the door open. I climbed down, and just before I shut the door, I glanced at each of them once more. They all looked a little too happy.

I was ready to get this over with, so I could focus on unpacking and working on my music. I slammed the door shut and stepped back. Isaac saluted Stone, whose confused face appeared in front of me as Isaac pulled out of the parking spot. He peeled out into traffic and disappeared.

Now alone with Stone, I turned my attention to him. His gaze was trained on the road as if he were willing Isaac to drive back. I wasn't sure what I was going to do. I didn't want to stay here and eat lunch with him, but my ride had just bugged out of here.

I could call Tilly, but I doubted that she would make the effort to come get me. To her, this was a brilliant idea, even if I was left to eat lunch with just Stone. She wouldn't see the problem.

Stone finally glanced over at me, and I couldn't read his expression. But he didn't look happy. Which perfectly reflected how I felt.

"I'll get a ride to take me back," I said as I shuffled around in my purse for my phone and then cursed out loud. Realizing what I'd just done, I pinched my lips together and glanced up at Stone.

His ridiculous half smile that used to make my knees weak appeared for a moment before it disappeared. "Everything okay?"

I sighed and shook my head as I silently willed my heart

to stop pounding. "I forgot my phone." I raised my hands and dropped them to my side. "I'm stranded."

Stone studied me before he dropped his gaze to the keys he had in his hands. "I wouldn't say you're stranded."

"Oh really? I have no phone and no car. What would you call it?"

He glanced up at me. "I'm here."

All thought left my mind as I studied him. I knew I shouldn't read into his words, but there was a tone to his voice and a softness to his gaze that had me questioning my assumptions. And then I remembered everything that happened to my family after he stole Cayden's scholarship. Talk about cold water in the face.

"You don't have to stay. I can take care of myself," I said as I started walking toward the restaurant. "I'll see if I can borrow someone's phone inside."

I didn't glance over my shoulder to see if he was following me. I just focused on getting inside. The smell of basil, tomato sauce, and garlic filled my nose as soon as I pulled open the door. The dining room was about half full of people dressed in business suits or construction clothes. I got in line behind a group of guys dressed in neon green shirts. There were six people between me and the counter.

I heard someone clear their throat behind me, and I turned to see Stone standing there with his hands shoved into his front pockets. He was staring at the menu above the cashiers. I narrowed my eyes.

"What are you doing?" I asked, hating that he was this

close to me. He smelled like sandalwood and musk. Did he wear cologne? What kind? I shook my head to get my thoughts right.

"This is a restaurant," he said as he leaned closer to me without taking his eyes off the menu.

"I know it's a restaurant." My entire body flushed from his proximity.

He flicked his gaze down to me before he straightened and sighed. "I'm hungry, so I'm deciding what to order." He frowned. "Unless you're not okay with that."

My lips parted. I wanted to say something quippy in return, but all I could manage out was a soft, "Oh."

He held my gaze. I hated that he could bother me like this. I wasn't sure how long we'd stood there, staring at each other, when Stone flicked his gaze behind me and said, "Line moved."

I whipped my head to glance behind me, and red-hot, searing pain rushed through my neck and down my shoulder. I winced as I brought my hand up to my neck. I was glad I was facing forward so Stone didn't witness my contorted face as I tried to breathe through the pain. I shuffled a few feet forward and stopped, waiting for the guy in front of me to finish his extremely long order.

"You know, it's stupid for you to spend money on a ride when I'm heading in the same direction." Stone's voice sounded inches away from me. I wanted to turn around to face him, but I also didn't want to find out that he was as close as he felt.

"I don't think that's a good idea," I said as I instinctually tipped my head to the side. My neck protested.

He was silent for a moment. "Not a good idea?" he asked. He sounded like he had no clue what I was talking about. "It's a ride, Em. Not a proposal."

Butterflies erupted in my stomach from the way he said my nickname. Like it was as normal as breathing.

"I know it's not a proposal," I said, this time keeping my face forward, so I didn't aggravate my neck again.

"Then why can't I give you a ride home?"

Heat prickled my skin. Why wouldn't he let this go? It was better for us to pretend that we didn't know each other. It was better for him to keep to himself and for me to keep to myself. Things were less complicated when we lived like the other person didn't exist.

"Because," I hissed.

"It's just a ride. A neighbor helping another neighbor out. Unless...*you* think it means something more."

I turned to face him, his last few words still lingering in the air. He stared down at me, almost daring me to respond. I narrowed my eyes, mentally telling myself not to let him goad me, but it was too late. He was daring me, and I was stupid enough to take the dare.

"I don't think it means something more," I said, enunciating each word.

His gaze drifted down to my lips, where it lingered. Then he leaned in, inches away from me, as he whispered, "Prove it."

8

STONE

This is what insanity looks like. I was officially insane. Standing in front of Emerson at Tony's Pizza, daring her to let me take her home. I'd lost my mind.

If I knew what was good for me, I would let her walk away. I wouldn't follow her into the restaurant, I certainly wouldn't get in line behind her, and I wouldn't *ever* allow my gaze to drift down to her perfectly pouty lips.

But I didn't know what's good for me, which is why I was standing in line with Emerson glaring at me as she chewed on my words. I thought she would reply, but she didn't. Instead, she turned, stepped up to the cashier, and ordered two pieces of pepperoni pizza and two fountain drinks.

She paid before I could say anything. When she shoved a cup into my hand, I realized what she'd done.

"I could have paid for my own food," I said as I followed her to the soda dispenser.

"It's my treat," she said as she filled her cup with ice and then pressed it against the lever under the Sprite spout. I didn't like that. I didn't want to owe her. I parted my lips, but she turned to meet my gaze. "After all, you helped me unload my truck." She smiled a sly, goading smile. "We're even."

"I was just helping a neighbor out. If you want to get technical, the guys helped out more than I did."

The cashier set our plates of pizza on the counter before she returned to the register to take an older man's order.

"Well, they told me that if I paid for your lunch, we were even." She nodded toward my slice as she picked up hers. "So... we're even."

She turned and headed to one of the empty seats. I should have just scarfed down the pizza and left. But impulse took over my body as I followed her. I set my plate and drink down across from her before she could protest.

She had picked up the pizza and brought it to her mouth as she watched me plop down on the seat. If she wanted me to leave, she was going to have to say the words.

We ate in silence. With my pizza mostly gone, I chewed as my gaze slipped over to her. I took a long swig of my drink and set my glass down. "So, is this how it's going to be?" I asked before I had time to police my words.

She met my gaze, little frown lines appearing between her brows. "How what's going to be?"

"This." I lifted my hand and motioned between us. "You and me. Are we going to spend the next six months fighting?"

She studied me. "How do you know that I'm only going to be here for six months?"

"I know Poppy. She told me she was subletting her apartment." Did she think I was stalking her?

"Oh." She took a bite of her pizza before wiping her lips with her napkin. She rolled her shoulders forward as she chewed thoughtfully. After she took a drink, she glanced up at me. "How about we agree to be cordial? We'll act like every other neighbor in the world. We nod when we see each other. We don't have conversations that last longer than a few minutes. And when we talk, we discuss the weather, work, or the latest sitcom." She wiped her fingers on her napkin before she extended her hand.

I eyed it. I was unsure if it was a good idea to touch her, but she looked determined that we make this pact, so I reached over before stopping an inch from her hand. "And we be each other's ride if we need it."

She frowned. "Besides today, I don't plan on being stranded anywhere."

I shook my head. "If you're ever stranded or drunk, you call me. I will be your designated driver." I lowered my eyes, so she knew that I was serious.

I wasn't going to tell her that I had ulterior motives. I'd seen the way my friends looked at her. I'd seen the way drunk guys looked at her last night. If she was going to get a ride home from anyone, it was going to be me. And if she was going to be inebriated as well, there was no way in hell I was going to let another man take her home.

For my sanity, I needed her to agree.

She studied my hand. I could tell that she was weighing the pros and cons of my offer. Finally, she closed the gap, and we shook on it.

Relief flooded my body. My fight mode had been activated merely from the thought of some other guy taking her home. If she hadn't agreed, I would've gone out of my mind.

We finished eating, and out of instinct, I grabbed her garbage with mine. Emerson paused like she was about to protest, but I shot her a look that dared her to fight me about her garbage, and she sighed in response. She followed as I dumped the plates in the trash and pushed through the door, holding it open for her behind me.

I could feel her resistance to that as well, but I just ignored it. I shoved my hands into the front pockets of my jacket and looked both ways as I headed over to my motorcycle.

"Wait a minute." Emerson's voice stopped me in my tracks.

I glanced over my shoulder at her. She was standing a few feet away, shaking her head.

"I'm not getting on that." She waggled her finger in my bike's direction.

"You shook on it," I said as I picked up my helmet and held it out for her.

"Yeah, well...I forgot you ride this thing."

I feigned hurt as I ran my hand over the seat. "Don't talk to Tabitha like that."

She quirked an eyebrow. "Tabitha?"

I nodded. "She's my girl, aren't you?" I changed my voice to make it sound like I was talking to a baby. I blew Tabitha a kiss and then glanced back at Emerson. She looked annoyed but hadn't come any closer. "You shook on it, Em. Come on, you're a woman of your word, right?"

She glowered at me. I could see her inner turmoil as she weighed her desire to keep her word against her desire to tell me off and storm back into the restaurant. I waited, allowing my gaze to be the silent dare she needed.

Suddenly, she let out a loud, exasperated sigh and marched toward me. "Only because I shook on it."

I smiled at her as she grabbed my helmet. "That's the Emerson I know."

She glared at me as she shoved my helmet on her head. "There."

"And this," I said as I shrugged off my leather jacket and held it up for her to slip her arms into.

She flipped the visor open. She looked adorable with her cheeks smooshed together, puckering her lips. Those goddamn lips that I couldn't stop staring at.

"I agreed to have you take me home, and I even put this on." She motioned toward her helmet. "But I'm not wearing your jacket."

I shrugged. "You're putting this on," I said as I shook it

out once more. She was going to learn that I was just as stubborn as she was.

She held my gaze, but it was having the opposite effect on me than she wanted. She wanted me to take her seriously, but all I could think about was how adorable she was. And it was killing me.

"Listen," I said, softening my voice and offering her a half smile. "My gran made me promise to wear a leather jacket when riding. I can only imagine what she would say if she found out I let a girl on my bike and didn't try to protect her." I squinted at her, hoping she would comply. "Help a guy out. A guy who wants to avoid a scolding from his grandmother."

Her gaze softened as she stared at me. Then she frowned and turned to pull her hair away from her neck. "That wasn't fair, you know," she said as she tipped her head ever so slightly in my direction. "Using your grandma to get me to do what you want."

I helped her as she fed her arms through the sleeves, and then I pulled it up onto her shoulders. I stepped back as she zipped up the front and glanced up to meet my gaze.

I had to fight the smile that wanted to emerge at the sight of her wearing my jacket and helmet. In this moment, she felt like she was...mine.

I cursed that thought and turned my attention to Tabitha. "Get on," I said, my voice coming out gruffer than I wanted it to. But my tone was the perfect representation of the turmoil going on inside of me.

Thankfully, Emerson didn't fight me. She swung her leg over Tabitha and settled on the seat. It took all my control to keep my thoughts clean as I motioned for her to scoot back.

She stared at me with a look that said, *are you serious?*

"Yep," I said as I swung my leg over. She scooted as far back as she could go, like the last thing she wanted was to be pressed up against me. Her hands gripped the seat beneath her, and I flicked my gaze to them before sighing. She really was going to fight me the entire ride. I hated and loved how stubborn she was.

I gripped the handles of my motorcycle before I turned the key and started up my bike.

"You're going to want to hold on," I said over my shoulder. Her reply came out muffled, and when she didn't wrap her arms around my waist, I shook my head. She was about to learn real quick. I took off out of the parking lot. From the corner of my eye, I saw her head and shoulders whip back. Suddenly, her arms were around my waist, and her chest pressed into my back. I smiled, enjoying how close she was to me now.

If I didn't keep my focus on the road, I was going to crash. So even though I could feel the warmth of her inner thighs through my jeans, I pushed my desire for her from my head and kept my gaze trained on the road as I sped toward our apartment complex.

It came too soon, and yet, not fast enough. After I punched in the code to the garage, I let go of the handlebars and straightened as I waited for the door to open. I half expected Emerson to climb off and shove my jacket and helmet into my arms before sprinting away.

But she didn't move. When the door was fully open, I leaned forward, caging her in as I made my way to my parking spot. She climbed off after I killed the engine and pulled back. I got off as well while she took off my helmet and jacket.

"Thanks," she said as she handed them over to me.

"Of course." I held the items to my chest and watched as she started to walk away. I didn't want to end on that note, so I called out to her before I could stop myself. "Emerson?"

She stopped walking, and seconds felt like minutes as she turned to face me. "Yeah?"

I needed to say something more coherent than the thoughts running through my mind. I had so many things I wanted to say, but I didn't know how to say any of them. I cursed at my thoughts as I stilled my mind and said the first thing that came out.

"I hope that, maybe someday, we can be friends."

I waited as she kept her focus on the ground. When she didn't respond right away, I started to fear that I'd said the wrong thing. It was true. We'd been friends once. I really hoped we could be friends again. Was everything so broken that she couldn't even imagine we could find a place where friendship could exist between us?

I parted my lips, ready to recant my wish, when Emerson glanced up at me and whispered, "Okay," before she turned and hurried over to the elevator.

I lingered by my bike long after she disappeared. Part of me wanted to get back on my bike and ride until these feelings brewing in my chest disappeared. But if the last few years were any indicator of how good I was at getting over Emerson, I was going to have to ride forever.

So, instead, I decided to type a scathing text to the guys, reaming them out for ditching me with Emerson. They just sent me smiley and kissy face emojis in response. I cursed and shoved my phone into my back pocket as I clung to my jacket and helmet and walked across the parking garage to slam my fist into the up button.

I kept my gaze on the ground as I unlocked my door and walked inside. I was weak. I wanted to look over at Emerson's place, but I forced myself to slam the door and stalk into my bedroom. After changing into my workout clothes, I grabbed my jump rope and headphones before I headed back out to the landing.

I was going to exercise until my muscles gave out. Maybe then I'd forget the feeling of Emerson's body pressed to mine.

Maybe then, I'd forget how I couldn't seem to forget her.

9

EMERSON

"Wait, let me get this straight. You ended up eating lunch with Stone, and then he took you home on his *motorcycle*?" Tilly's voice was so loud that I had to pull the phone away to save my eardrums.

"Yes. That's literally what I just said to you," I said as I sandwiched my phone between my shoulder and cheek, so I could strum a chord I'd just written.

"This is perfect." Tilly's voice was low like she was whispering to herself and hadn't meant for me to hear.

"I'd say it's the exact opposite of perfect," I responded. I contemplated asking her what she meant, but I knew it was safer for me not to pry. Tilly always seemed to have plans for me, and it was better if I didn't know what they were.

Noise from the landing drew my attention to my door, so I stood and made my way over to peek through my peephole. "Are you here?" I asked, not putting it past my best friend to suddenly appear out of thin air.

"Huh?" Her voice echoed in my ear as I squinted to see better.

Suddenly, a very shirtless and sweaty Stone came into view. He was doing some crazy jump rope routine on the landing. My gaze drifted down his chest to his abs. The way the band of his pants slid further and further down his waist each time he jumped had my heart pounding.

Memories of the feeling of his body pressed against mine came rushing back to me, and I had to pull myself away from the door before the whole complex caught fire and all that was left was me, standing in front of my door, staring at Stone.

It would be just my luck.

"Are you there?" Tilly's voice made its way through my cloudy mind, and I blinked a few times to center myself. I vowed right there and then to never look through my peephole, ever again.

"Yeah, I'm here," I whispered.

"What happened? Why do you sound different?"

I cleared my throat. "I don't sound different."

"Ha. Did you just see him?" She paused. "You saw him, didn't you?"

I rolled my eyes. "Can we talk about something else?"

She laughed, telling me that she knew she'd caught me red-handed. Thankfully, she dropped the topic and started going over plans for the rest of the weekend. I had a gig tonight at Festivia, and we were still waiting to hear back from Fusion Boozin' about tomorrow.

She told me that Troy from Night Spirits said I did well and was willing to have me back if a slot opened up. I was a little disappointed that nothing came from the set I played last night. I'd heard whispers that a scout from Cherry Red Records had been there, but no one came looking for me after, and Tilly hadn't mentioned a call or email. She wouldn't be able to keep something like that a secret.

I blew out my breath as I straightened and headed back to my guitar and music. I was struggling to get this song right. Part of me wanted to showcase it tonight, but with the way Stone kept floating in and out of my mind, I was too distracted to focus on it.

"Tilly?" I asked, turning my attention to the phone.

"Yeah?"

"Can I let you go? I'll see you tonight."

"Um-hmm, yeah."

We said our goodbyes. I hung up before I dropped my phone on the couch and then collapsed on the cushions next to it. I closed my eyes and tipped my head back, taking in a deep breath.

I needed a shower. That would help me center my mind and focus. I grabbed my phone and stood. I was in my bathroom, stripped down to just my underwear when I got a text from Tilly.

Tilly: I made you a flaxseed hair serum. It's on your kitchen counter. Use it after your shower.

I sighed as I shook my head. Tilly seemed convinced that it did something for my hair, but I was unsure. She was also superstitious, having me do these strange routines with hopes that it would be the thing that turned my luck around.

I opened my bathroom door. I thought about covering up, but I was only going to be in the kitchen for a second. Besides, I was alone. What did it matter if I walked around topless?

I padded through the living room to the kitchen. I scoured the counters until I found the small Mason jar full of brown goo. I cheered as I reached over my sink and scooped it up. Just then, my gaze flicked up to the window, and my entire body froze.

Stone was standing there, still sweaty and shirtless, staring at me. He looked as frozen as I felt.

I screamed—loud enough to wake generations of my ancestors—and dropped down to the ground. My arm instantly went to cover my breasts even though there was no way he could see them now. I closed my eyes and shook my head as I whispered, "Oh, no. No, no, no." Over and over again.

That didn't just happen. Did it? No, it didn't happen. I didn't just flash my brother's ex-best friend...did I?

I set the jar down, cursing Tilly and her superstitions, and then used both hands to cover my face. I breathed through my nose and out my mouth about a thousand times, before I grabbed the jar and crawled through my apartment into my bathroom, locking the door before I stood.

I stared at myself in the mirror, trying to determine if Stone had really seen everything. The window in the kitchen was small. There was a chance he just got a peek. I shook my head, my entire body flushing in embarrassment. There was no use trying to lie to myself. He'd seen me shirtless. And he'd seen everything.

Me: I just flashed Stone.

I sent the text off to Tilly before I undressed the rest of the way and climbed into the shower. I thought the heat from the water and the lavender soap would make me feel better—it didn't.

My insides were as discombobulated as they were when I got in. I turned off the water and wrapped my hair in a ratty t-shirt. I slipped on my satin robe, made sure I was completely covered, and picked up my phone.

Tilly had blown up my text messages. She sent me demands for more information, GIFs, and emojis all depicting how confused she was. I shot her a quick text that said I'd tell her tonight and that I needed to get ready.

She sent me a grumpy emoji before she sent a thumbs-up.

I channeled all my anxious energy into doing my makeup and hair. With my face done and my hair up in big rollers, I made my way into my room. I spent the next half hour unpacking boxes and hanging my clothes up in the closet. When I got to my orange-and-black-patterned ruffled dress with a deep V, I abandoned the rest of the boxes and got dressed. After accessorizing with a black chunky belt, I headed back into the bathroom to finish getting ready.

I found my white cowboy boots in a box marked *shoes* before grabbing a few necklaces and bracelets. I set my boots by the front door and then sat down on the couch and grabbed my guitar. I kept my oath to myself and didn't peek to see if Stone was still on the landing. I had half a mind to solder the peephole shut.

I got lost in playing and singing. I only stopped when my phone chimed, and I glanced down. Tilly was making her way toward Festivia and she'd see me there. My time slot was earlier tonight, so I placed my guitar into its case.

I had twenty minutes before I had to leave since Festivia was only five minutes down the road from me. I fixed myself a quick bowl of cereal and leaned against the counter while I ate.

Suddenly, Stone's door opened, and he came out wearing his leather jacket. His helmet was perched under his arm as he turned to lock the door. I knew I should pull my gaze away, but I didn't. Instead, I watched him—studied him—as he turned and started to make his way to the elevator.

He stood there, staring down at his phone, and I wondered where he was going. Was he meeting girls? He was probably meeting girls. He was wearing a pair of dark jeans. His hair was styled, and I didn't have to stand next to him to know exactly what he smelled like.

As if he sensed that I was watching him, he turned his

head and met my gaze. I told myself to look away, but my body didn't listen. Instead, I just stood there, holding his gaze. I had so many questions. And for some reason, I thought that studying him would give me answers.

Why did he crush my brother's dreams? What had happened since he walked away from our small town? Had he thought about me? Did he still have the keychain I gave him? Why didn't he ever reach out?

There were times back in high school when I thought he liked me. I'd catch him looking at me like I meant something to him. But he never made a move. I wanted to know if it had been real, or if I'd misread everything.

The elevator doors opened, and Stone pulled his gaze away and glanced inside. He paused before he boarded the car. The doors shut, and he was gone.

I blew out my breath as I dumped the rest of my cereal down the sink and rinsed out my bowl. I wasn't hungry anymore, and it was probably better if I didn't stuff my face before I went onstage.

I grabbed my purse and my guitar before locking up my apartment and taking the elevator down to the first floor. The sun had disappeared, leaving a black sky full of stars. The air was cool, and I appreciated that. I didn't want to show up sweaty and gross for my slot.

The city had come to life. People were wandering the sidewalks either on their way to a dinner reservation or coming from one. I took in a deep breath as I followed the directions on my phone. Festivia was a small bar, but it was bursting with people. The walls were fitted with large accordion doors that had been pushed open, and people were eating inside and out on the patio.

I smiled at the hostess and told her who I was. There was currently a man in a cowboy hat singing into the microphone onstage. She nodded as she waved for me to follow her. I kept close as she weaved in between the tables and the waitresses taking orders.

She took me through to the back and opened a small door. The room held a compact vanity with a chair in front of it. She smiled and said they would come get me when it was time.

I thanked her and sat down, trying to calm my nerves while I waited. I'd just pulled out my guitar when the door opened, and Tilly appeared. She smiled at me as she shut the door.

"I need details," she said before I could even say hello.

I shook my head. "No Stone talk until after my time slot."

She scowled at me before she sighed and nodded. "Fine." She grabbed the only other chair in the room and pulled it close. "I think we have another note from the philanthropist who is your biggest fan."

I frowned. "The who that is my what?"

She looked at me like I had three eyes. "The philanthropist who is your biggest fan."

I raised my eyebrows. "Saying it again doesn't make it make more sense."

She shook her head as she reached into her purse and pulled out a small white envelope. "The guy that paid for your apartment."

My stomach twisted at the reminder. As much as I appreciated that this fan wanted to help, I was still suspicious of his motives. Why did he want to help me? What was he expecting in return? Had Tilly vetted this person? She tended to believe the best in people.

"This was taped to my door when I got home from watching my niece." She handed me the envelope, and I picked it up with the tips of my forefinger and thumb. "Tilly," I said, with the tone of voice my mother used to give me. "Why would you bring this here? What if there's drugs or something in there?"

She stared at me before she rolled her eyes. "There are not drugs in there."

"Did you test it?" I stared at the envelope, fighting the urge to toss it across the room.

She shook her head. "You're so suspicious of everything." She took it from me and pulled the flap out from where the sender had tucked it into the envelope. She pulled out a note along with what looked like a small elephant.

She looked up at me with her lips flat and an annoyed look in her eyes. "Strange lookin' drugs," she said before she flipped the piece of paper over and read the note. "Dear Emerson, In Thailand and India, the elephant is a symbol for luck. I hope you have an amazing performance. Good luck." She looked up at me. "Aww. That's sweet."

I gingerly took the elephant from her and held it in my palm. "That is nice," I admitted.

"See? And you thought it was something nefarious."

"Have you not seen the news? Every day someone is getting abducted or drugged." I slipped the elephant into my guitar case before shutting it. "I'm realistic."

Tilly shook her head. "Well, I choose to believe that there is more good than bad out there. It's all about keeping your aura clean so it welcomes goodness." She leaned back in the chair and sighed. "Alright, show me what you're going to play tonight."

My entire body relaxed as I began to strum my guitar. All the stress from my day just melted away as I closed my eyes and began to sing.

This was my happy place.

This was where I belonged.

10

STONE

I woke the next morning with a crick in my neck. I groaned as I sat up from where I'd passed out on my couch. I managed to get myself into a sitting position with my elbows resting on my knees. My head felt like it weighed a million pounds as I let it hang down, unable to find the strength to lift it up.

I started to massage my neck before moving to my shoulder and wincing. I shouldn't have let Isaac push me to drink that much last night. But I had things that I needed to forget. Namely, the girl that lived next door. She had built a mansion in my mind, and no matter what I did, I couldn't forget her. I was already struggling before I saw her standing topless in her kitchen. Now, she was all I saw when I closed my eyes.

I groaned in frustration when the image of her standing there with her hair falling down her bare shoulders flashed in my mind once more. Her eyes wide. Her skin soft and creamy. And her...

I punched the couch to ground myself as I shoved her from my mind. She wasn't mine to look at like that. She wasn't mine to fantasize about. She would never be mine. And allowing myself to think about her like that was wrong.

She deserved better.

I heaved my body off the couch and stumbled into the bathroom, where I turned the shower on. Fifteen minutes later, I was clean, but my head still felt as if a cloud had taken up residence.

I got out of the shower, dried off, and tied the towel around my waist. I made my way into the kitchen and started some coffee. I leaned against the counter and closed my eyes, dreading today. It was playoff season, and I should have never had that much alcohol.

"Idiot," I said as I opened my eyes and focused on getting a mug from the cupboard. Just as I set it down on the counter next to the coffee machine, my phone buzzed. I walked into the living room and grabbed it off the side table.

Hayden: Hey boss! How was last night?

I sent her a puke-face emoji as I walked back into the kitchen.

Hayden: Haha, I figured from the calls last night.

Me: I called you?

Hayden: Yeah, a few times.

Me: Shoot

Hayden: The package was delivered last night with the note.

Me: You're amazing

She went into breaking down the interviews I had tonight. She told me she'd meet me outside the locker room to remind me.

I sent her a thumbs-up emoji before pressing the side button and the screen went dark. I set the phone down and poured myself a mug of coffee. My gaze drifted over to Emerson's apartment, and I allowed myself to wonder how she felt about my gift.

I'd never had the guts to tell her that my dad tried to pawn the gold keychain she'd given me that night. When he discovered that it wasn't worth anything, he threw it in the street trash can. By the time I'd discovered that it was missing, it was gone.

That was the night I moved out and never spoke to him again. I moved in with Gran and moved on with my life. I hated that he took something that meant so much to her. I knew how much she believed in its luck, and I'd do anything to help her find something to replace it.

Last night, I had Hayden drop off an envelope with an elephant charm in it. I'd studied different forms of lucky charms around the world. And now that I knew where she was, I was determined not to stop until she found the kind of luck she'd given me.

By the time my mug of coffee was finished, I felt better. I changed into a pair of sweats and a sweatshirt before grabbing my jacket, keys, and backpack. I slipped my phone into a zippered pocket as I pulled open the door. I had a busy day.

By the time I got to the stadium, my adrenaline was pumping. I parked in my spot and climbed off my bike. I walked under the awning and punched in the code to get into the stadium. The energy was buzzing when I walked into the locker room. Everyone was talking and laughing as they pumped themselves up for the game tonight.

Coach talked to us before we went into the weight room to warm up our muscles. George and I practiced plays on the field until the rest of the team came out. We went through plays, everyone laser-focused on what Coach wanted us to do.

By the time we went back into the locker room to change, my nerves were at an all-time high. I always got this way before a game. Once I got out on the field, all my anxiety melted away, and it was just me and the ball. But the anticipation before always made my stomach queasy.

We were playing the Pittsburgh Pirates. It started out intense—I was worried that we might not win. But then George and I fell into a rhythm, and we closed the gap. By third quarter, we'd taken the lead.

After every touchdown, I'd throw the ball to the ground and break out into a dance. I could hear the cheer of the crowd as they joined me. I pointed my finger at the camera as I pulled off my helmet and smiled.

God, I loved my job.

We won 27 to 21. When the final buzzer rang, the Tigers gathered together, cheering, chest bumping, and slapping each other's helmets. My heart was pounding as the echo of our victory rang through the stadium.

The locker room was abuzz as we ran inside. Coach went over how well we played, where we struggled, and said that we had a week of work ahead of us. Then he told us to get dressed; it was time for interviews.

I showered and dressed in my suit and tie. Hayden was waiting for me when I walked out of the locker room. She was a short girl with long red hair, which she always pulled back into a braid, and glasses perched on her nose.

She went over my talking points as we walked down the long hallway to the press corridor. Then I smiled for the cameras and avoided Priscilla's provocative looks as I fielded questions. When I was finally done, I was exhausted.

The guys were headed to Fusion Boozin' tonight to celebrate. I brushed them off, telling them that I was too tired. Truth was, I wasn't really interested in doing anything other than lying on the couch and pretending that I didn't care about who lived next door to me. Or the parts of her that I'd seen yesterday.

Hayden was waiting for me when I walked out of the locker room for the second time. I was wearing my leather jacket and had my bag strapped to my back. I nodded at her as she fell into step with me.

"I just heard that Emerson is playing tonight."

I stopped, my entire body responding to the sound of

her name. I glanced down at Hayden, hoping she didn't see my sudden change. If she did, she didn't acknowledge it. "Yeah?"

"I guess she got a spot at Fusion Boozin'." She glanced up at me. "Did you want me to send another charm?"

I pushed my hand through my hair. Crap. The guys were going there. That spelled disaster. "Yeah, let's do a dream catcher." Then I winced. "Do you think you can find one in time?"

Hayden gave me a pointed look. "I'm your assistant. That's my job." She focused on her phone as she typed out *dream catcher.* "Got it. I'll get started looking."

I smiled at her. "Thanks." I'd stopped in the hallway, knowing that I needed to head back to the locker room. I didn't want to just show up at the bar by myself and run into Emerson. The guys gossiped enough. I didn't need them drawing conclusions that I couldn't dig myself out of. It would be better if I showed up with them.

Hayden hurried off to find a dream catcher and get it to her in time. I went back into the locker room and hung out with the guys until everyone was ready. Then we walked out together, each of us getting into our separate cars.

I rode my bike the fifteen minutes to the bar. It was busy when we pulled into the back. Craig, the owner, gave us our own spots. We walked in through the back, past the stage, and filed through the bar. A guy and his band were currently playing. The crowd was either dancing or sitting at the small tables on the outskirts.

A roar sounded when the other patrons realized we'd arrived. We took some time to sign autographs and to get clapped on the shoulder by half-drunk fans thanking us for the win. This was why I avoided going out with the guys. Alone, I was inconspicuous. Together, we were a giant neon sign that read, *Tennessee Tigers*.

Luckily, the crowd's excitement died down, and all of us were settled in the reserved section with our drinks. I kept glancing over at the stage, wondering where Emerson was and when she was going to perform.

It felt like an eternity before she was finally announced. My entire body tensed at the sound of her name on the MC's lips. I wasn't sure where to look, but it felt impossible to pull my gaze from the stage. I sat there like a deer in headlights.

"Dude!" Isaac gripped my shoulders and shook me. "Did that guy just say Emerson?"

I shushed him, but the noise level was too high. Even if he had heard me, I doubted he cared. When Emerson walked out onto the stage dressed in a floral jumper that hugged her in all the right places, the entire table erupted in cheers.

For my teammates who didn't know who she was, George, Isaac, Colt, and Jayden quickly filled them in. Suddenly they were all whooping and hollering. Emerson glanced in our direction, her cheeks pink as she studied us for a moment before recognition passed over her face.

And then her gaze slipped to mine. She held it for a

moment. I knew I should pull back. I knew I shouldn't look at her, but I wanted to. I needed to.

Before I could act, she broke our contact and glanced over at the MC, who turned the stage over to her. She strummed her guitar a few times before she closed her eyes and started singing. The entire bar grew quiet as we listened to her song.

My heart pounded as I watched her sing. Her voice was soft and soothing. When she smiled and nodded to people in the crowd, I felt jealous. I wanted to be the only person she looked at like that.

I growled under my breath as I sat back in my seat. I downed my whiskey and ordered another one. I hated the feelings that were brewing inside of me. I needed to dull them. I needed to dull the pain.

I hated that she looked this beautiful. I hated that I wanted to touch her. I hated that other men in the bar were looking at her like I was. I hated it because they had the chance that I was never going to have. It was torture.

Unable to sit there, wallowing in my self-pity, I excused myself. I needed to get out of here before the walls closed in on me and I could no longer breathe.

I pushed through the crowd until I got to the door that led backstage. I needed to get to my motorcycle and ride until my body returned to its normal temperature. Thankfully, backstage was empty as I walked through. I caught a glimpse of Emerson still on the stage, but she'd transitioned to a new song.

I knew I shouldn't look, but I couldn't help but stare as I walked past her.

I felt my foot come down on something followed by a feminine, "Ouch!"

I whipped my gaze over to see Tilly, Emerson's friend, standing there with a pained expression on her face. She had lifted her foot and was holding it with her hand. "Stone?" she asked.

"I'm so sorry," I whispered as I glanced down to her foot. "Are you okay?"

She nodded as she rubbed her foot a few times before setting it back down on the ground. "I didn't know that you were going to be here."

She was holding a folder, and I could see some feathers peeking out from the bottom. I wondered if it was the dream catcher that Hayden had found.

"Yeah, I'm here with a few of the guys."

She glanced toward the stage like she was looking for them in the crowd. "That's amazing," she whispered.

I frowned. Did Emerson want us here? "Yeah?" I asked.

She snapped her gaze back to me, her eyes wide like she hadn't meant to say anything. "I—er—umm." She blew out her breath. "I just think it's awesome that an NFL team is supporting a local artist." She smiled a bit too wide. Like she was plotting something.

"Really?"

Her smile remained for a few more seconds before she sighed and waved toward Emerson. "Poor girl is trying. She's worked so hard to get discovered, but it seems like she can't ever catch a break." Tilly hugged the folder to her chest. "I just want the best for her."

I glanced toward Emerson. Tilly's words were rolling around in my mind. "You think that if she's tied to an NFL team, she might draw attention to herself?"

Tilly glanced over at me. "Or tied to an NFL player..." She dragged her gaze over me before meeting my eyes.

"Me?" I asked, pointing to myself.

She shrugged. "It wouldn't have to be for real. And you have history. You'll protect her." Then she narrowed her eyes. "Right?"

If she only knew how much I wanted to protect Emerson. My mind was whirling. "So, you think I should get into a relationship with Emerson?" I needed her to be clear. There was no way I wanted to misinterpret what she was saying.

She raised her finger. "A fake relationship, yes."

I glanced over at the stage. "Does she want this?" I was having a hard time believing that Emerson would be up for dating me. I could only assume Emerson didn't know.

"Eh." Tilly's response solidified my thoughts. I glanced over at her, hating that I wanted this as much as I did. Tilly shot me a smile. "Emerson can be convinced."

Reality came crashing down around me. As much as Tilly hoped Emerson would agree to this, I knew better. Emerson could barely talk to me, much less fake a relationship with me. This was over before it started.

The desire to leave grew even stronger. I wished I'd never stopped to talk to Tilly. I'd just gone on an emotional rollercoaster that came crashing to Earth in a fiery ball of disappointment. I pushed my hand through my hair, gripped my motorcycle helmet, and shrugged.

"She'll never say yes," I said. "But if you can convince her, I might be willing to give it a shot." I gave Tilly a forced smile and turned. I wasn't waiting for her to say anything more.

I headed to the back door and pushed it open. Darkness surrounded me as I walked over to my bike and climbed on. I shoved my helmet on my head, started the engine, and peeled out.

Streetlights and people whipped past me as I made my way down the road. I was on autopilot until I ran out of gas and pulled into a gas station.

As I stood there, filling my tank, I let my thoughts return to my conversation with Tilly. I couldn't lie to myself, I wanted this. I wanted to pull Emerson close. I wanted to hold her hand. I wanted to be important to her...even if it was all fake.

But she was never going to say yes, and I was going to be tortured by watching her fake a relationship with someone else. From the determined look on Tilly's face, this was happening whether it was with me or not.

I was about to enter my personal circle of hell. I was her neighbor, and that meant I would have a front-row seat to her relationships, fake or otherwise.

And I wasn't going to do anything to stop it. Even if it hurt, it didn't matter. I wasn't going to move. I was here to stay.

The gas pump clicked, so I turned back to my bike and pulled the nozzle from my gas tank. My phone buzzed in my back pocket. I screwed the cap on the gas tank before I pulled my phone from my pocket.

George: Dude. Get back here. Someone's creeping on your girl.

11

EMERSON

The rush that I got from the audience's cheers as I finished my set left my cheeks warm and my heart pounding. I bowed once more as I grabbed the neck of my guitar and headed offstage.

Tilly was there to greet me. She pulled me into a hug. My ears were ringing, so I couldn't quite make out what she was saying, but from the tone in her voice and the way her eyes lit up, she was happy for me.

"I think that was the best set ever," she said.

Her words finally made their way through the cloud that had settled in my brain. "Really?" I asked as I made my way into the dressing room and over to my guitar case, which I'd propped up in the corner.

"Amazing, girl." She paused, and I glanced up at her. "I can feel the contract coming soon."

I smiled at her, but when I turned my attention back to

my guitar, that smile faded. I knew that she was trying to hype me up, but I'd been here before. I thought my chance was coming, but every performance fell flat. No scouts. No contracts. No forward movement.

I loved singing. I loved pouring my heart into my music. But I hated that even though I wanted it to turn into something, it never did. I worried that the crushing defeat would eventually stomp out my love for what I was doing.

I forced those thoughts from my mind as I snapped the clasps of the case into place and wrapped my fingers around the handle before I stood. "Well, let's not get ahead of ourselves. We'll just take it night by night." I gave her a smile. "It's a game of odds. Eventually, it'll happen."

Tilly returned my smile, but there was a glint in her eyes that I'd never seen before. I narrowed my eyes at her. She was up to something.

"What?" I asked slowly.

She wiggled her eyebrows before hooking her arm through mine. "Let's put your guitar in my car and then come back and get a drink." She started guiding me through the room to the door.

I paused as I looked down at her. "Are you trying to get me drunk?"

She shrugged as we headed toward the hallway that led to the back door. "So, what if I am?"

I rolled my eyes. "Whatever you are plotting, the answer is no."

She laughed as she held the door so I could walk through. "You haven't heard my idea."

I shook my head as we walked over to her car. I waited at the trunk while she opened the driver's door and pulled the trunk release. "I don't need to hear it. I already know it's crazy."

I aimlessly looked around at the cars around us. I'd seen Stone in the crowd, and I half expected to see his motorcycle parked out here. But from my quick survey, it didn't look like he was here. Had I imagined it?

No. I'd seen him. His gaze was dark and piercing as he stared back at me. Even the memory of his intense gaze made my heart pound. I swallowed, hoping that was all it took to regulate my body temperature as I turned back to Tilly.

She'd come back and pulled the trunk open. I set my guitar inside, and she shut the trunk and turned to face me. "I come up with great ideas," she said, completely oblivious to the mini mental breakdown I just went through when I let my thoughts turn to Stone and the way he made me feel.

Thank goodness my best friend couldn't read minds.

"I beg to differ," I said as I followed her back into the bar.

We made our way to the bar, where Tilly ordered me something fruity and full of alcohol. I studied her, contemplating if I should change the order. I didn't want to get so drunk that I had to show up at The Jumping Bean tomorrow completely hungover. But I also couldn't keep my thoughts away from Stone. Maybe some booze would help with that.

When the bartender slid the drink into my hand, I took it. The alcohol hit me like a ton of bricks as soon as I took the first sip. Eventually, my body relaxed, and all I could taste was the fruit.

"This is amazing," I yelled at Tilly, who had already ordered a second round of drinks.

"Right?" she replied. She was dancing to the music.

I hopped off my barstool and joined her. We were laughing as we bumped into each other. The second drink was down, and my inhibitions were completely gone. I was dancing with Tilly and everyone around me.

A guy who I'd seen at my previous shows appeared next to me. His arm slipped around my waist as he pulled me closer. We danced together in a way I didn't normally like, but I didn't care. I was drunk, and I wanted to forget Stone and his dark blue eyes as they stared at me during my set and yesterday afternoon when I stood topless in my kitchen.

He'd seen my breasts. And I hated that I wanted to know what he thought. He was so unreadable that I was never going to find out.

"I wanted to tell you how talented I think you are," the mysterious guy said as he leaned forward. His breath was hot and sticky on my skin.

"Thanks," I said. I moved to the side, but my foot hooked on someone else's, and suddenly I was falling forward.

Mystery guy's arm tightened around me as he kept me upright. I giggled and looked sheepishly up at him.

"Sorry," I said. My words were slurred, and my tongue felt like molasses in my mouth.

He didn't look put off as he smiled down at me. "Name's Brett."

I nodded. "Nice to meet you, Brett. I'm Emerson." I stuck my hand out, and he laughed as he took it.

"I know that." Then he looked sheepish. "I promise I'm not a stalker, but I've come to every one of your sets." He gave me an embarrassed smile.

He was cute. He had dirty blond hair that was tousled in a purposeful way. He had dark brown eyes, and they were inviting as he studied me. He looked like the perfect guy to help me forget Stone and my stupid thoughts.

"I don't think you're a stalker," I whispered as I leaned forward. I wiggled my eyebrows and stared up at him through my eyelashes. I was going to flirt with this guy until Stone was a distant memory.

"Is it creepy if I say that I'm your biggest fan?" he asked.

He looked so bashful and adorable that I reached forward and pinched his cheek. Not something that I would normally do, but I was throwing all my inhibitions out of the window.

"That's adorable," I said as I reached up and pinched his other cheek.

He was smiling down at me. I released his cheeks but kept

my hands on his face. Suddenly, I felt the warmth of his palms on my waist as he rested them just above my hips. Then, he slid them ever so slightly to my back and pulled me closer.

My gaze drifted to his lips as my body stilled. I wanted to kiss him. But not because I *wanted* to kiss him. I just wanted to forget Stone. And the best way to do that was to entangle myself with someone else.

Or at least, that was what I thought I should do.

"Emerson," Brett whispered. The tone of his voice sent shivers down my back.

I leaned forward, wondering if he was going to meet my lips. My head was swimming, and my eyesight was wonky, but I swear he leaned in as well.

"Excuse me," a deep voice sounded beside us. A deep, familiar voice.

Before I could even look to see who it was, my hands were pulled from Brett's face, and suddenly I was spun against a tall, muscular chest. I parted my lips to protest, but Brett beat me to it. "Hey, dude."

I glanced up to see Stone grip Brett's shoulder. "I'm going to stop you right there," Stone said, his voice low and menacing. "It's never going to happen." Stone's hand found my waist and pulled me close. "She's not available."

I frowned and parted my lips to protest, but Stone didn't wait for me to respond. Instead, he held me as he moved me away from Brett. I wondered where Tilly had gone. I wiggled, trying to break his hold on me, but he was stronger.

He kept me close as he danced us into the corner, away from the crowd.

I pressed on his chest, trying to get away, but it was futile. He wasn't interested in letting me go.

"Will you just dance with me?" he finally asked. Both of his arms were wrapped around me, and I was closer to him than I'd ever been before.

The alcohol and his cologne had my head swirling. I wanted to fight, but I was too tired. I collapsed against his chest, exhausted and ready to feel normal again. I felt his arms relax as well, but he didn't release me. Instead, his right hand found my left, and he cradled it as he brought it up next to his chest and swayed side to side.

"What are you doing?" I finally managed out. I glanced up at him to see that he was staring straight ahead.

"Stopping you from making a mistake."

I frowned. "That's not your job."

He flicked his gaze down at me. "I don't want it to be my job, but you're making it impossible to ignore you."

I sighed as I dropped his gaze and glanced around. "I don't need you to protect me. I've been just fine on my own." I felt his body tense. His response intrigued me, but I didn't have the courage to ask him what it meant.

"That guy wanted more from you, Emerson," he said, his voice low and threatening like just the thought of another guy wanting to be with me was causing him pain.

He was being ridiculous. He wasn't my boyfriend, my brother, or my...anything. He needed to let me live my life.

"You don't think I know that?" I glanced up at him. "Maybe I want him to want me."

Stone's jaw flinched. His gaze was deep and raw, and it made me want to pull back, but I didn't. Instead, I remained, daring him to break my gaze.

"You want him?" Stone asked. His tone had turned daring.

I swallowed, my mouth feeling dry and sticky. I hated drinking, and I hated that I was drunk during this conversation. I would be able to hold my ground so much better if my thoughts weren't so jumbled. "Maybe."

He studied me. "Have you talked to Tilly?"

I frowned. I had not anticipated him changing the subject like that. "Yeah, I've talked to Tilly."

He paused and searched my gaze as if he were looking for an answer to a question. But I didn't know what that question was. I pulled my eyebrows together as I waited for further explanation, but it never came. He pulled his gaze from mine and focused on something above my head.

A drunk group of women came our way, and I felt his hand tighten on my back as he pulled me closer and turned me slightly. Almost like he wanted to protect me from their flailing arms and boisterous voices.

I felt very confused with what was happening. I could've sworn I hadn't seen his motorcycle, and I hadn't noticed him sitting with his friends at the end of my set. Had he always been here? Maybe he'd left earlier, but now he was back. Why was he back?

Was it for me?

I shook my head. That was a stupid thought. Of course, he hadn't come back for me. That would be ridiculous. Maybe he left to pick up a friend...or a girl?

My stomach churned at that thought. I didn't like it at all, so I tossed it out of my mind. No, he probably left to pick up a friend and just got back. That was the story I was going to tell myself.

The last notes of the song slowly faded away, and the crowd erupted into cheers. I pulled away from Stone and turned to face the stage, clapping and cheering along with everyone else. Stone's hand lingered on my waist for a moment longer than expected, but by the time I turned to face him, he'd removed it and was waving to his teammates who were still sitting at the reserved table.

Before I could say anything, he left my side to join them. Brett had disappeared, and I was now alone. I glanced through the crowd. Where was Tilly? After a few minutes of dodging dancers and drunk men, I finally found her making out with a guy I'd never seen before.

I cleared my throat, hoping that would get her attention —I was wrong. I tapped her shoulder, and she finally pulled away from the guy and glanced up at me.

"Emerson," she said, her voice slurred. She pressed on the guy's shoulders and moved to stand. She took one step toward me, but her legs gave out, and suddenly she stumbled into my arms.

I was almost too late to catch her, but thankfully, I was a

bit more sober than her. I stumbled but stayed upright as I held my friend in my arms.

"Tilly," I said.

"I'm so sorry, Emerson," she said as she attempted to get her feet under her.

I didn't like the way I felt. My head was cloudy. My stomach hurt. My interaction with Stone had me confused, and all I wanted to do was go home and crawl under my covers. "Can we go home?" I asked.

She stared up at me with her eyes wide. Then she nodded. "Yeah."

I turned until we were hip to hip. I wrapped my arm around her waist to help her stay upright. We shuffled through the crowd, using each other as support until we got to the front door. I moved to push the door open, but Stone's voice stopped me.

"Let me give you a ride home," he said in a way that told me he wasn't really open to negotiation.

I wanted to say no. I wanted him to stay away. But I was too tired, and I was ready to be home, so I just nodded. He studied me for a moment before he moved to pick up Tilly. She gasped, but when she saw Stone, she wrapped her arms around his neck and rested her head on his shoulder.

"Wait here for me," he said. He held my gaze, and my knees turned weak from the desperate look in his eyes. All I could do was nod. He studied me for a moment longer before he pushed through the door and walked around the building. I rested against the wall, closing my eyes as the coolness of the brick seeped through to my skin.

I did not feel good. My body felt hot, and my stomach churned. I hated that I drank this much. I was never going to do it in the future.

"Ready?" Stone's voice broke through my thoughts.

I opened my eyes to see him studying me. I nodded, and as I moved to take a step, my leg gave way, and I stumbled to catch myself. Stone's arms were around my waist and under my knees before I knew what was going on.

He pulled me to his chest like I was weightless. "Whoa," he said, softly. "I've got you."

I wanted to fight him. I wanted to tell him to put me down. That I didn't need his help. But I was too tired to fight him, and his arms wrapped protectively around me felt too good.

I'd be stronger tomorrow. Tonight, I was going to let him carry me to Tilly's car. I was going to let him take care of me. I could feel his heart pound against my arm. I leaned my head against his shoulder, the warmth of his body washed over me in a way that felt like home. Like this was where I was meant to be.

When he got to Tilly's car, he gently put my feet onto the ground and pulled open the passenger door. He helped me sit, and I turned to buckle my seatbelt, but he beat me to it. He pulled on the latch plate and leaned forward to slide it into the buckle.

His cologne filled my senses, and I leaned my head back and murmured, "You smell so good."

He hesitated as he hovered over me. "I do?"

I nodded. "It's not fair. You smell like a Greek god."

He chuckled as he pulled back and shut my door. I kept my eyes closed as he opened the driver's door and started the engine. I wanted to ask him what he was going to do about his motorcycle, but I was too tired to talk.

Somewhere in the cloud that was my brain, I heard him ask Tilly where she lived. She said something about having her license in her purse. I gave her a weak goodbye when Stone pulled up to her apartment and climbed into the back to help her out. She mumbled something about calling me tomorrow, and I raised my hand to her in acknowledgement.

I was jostled awake when Stone got back into the driver's seat. I moaned but kept my eyes closed as he pulled out of the parking lot. I wasn't sure how long it took before he pulled into our garage and turned off the engine.

"We're here," he whispered.

I nodded and moved to unbuckle my seatbelt. By the time he opened my door, I'd managed to find the release and push on it. I turned to climb out of the car by myself, but he shook his head.

"I've got you," he said as I felt his arms slide under my knees and around my back.

He lifted me up, and the desire to fight him never came. Instead, I rested against his chest like this was where I belonged.

"You're not fair," I mumbled into his neck.

I could feel the rumble of his laugh followed by the sound of the car door closing. "I'm not fair?" he asked.

I shook my head against his shoulder. "You're always around." I sighed. "Why are you always around?"

"I'm around?" he asked. The elevator chimed.

"Always," I whispered.

"Would you be happier if I left?"

"No," I said, drawing out the word. "No. You left once." I hiccupped as the memories of him leaving washed through me. I still didn't understand what happened between him and Cayden. I had a hard time believing that he just stole my brother's scholarship. It didn't match the reality that I'd lived. I'd seen their friendship.

He was quiet for a moment. I cracked an eye and glanced up just to make sure he was still there. "I'm sorry. I wanted to tell you, but..." He didn't finish his thought. After the elevator rang and he carried me out, he never brought it back up.

Now on our landing, he set me down on my feet. "Think you can make it inside?"

I opened my eyes and stared at my door. It felt like it was a million miles away. But I didn't want him to think that I was weak, so I nodded. "I got this," I mumbled.

Apparently, I didn't have it. Seconds later, he wrapped his arm around my waist and pulled me against him. "Let me help," he said.

I motioned to my purse and told him the keys were in

there. He dug around for a moment before emerging triumphant. After the door was unlocked, he helped me inside. I thought he was going to leave me as soon as I crossed the living room, but he stayed by my side as he walked me into my room.

I collapsed on my bed, flopping back while my legs dangled off the edge. "Help me get into my pajamas," I said as I lifted my arm and let it drop to show him how tired I was. When he didn't answer, I curled to the side. "It's not like you haven't seen my boobs." I closed my eyes. "You haven't said anything about that. Were they that hideous?"

It felt like an eternity before I heard the sound of my dresser drawers opening and closing.

"Sit up," he commanded, his voice suddenly next to me.

I obeyed. After unbuttoning my jumper, I pulled it down around my waist. I moved to unhook my bra, but his voice was raspy when he said, "Don't."

I glanced up at him and saw heat in his gaze as he held up my shirt. I studied him. His expression was pained as he helped me slip my arms through the shirt and pulled it over my head.

As soon as my head was through, I returned my gaze to him, but he didn't look at me again.

He helped me slip out of the jumper the rest of the way. Then he knelt in front of me before sliding my feet into the matching pair of shorts. My skin warmed under his gaze as he pulled the shorts up my legs and stopped just before my thighs.

"Can you get them the rest of the way?" he asked. His voice was deep, and he didn't look up at me.

"Yeah," I said as I stood slightly and shimmed the shorts up the rest of the way. Now dressed in my pajamas, I climbed up to my pillows and snuggled under my comforter. The whole world melted away as I lay there.

"I'll be right back," Stone said and left before I could say anything.

I wasn't sure if he returned. I thought I heard someone moving around in my room, but by the time I could get my eyes open, my room was empty.

I settled back into my pillows, closed my eyes, and passed out.

12

STONE

I slept like shit.

I tossed and turned in my bed all night. I wanted to say that it was from the adrenaline still coursing through my veins after yesterday's game, but I knew better.

I couldn't sleep because I couldn't stop thinking about Emerson.

This was torture.

At seven, I finally ripped my eyes open, pulled off my comforter, and slipped into my gym shorts. I needed to exercise, or the feelings that were coursing through my veins were going to consume me.

I grabbed my jump rope and headed out onto the landing. I blared my music in my headphones, and thirty minutes later, I was covered in sweat and my legs were numb. I went inside, grabbed a glass of water, and took a shower.

I was out the door by eight. Thankfully, George drove my motorcycle here last night so I didn't have to head back to Fusion Boozin' to get it. I walked into the locker room at nine. Even though we won last night, coach was going to work us hard today. By the time practice was over, I'd finally cleared my mind enough to focus on something other than Emerson.

The guys tried to tease me in the locker room, but thankfully, one look from me and they shut up. I showered and changed. Then I grabbed my jacket and helmet and headed out to the parking lot where I climbed on my bike and headed to China Cavern for some to-go lo mein.

They knew me there, and as soon as I walked in, they had my order started. Fifteen minutes later, I was leaving with a plastic bag full of food. I rode home and tapped my foot while I waited for the elevator to come down to the parking garage.

I rode the elevator to my floor and stepped out onto the landing. I nearly ran right into Emerson, who had come up the stairs, but thankfully, I caught myself before that happened.

"Sorry," she said as she sidestepped me and my bag of food. She was wearing a green polo with The Jumping Bean embroidered on it. In her hand, she was carrying a hat with the same logo. Her hair was flattened like she'd been wearing the hat all day.

I pulled the bag of food out of her way and smiled

sheepishly. "No harm, no foul." I lifted the bag and held the warm food against my chest.

When Emerson didn't leave right away, I lingered. She looked like she had something she wanted to say. I must be a glutton for punishment, 'cause I wanted to hear it.

"I wanted to thank you for what you did for me last night." Her cheeks flushed as she glanced at everything else but me. "And thanks for the pain meds and water on my nightstand. I didn't even notice that you'd brought it in." She flicked her gaze toward me before studying the ground.

"Sure. I was happy to help." There was so much more that I wanted to say, but I couldn't seem to find the words.

She glanced up at me and held my gaze for a moment before she sighed and motioned toward her door. "I should get going. I've got to make dinner, and I'm exhausted." She leaned toward me, her scent wafting with the movement. "Don't let me drink like that again."

"I have enough food for a family of four. Wanna eat dinner with me?" I held up the food as proof. When I realized what I'd just asked, I silently cursed myself. I needed to backtrack. "I mean, if you want."

She eyed my food and then her gaze drifted to my door. She chewed her bottom lip and I could see the unrest rushing through her. She wanted to say no but I could tell she was hungry with the way she was staring at the bag of food.

"Come on," I said as I nodded toward my door. "It's just food." I started walking, praying that she'd follow me. When

I got to my door, I grabbed my keys from my pocket, slipped the key into the lock, and turned. I peeked over my shoulder to see that Emerson was still standing there.

I took that as a good sign. I pushed open my door and walked into the kitchen. After setting the food down on the counter, I walked back to the open door and glanced out. Emerson was chewing her thumbnail now.

I waved at her. "Come on. I won't bite." I folded my arms and leaned against the doorframe. "It's just dinner, Em."

She narrowed her eyes before she sighed and dropped her arms to her side. "Fine." She crossed the space between us and paused right before she walked past me. "It's just dinner."

I watched as she entered my apartment. I was silently cheering inside. I nodded as I moved to follow her, grabbing the door handle to swing the door shut. "Yep, just dinner," I replied.

I hurried around her as she made her way into the kitchen. I opened a cupboard. "You can get a plate here," I said as I motioned toward Gran's floral plates.

Emerson pulled one down and glanced at the design. "I never pegged you for a floral china kind of guy."

I laughed as I got a plate as well. "It's my Gran's. In fact, this whole apartment is hers. I'm watching it while she's on a cruise."

Emerson raised her eyebrows. "Your Gran?"

I nodded. "Yeah. She and I rebuilt our relationship after

I left my dad's house. I needed a place to stay, and she welcomed me in with open arms." I paused, a smile spreading across my lips at the memories that flooded my mind. "It was the first time I felt like I could live without strings attached."

Emerson was hugging the plate to her chest as she watched me. I couldn't quite tell what she was thinking, and I wasn't sure I wanted to know. We had history, and I could only imagine my words were bringing back some uncomfortable memories.

"I'm sorry," she whispered.

I'd set my plate down on the counter and started the process of untying the plastic bag so I could pull out the white to-go boxes. "For what?" I asked.

She shrugged. "For my parents kicking you out. I know you wanted my house to be a safe place to land."

I opened the sesame chicken and got sauce on my fingers. I glanced up at her. Her words hit me harder than I think she realized. "It's okay," I said as I rounded the counter and turned on the faucet.

"Was it?" she asked, leaning forward and catching my gaze. "You and Cayden were inseparable, and you needed a safe place. I'm sorry my parents weren't that for you."

I turned off the water as I chewed on her words. I shook off my hands before grabbing the towel hanging from the oven handle. After my hands were dry, I moved back over to finish opening the containers of food.

"Thanks," was all I could think to say. Truth was, it

hadn't been her decision to make. Her parents were the ones who told me to leave. She was collateral damage from their desire to make their son into a football star. I hated that for her. "You're sweet to care."

Her gaze landed on me once more. She studied me like she had more she wanted to say, but we didn't have that kind of relationship. Truth was, I didn't know how to define our relationship. The girl I knew in high school? My ex-best-friend's sister? And what was I to her?

Not wanting to get into too deep a conversation, I decided to pivot. "Tell me about your music," I said as I dumped some chicken lo mein onto my plate.

She'd just filled her plate with rice and sesame chicken. Some of the sauce had gotten on the handle of her spoon and on her fingers. She licked them as she watched me.

"I tried the college route," she said.

"Didn't work?"

She shook her head. "Turns out the only thing I'm good at is singing." She sighed. "And even then, I feel like nothing I do is good enough." She added some white rice to her plate and then picked it up.

I paused, taking the time to stare at her. I wanted her to know how ridiculous that was. "That's not true," I said. My tone had come out deep and commanding. She had to know that was a lie. "From what I've seen, you're incredible."

She held my gaze. Her eyes were wide as she studied me. Was she shocked by my words? They were true, and I would say them over and over again until she started to believe them.

"Follow me," I said, taking my plate overflowing with food over to the living room and setting it down on the coffee table. I needed to focus on something other than Emerson. "Want a soda?" I asked as I straightened and turned to head back to the fridge.

"What do you have?"

I listed off what I could remember having and she picked a Sprite. I grabbed a Coke. By the time I got back to the living room, she was sitting on the chair perpendicular to the couch. I set her drink down on the coffee table by her plate before collapsing on the couch.

The sound of the tabs cracking filled the air. We kept quiet as we ate. I didn't realize how hungry I was until the first bite passed my lips. Then I was unstoppable.

Emerson ate a few bites before she set her plate down. She wiped her lips with a napkin and glanced over at me. "What about you? I mean, I know you have the Tigers, but is there anything else?"

"Like what?" I asked through a mouthful of food.

Emerson's cheeks flushed as she dropped her gaze. She picked up her fork and skewered a piece of chicken. She slipped it into her mouth and chewed thoughtfully. "Like... your personal life?" She glanced over at me.

Was she asking me if I was dating anyone? That was cute. I chuckled and shook my head. "I'm not dating anyone if that's what you're asking."

She raised her eyebrows. "Really?"

"Did you know that I was voted MEP last year?"

She frowned. "MEP?"

"Most eligible player." Then I paused. "Player as in football player. Not player in the dating sense." Why had this been the first time I realized how ridiculous that sounded? The last thing I wanted people to think was that I was out dating anyone and everyone. That wasn't my style.

"I figured that," she said, her lips tipping up into a shy smile. "And no, I didn't know that you were voted MEP."

I shrugged. Silence fell between us. I glanced over at her, wondering why she hadn't offered the same information.

"And you?" I asked as I spun my fork around in my lo mein.

"Me?"

I was in the middle of chewing, so I just nodded.

She sighed as she slumped forward. "No. I'm not dating anyone." She took a sip of her soda.

As much as those words caused my heart to sing, I was confused. Why wasn't she dating anyone? She was the complete package. She was gorgeous, smart, funny, talented. The rest of the male population must have their heads in the sand. She should have guys knocking down her door. Even though that thought made my skin prick with jealousy, it still pissed me off that it wasn't happening.

Her gaze drifted over to me. She must have seen my

confused expression because she just shrugged. "I mean, I've dated, but nothing lasted."

"Why not?" I asked as I picked up my drink and took a big swig.

She pushed some rice around on her plate with her fork. "I guess I have this curse of comparing my relationships to what my grandparents had. Nothing ever seems to measure up."

I was jealous that Emerson had such an amazing example of a loving relationship. My parents seemed to show affection by beating and leaving each other. My thoughts shifted to the keychain she gave me the night I showed up with a bloodied face. Shame that I lost her gift rushed through me, and suddenly, I needed to change the subject. I didn't want her to ask me where it was.

I didn't want to have to tell her that it was gone.

Emerson's phone chimed, and I blew out my breath as I watched her pull her phone from her pocket. She studied the screen with a frown before she glanced up at me.

"Tilly's here. She's hoping she can get her car from you."

I stood and made my way into the kitchen and fished her keys from the bowl I'd set them in when I got back last night. "Yep," I said as I held them up in the air.

Emerson nodded and typed on her phone, but a knock sounded on my door before she finished. I rounded the counter peninsula and pulled open the door. Tilly's smile was wide as she nodded at me.

"How's it going, Stone?" she asked. She didn't wait for

an invitation. She just pushed past me and scanned the room until her gaze landed on Emerson.

"Good, you're both here," she said as she moved to drop down onto the couch right where I'd been sitting.

"Come on in," I said as I moved to shut the door behind her. I motioned toward the food on the counter. "Are you hungry, Tilly?" I asked.

She glanced up at me and then to the boxes of food. She shook her head and waved her hand. "I grabbed some fast food after work. I'm stuffed." She leaned forward, her focus trained on Emerson.

Emerson had pulled back slightly as she stared at her friend. "What is that look for?" she asked before flicking her gaze to me.

"I had a genius idea, and I want you to agree with it," Tilly said as she leaned forward and grabbed a piece of sesame chicken off of Emerson's plate.

Emerson looked uneasy. "Okay," she said slowly.

Tilly glanced over at me before she patted the seat next to her. "Sit," she commanded.

Tilly was tiny but mighty. I moved to join her because I didn't want to see what would happen if I tried to defy her. She looked at me and then studied Emerson, who was watching her with wide eyes.

"I already talked to Stone about this"—Emerson snapped her gaze to me—"but I wanted to have the two of you together when I pitched this to Emerson." She smiled sheepishly at her friend.

"Tilly." Emerson's voice was low and full of warning.

"I haven't finished." Tilly paused for what felt like an eternity before she sucked in her breath. "I think the two of you should fake a relationship."

"Tilly!" Emerson's face turned red as she stared at her friend. She glanced over at me with an apologetic expression. "I'm so sorry. You do not have to do that."

"Hear me out." Tilly raised her hands. "You need the visibility. Linking yourself with someone famous would get eyes on you."

Emerson's face reddened. "I don't need a famous person to help me." Her voice was soft, and my heart hurt for her. I knew what it was like to feel like your life was hanging in the balance as you waited for someone to finally believe in you.

"I'll do it," I said. The words echoed as both girls turned to look at me. Emerson's eyes were wider than I'd ever seen them.

"You don't have to, because I'm not doing this." Emerson stood abruptly. She knocked into her plate, almost flinging it to the ground, but she caught it before it fell. "I'm sorry, I have to go," she whispered as she made her way through my apartment and opened the front door.

I watched her until she disappeared onto the landing, then I turned to look at Tilly. The last thing I needed was for Emerson to pull away from me. She was already so distant. I was gradually chipping away at her cold exterior, and I didn't need her to retreat again.

"I'll talk to her," Tilly said as she patted my knee. She closed the front door behind her, and I was left in my apartment alone.

Unable to sit with all the nervous energy vibrating through my body, I stood and began pacing back and forth. I thought about checking how things were going through the peephole, but decided that it would only make me more anxious. So I focused on trying to think about anything other than Emerson suddenly hating me more than she already did.

Seconds felt like hours, but eventually, my front door opened and Emerson and Tilly appeared. Tilly was smiling, and Emerson looked stoic as she stood behind her friend.

I stopped pacing and turned my attention to them.

Tilly pumped her fists in the air. "Operation Get Emerson Discovered is a go!"

13

EMERSON

1 5 hours later and I still felt unsure about Tilly's plan. When I texted her and tried to use my family and what they would think as an excuse, she sidestepped my worries by saying all I had to do was tell them I was using Stone for his fame, and they would definitely be on board. I parted my lips to protest, but then closed them. She did have a point.

She also promised me that I'd only have to fake date Stone for a few games and a few shows. All we needed was to get the press and tabloids talking about me. A talent scout would have to take notice. Then I could break things off with Stone once the ball was already rolling.

I hated the idea that I needed to use Stone to start my career, but he seemed willing, and I was desperate. I'd already tried to get discovered the organic way, but it seemed like nothing was working. It was fake a relationship with Stone Walker or accept my fate as a barista at The Jumping Bean forever.

"What can it hurt?" I repeated Tilly's question under my breath as I pushed against the counter and straightened. There was a lull at work. And when things slowed, all my thoughts and fears came rushing back into my mind.

"What can't hurt?" Rachel, my co-worker, asked as she dumped that morning's coffee out into the sink. She rinsed the pot out and returned it to the coffee machine to make a fresh batch.

I glanced over at her. "Nothing."

She frowned at me. "You just muttered something under your breath." She narrowed her eyes. "Are you keeping a secret from me?"

"Nope," I lied.

She eyed me. I could tell that she didn't believe me, but I just smiled at her and turned my attention back to the front of the store. What did it mean to fake date someone? What were the rules? Were we supposed to kiss? People who dated kissed. Would people suspect that my relationship with Stone wasn't real if we didn't?

If we kissed, how much kissing was required? Did I even want to?

"Emerson?" a deep voice invaded my thoughts.

I yelped and turned, heat flooding my entire body as I pushed the thoughts of kissing Stone from my mind. "Yep?" I asked, focusing my attention on the customer standing in front of me. "Brett?"

Brett was standing there wearing a pair of jeans and a lime-green construction shirt. He looked embarrassed as he pushed his hand through his hair and met my gaze. "Yeah. Sorry, did I startle you?"

I needed someplace for my nervous energy to go, so I brushed off the counter with my hand. "Sorry, I was just lost in thought."

He studied me. "Was it a song?"

"Huh?"

"You said you were lost in thought. I thought, maybe you were thinking about a new song."

I pinched my lips together as my mind returned to what I had actually been thinking about. There was no way I was going to speak those words, so I just slowly nodded. "Yep. That's what I was thinking about. Lyrics."

He shoved his hands into his front pockets. "Amazing." Then he shrugged. "Can I hear some of it?"

It was like I'd picked up a shovel and was digging a deeper and deeper hole for myself. "You know, I don't really like sharing my songs before they are solidified in my mind."

He nodded. "Ah. Gotcha." Then he smiled. It was soft and uncomplicated, unlike Stone.

I glanced around. "Did you come for some coffee?" I motioned toward the register.

Brett smiled and stepped closer. "Coffee and..." He paused as he met my gaze. "And the coffee maker."

My cheeks heated. I had not expected that answer. "Oh, yeah?" I asked.

He nodded. "I feel bad for how things went down the other night. I wanted to talk to you to see if you could forgive me."

I waved away his concern. "Don't even worry about it. Alcohol was involved."

He smiled at me. "Yeah. It makes you do crazy things."

I nodded. "That it does. In fact, there are a ton of songs about the things it makes us do."

"That's true."

I leaned forward and lowered my voice. "If you want to keep standing here, you'll have to order something." I smiled. The sound of the front doorbell filled the air, and I straightened, hoping it wasn't Wanda, the shop owner. "Can I take your order?" I asked, a little louder than I would normally.

"Yes, ma'am," Brett said as he stepped closer to the counter. "I would like a regular coffee with cream."

"Got it," I said as I glanced over at him and smiled. Standing here, talking to Brett, felt easy.

Things with him were uncomplicated. It was nice. Sure, he didn't give me the kind of butterflies that Stone did, but it was nice to not have to worry about my family when flirting with him.

The sound of someone clearing his throat behind Brett had the two of us glancing behind him. As soon as I saw Stone's icy glare, my blood ran cold. I pursed my lips, my body instantly reacting to his presence. Brett glanced at me before he glanced back at Stone.

"What are you doing here?" I asked before I realized the words left my lips.

Stone raised his eyebrows. "Getting coffee," he said as he met my gaze head-on.

I glanced over at Brett and gave him a quick smile before I turned my focus back to Stone. "That's so strange. You've never gotten coffee here before."

Stone looked unbothered by my observation. He shifted his bike helmet from one hand to the other. "I like to switch it up."

Heat pricked my skin. I hated that he seemed cool and collected while I felt so discombobulated.

"Hey, you're that guy from the bar." Brett turned to face him fully. "I wanted to apologize for my behavior that night. I should have never drunk that much. I never meant anything untoward with Emerson." He stuck out his hand and waited for Stone to take it.

Stone's eyebrows went up. He pulled his gaze from me and just stared at Brett as if he were daring him to keep talking.

Brett laughed for a second before he wiggled his fingers. When it became apparent that Stone wasn't going to accept his handshake, he curled his fingers into his palm and dropped his hand. "Anyways..." Brett snapped his fingers before he clapped his hands.

I stared at Stone, confused why he was acting this way toward Brett. I could tell that he was making Brett feel nervous, and it was making me mad. Why was he acting like his? Nothing happened that night. It wasn't like Brett treated me bad.

I pulled my gaze from Stone and smiled up at Brett. "Rachel will fill your order. Will you excuse me?"

Brett looked like he wanted to protest, but I moved from behind the register before he could respond. He was down by the pickup place by the time I rounded the counter and grabbed Stone's arm.

He seemed confused as I motioned for him to follow me. Thankfully, he didn't protest, and he let me lead him into the nearby supply closet right next to the bathrooms. I shoved him inside, turning the light on once we were both in.

"What the heck?" I asked, turning to face him. All I was staring at was his broad chest.

I moved to step back but when I ran into the door I'd just shut, I realized that coming into the closet wasn't the smartest idea I'd ever had. If he was a normal-sized human, it would have been fine. But Stone wasn't normal. He was tall and broad, and being in this tiny closet just amplified the size difference between us.

He was staring down at me when I finally brought my gaze up to meet his. I studied him, unable to break away. The air around us sizzled with electricity. It was as if he was daring me. It always felt like he was daring me.

I finally found my voice. "Why did you do that?"

He frowned. "Do what?"

I sighed as I moved my gaze to stare at his chest. Even

though he was wearing a shirt, I could see his muscle defini-
tion, and it made my heart pound. "You're not my brother.
You're not my protector. You have no moral obligation to
keep guys away from me." I hated that when I was around
him, my head felt cloudy and thoughts were hard to
express.

He lifted his hand and rested it on the rack of cleaning
supplies next to me. He drummed his fingers on the plastic
liner that sat on top of the shelves. I was grateful for something else to look at other than his deep blue eyes that
seemed to suck me in every time he looked at me.

"Doesn't a boyfriend have an obligation to protect his
girlfriend?"

Goosebumps erupted across my skin. I swallowed,
hating and loving the sound of those words on his lips. Why
did I like it so much? He wasn't my boyfriend. I wasn't his
girlfriend. This was a purely contractual agreement.

"Of course, he does," I said, slowly bringing my gaze
back up to meet his. "But that's if it's real. This"—I
motioned between his chest and mine—"is fake." I blew out
my breath, grateful that I'd said those words. They were
helping to ground me in reality. "And we haven't even
started this relationship yet."

I could feel his stare. It was boring into me. He had so
much he wanted to say, but he wasn't saying any of it. And
from the intensity of his stare, I wasn't sure I wanted him to
tell me.

"So, please. Don't drive off a guy who may want me

once this arrangement between us is over." I glanced up at him.

His eyes had darkened. His eyebrows were drawn together as if he were trying to process what I'd just said to him.

"You want to date that guy when our fake relationship is done?" His tone was daring as he held my gaze.

I wanted to pull away. I didn't want Stone to see the truth. I was confused and conflicted. All I knew was that, one day, Stone was going to walk away. He always left, and I needed to be prepared for that. I needed to be able to pick up the pieces and move forward. Or I would crumble and never recover.

"Yes," I finally whispered.

That seemed to surprise Stone. He grew quiet as he studied me. Then he sighed, pushed his hand through his hair, and shrugged.

"Fine. I'll be nice. But that doesn't mean I'm going to go out of my way to talk to him. We won't be friends."

"Of course."

He scrubbed his face and glanced up at the ceiling before dropping his gaze to meet mine. "Under one condition." He took a step closer to me. His cologne filled my nose and made my head swim.

"Okay," I whispered, staring at his chest, unable to focus on anything else but how close he was to me.

He slid the pad of his forefinger to my chin and pressed up until my gaze met his. He leaned into me. My heart was pounding so hard that I feared he'd know exactly what he was doing to me. He would know the feelings that were coursing through my body.

"When we are dating..." He paused as his gaze flicked down to my lips. "You are mine." He glanced up at me. "Even if it's fake."

He leaned in, and my whole body stilled, waiting for him to touch me. His arm brushed mine, and suddenly, the pressure of the door against my back disappeared as the door swung out. He raised his eyebrows.

I swallowed in an attempt to ground myself in the present. I hated that I was more flustered by this interaction than he was. I nodded and turned to leave. Brett was lingering by the front door when I walked around the corner. He frowned as he came over to me.

"Everything okay?" he asked. He glanced over at Stone, who walked past but didn't bother to look over at him.

"Peachy keen," Stone said as he stepped up to the register and gave his order to Rachel.

Brett looked over at me, and I smiled. "Everything is fine. I just had something I needed to talk to him about."

"Who is he?" Brett asked as he glanced back at Stone.

"He's my neighbor." It was true. Sure, we had more history than that, but I didn't want to get into it with Brett, certainly not here.

Thankfully, that seemed to appease him. He nodded before he brought his hand up to my elbow and motioned for me to step to the side. I followed his lead until we were standing next to the front windows.

"Did you used to date him?" Brett asked, his voice low.

"Stone?"

He nodded.

"No. He used to be best friends with my brother before..." I didn't want to repeat my parents' normal talking points. I didn't think what happened back then was as black-and-white as they did. "They had a falling out."

Brett glanced up at Stone, who was standing by the pickup window. He was scrolling on his phone. If he was bothered by the fact that Brett and I were having this conversation, he didn't show it.

"It was in the past, and we've all moved forward."

Brett glanced down at me. "Really?"

I nodded. "Really." I smiled. "We just help each other out. That's it."

Brett looked relieved as he focused back on me. "That's good to hear."

I raised my eyebrows. "Oh yeah?"

He smiled. "Yeah." He pulled out his phone. "Any chance I can get your number?"

"What for?"

"Well, I'm thinking I have to eat dinner, and you have to eat dinner..."

"Of course."

He winked as he pushed his phone in my direction.

"What are the chances that the two of us end up at the same restaurant?"

I took his phone and punched in my number. "I think there's a high probability." I handed his phone back to him. "I'm pretty open unless I'm at a gig."

He took his phone and slipped it into his back pocket. "I'll reach out to you."

I smiled. "You do that."

He took a sip of his coffee and set the bottom of the cup into his palm. He grinned at me before he glanced at his watch. "I gotta head back to work. I'll text you later."

"Sounds like a date."

I watched as he walked through the front doors and then stopped to wave before he let the doors swing shut behind him. I waved back, and once he was gone, I blew out my breath and turned.

Stone was standing behind me, holding his coffee cup. His gaze was on the door as if he too were watching Brett leave.

"That was sweet," he said and then took a drink of his coffee.

I glared up at him as I moved to step around him. "Brett is nice."

"Too bad you're going to have to break it off in a few days."

I stopped moving.

"I mean it, Emerson. To make this work, you can't have a

sidepiece. You don't want that kind of publicity." He glanced down at me.

I turned my attention to the menu above the register. "I know." I took in a deep breath and turned to focus on him. "I promise you, on Friday, it will be just me and you."

His expression softened. "It's best not to embroil your-self in a scandal. You don't want that."

I held his gaze and nodded. "I know."

He pursed his lips and held my gaze for a moment longer before he dropped it and left. The sound of the door-bell hitting the glass marked his departure.

Rachel was staring at me when I joined her behind the counter.

"*What* was that?" she asked. "Who were they? Why did you take that tall, hunky one into the closet?"

I rested my arms on the counter next to the register before I stepped back and leaned my head forward, stretching my arms out. I could feel Rachel circling around me. "Rachel?"

"Yeah?"

I tipped my head to the side so I could look up at her. "If I promise to tell you everything, can you promise me something?"

Her eyes were wide, and she nodded.

"Don't make me tell you right now."

14

STONE

The roar of my motorcycle filled the garage as I pulled into my parking spot and killed the engine. I swung my leg off my bike, and my leg nearly gave out. Coach was not happy when I showed up late because I was getting coffee, and he let me know it when I ran onto the field during practice.

He had me run and squat more than I'd ever done in the past. Which I accepted. It helped me work off my interaction with Emerson. I left the coffee shop feeling so confused.

I hated that she was looking forward to when our fake relationship would be over. I guess I'd lulled myself into this idea that Emerson was going to be mine. All mine. Forever. I didn't have an end date on my calendar for our fake relationship. Apparently, she thought different.

And her thoughts were like a gut punch.

I climbed off my bike and walked over to the elevator. I

hit the up button and waited for the doors to open. I jumped in the shower when I got home. Once I was clean, I wrapped a towel around my waist and headed out to the kitchen to find my phone.

Hayden had sent me a text. Emerson had a gig tonight, and she was wondering if I wanted to send her a lucky charm.

Me: Let's go with the Chinese coin. It's a good luck charm that symbolizes wealth and prosperity.

Hayden: Got it. I'll find one and write the note.

I texted back a thank you and set my phone down. With Emerson at a gig tonight, she wouldn't be out with *Brett*. I didn't get a good vibe from that guy. I knew I didn't really have a say in who she dated. But with the reveal of our relationship coming up, I felt like it was my business— for now.

Just as I moved to set my phone down, it buzzed. I turned it so I could see the screen, expecting it to be a text from Hayden, but I frowned when I saw it was from Priscilla. I unlocked my phone so I could read the message.

Priscilla: We haven't hung out in a while. I have a reservation at Etch tonight. My date bailed on me. Wanna be my plus one?

I chewed on her question, and just when I went to text *thanks, but no thanks*, a message popped up.

Priscilla: Strictly as friends and colleagues.

I scrubbed my face with my hand. What would it hurt? After all, Emerson was very clear that she just saw our relationship as fake, and she was determined to keep all her other relationship avenues open. Shouldn't I do the same?

I wanted my relationship with Emerson to be more than fake. But I couldn't hold onto her when she so openly told me that she had no intention of keeping this going past a few games and a few gigs. I needed to take that woman at her word.

I needed to protect my heart.

Me: Give me twenty minutes, and I'll pick you up.

Priscilla: I've seen the death trap you drive around. I'll come get you.

I didn't like the idea of Priscilla picking me up for a date, but I knew that there was no way she would get on my bike if I showed up at her place. I texted her a thumbs-up and set my phone back down.

I settled on a pair of gray slacks and a white button-down shirt. I rolled the sleeves and found a pair of dress shoes in my closet. I went into the bathroom and styled my hair before spritzing some cologne. I went back to the kitchen to find a text from Priscilla saying she was five minutes out.

I checked the time and saw she sent that text seven minutes ago. I grabbed my wallet and slipped it into my back pocket. Just as I rounded the peninsula, there was a knock on the door. Hating that I made Priscilla get out of her car to come get me, I hurried to unlock the door and pulled it open.

Priscilla looked slightly annoyed when her deep brown

eyes met mine. She was wearing a navy-blue satin dress and black heels. Her hair was pulled back, and she had a black fur shawl around her shoulders. Her red lips tipped up into a smile when she saw me.

"You kept me waiting, silly goose." I could hear the annoyance in her voice, but I chose to ignore it.

"Yeah, sorry," I said as I grabbed my keys and moved to join her on the landing. She stepped to the side and watched as I locked my apartment and turned to face her. "Ready?"

She nodded as she slipped her arm through mine. "Your stairs as so slippery," she said as she pressed her body against mine.

I pointed to the elevator. "Do you want to take the elevator down?"

She glanced over at it but shook her head. "It's okay. I don't mind the walk."

I didn't have to ask what her real intentions were. It was clear from the death grip she had on my arm. She wanted to go down the stairs, so she had an excuse to hold onto me.

I didn't have the energy to push back. Instead, I just let her hold onto me as we made our way to the stairs. Just as we got to the top, I saw Emerson and stopped dead in my tracks.

She was staring at her phone as she was coming up the stairs. She was wearing her green polo and khaki pants from work. Her keys dangled from the hand that was holding her phone. I had half a mind to yank Priscilla back toward my apartment. But she would no doubt protest, and with the door locked, we would be found out before I could get her inside. It was best to just stand here and face Emerson.

Plus, she should know that if she was keeping her options open, so was I.

It took a second for Emerson to notice that we were standing at the top of the stairs. She glanced up for a moment, whispered, "Excuse me," and then paused and lifted her gaze to meet mine before she glanced over at Priscilla. Her lips parted as she turned to look at me.

"Emerson," I said as I nodded in her direction.

"Stone." Her voice came out breathy and confused.

We stood there, studying each other before Priscilla leaned forward. "I'm Priscilla," she said, extending her hand toward Emerson.

Emerson took it, and they shook before Emerson pulled her hand back. "Emerson," she said.

"Emerson," Priscilla repeated. Then she flicked her gaze between Emerson and me. "And how do you know Stone?"

Emerson glanced at me before she nodded toward her door. "I'm subletting that apartment."

Priscilla followed her gesture. "Poppy left?"

I shook my head. "She's gone for six months to photograph birds in Europe."

"Oh." Priscilla turned her attention back to Emerson. "That's nice." Except the bite to her tone made it clear she thought it was anything but nice. "Well, just make sure that you keep Stone's residence under wraps. He likes his anonymity. I know it must feel crazy to live across from someone who is famous, but we have to do what we can to keep the paparazzi away from him." She was waggling her finger toward Emerson and ended her statement by placing her hand on my chest like she was claiming me.

Emerson's eyes widened as she glanced between us. "Do you know what's funny—it's Priscilla, right?" She pointed her finger at Priscilla.

She nodded. "Priscilla."

"Right. Stone's never mentioned you. Not the time he wrapped his arms around me and gave me a ride home on his motorcycle. And not last night when he fed me dinner in his apartment."

Priscilla gasped, but Emerson didn't miss a beat. Her expression deadpanned as she settled her gaze on me. Then she moved to climb the stairs. "Excuse me," she said, not really waiting for us to move to the side.

I had to press Priscilla against the wall to let Emerson slip by. I watched her as she crossed the landing and pulled out her keys to unlock her door.

"Let's go," Priscilla hissed, her nails digging ever so slightly into my forearm.

I pulled my attention from Emerson and glanced down at Priscilla. She looked perturbed, but she didn't say anything as we walked down the stairs until we got to the parking lot.

Priscilla tried to engage me in conversation about Emerson while we sat in the back of the luxury ride share she'd rented, but I wasn't really interested in talking to her about Emerson. I wasn't interested in hearing Priscilla talk bad about her, and I certainly didn't want to try dissecting my feelings for Emerson in front of Priscilla.

Once we were at the restaurant, I dodged her questions and comments by changing the subject and ordering alcohol. When our food came, I kept my mouth full, so conversation was hard. I honestly didn't want to be there. I felt like an idiot for even agreeing in the first place. Priscilla didn't seem to mind and carried on the conversation by herself while I responded with a few nods and basic responses.

I paid the check and moved to stand, feeling a little tipsy from the two bottles of wine we drank. When we got outside, I told Priscilla I'd get my own ride home. She pouted as she leaned into me. I wanted to step to the side to put more distance between us, but I knew she'd just follow me if I moved, so I let her lean on me.

Her car came to pick her up first. I made sure she got into the back seat and buckled her in. She slurred her words when she told the driver where she wanted to go. I clarified with him, and he nodded and promised to get her home in one piece. I stepped away from the car before concern filled my chest, and I knocked on the hood of the car, telling the driver to wait.

There was no way I wanted her riding home by herself. Thankfully, the driver didn't pull away. I jiggled the door handle, and he unlocked the doors so I could climb into the back seat with Priscilla. She sighed and laid her head on my shoulder as the driver pulled away from the curb and into the busy city traffic.

By the time he pulled into the circle drive of her apartment complex, Priscilla was passed out. I told him I could take it from here and gently shifted her off my shoulder as I climbed out of the car. I rounded the trunk and opened her door. She mumbled something but didn't open her eyes. I asked the driver to wait-- I'd be back down in five minutes, max. He just nodded as he grabbed his phone from the cupholder and started scrolling.

It took some work to get Priscilla into position so I could wrap my arm around her back to support her upper body and get my other arm under her knees. She was pressed against my chest as I carried her to the automatic doors.

Thankfully, her doorman, Bob, knew me. He nodded to me as he met me at the elevator and swiped his card. He thanked me for the great game on Sunday—he'd doubled his money in a bet—and then stepped to the side so I could board the elevator car.

Once I got Priscilla into bed with a water and a bottle of pain meds on her nightstand, I turned off her lights, locked her door, and headed back out to the elevator.

Bob wished me a good night as I walked through the automatic doors and back outside. The driver was idling a bit further down the drive. I opened the back door, told him to drop me off a block away from my apartment, and closed my eyes as I rested against the head rest.

He dropped me off at the convenience store on the

corner. I could tell that he didn't believe this was where I lived, but I just threw a couple of hundreds in his direction and got out.

I kept to the shadows as I made my way to my apartment. I was exhausted when I finally got inside. Oscar was waiting for me at the door. I'd forgotten to feed him, and he was hungry. I grabbed a can from under the sink and cracked the lid. I set it on a paper plate on the kitchen floor, and he happily dove in.

I flipped off the kitchen light and stumbled to my room. I stripped down to my boxers, set my phone on the charger on my nightstand, and climbed into bed. I was asleep before my head hit the pillow.

RINGING. Strange ringing.

I turned my head to hear better, but the movement caused my head to feel as if it were splitting apart. I moaned as I reached up to keep my head together. Maybe I was just dreaming.

That was it. If I lay still, it would go away.

My body started to relax and feel heavy. Sleep was moments away...

Ringing. Again.

I peeked out through one eye. Were aliens attacking? I shifted my eye around the room, but I was alone. I turned to my side and slowly peeled both eyes open. My phone was lighting up on the charger.

An alert.

I cursed under my breath as I heaved my hand at it. Thankfully, my aim was better now that I wasn't drunk, and I was able to pull my phone off the charger and swipe it on.

"Poppy's doorbell?" I asked as I read the alert out loud. Dammit. That woman was going to be the death of me.

I moved to put my phone into sleep mode when my mind finally caught up with what was going on. Poppy's doorbell was now Emerson's doorbell. And it was going off. At eight in the morning.

Where was Emerson?

I went back and forth on whether I should look or not until I settled on looking. Worst case scenario, it could be her kidnappers dropping off a ransom note. This could be my only chance at witnessing the culprits.

I clicked on the app as I sat up on my bed. My head was throbbing, but it managed to clear to the point where I could actually process my thoughts. Which was an upgrade.

It took a moment to connect, but suddenly, I was staring at a close-up of Brett. He was standing outside of Emerson's apartment. He looked disheveled. His head was tipped forward, and both hands were resting on the doorframe.

"Emerson?" he called as he reached over to push on the doorbell once more. He focused on the doorbell and muttered, "She has one of those camera doorbells."

He stepped back and looked straight at the camera.

"Emerson, you left before I could say what I wanted to say. So, I hope you don't mind that I came over first thing."

I sat up straighter. She left? Left where? The gig? His house? His *bed*? My blood was boiling now as I glared at my phone.

"Listen, I know you're nervous about you and me, but I have to say, we are vibing. Like, let's see where this goes." He drug his hand down his face and tipped it to the sky. "I didn't want to tell you this, but I'm the guy."

I frowned. What the hell did that mean?

He waved to his chest. "I'm the guy who believes in you. I've always believed in you."

Bullshit. What did he know about Emerson? *He's* the one who believes in her? Since when? They just met. Why was he talking like he had the kind of history we had? This guy had weasel written all over him. I hated that he was manipulating her like this.

"I've had a lot of girls in my life, but no one's been like you. I just want to see if we can make this work."

He did this ridiculous half-smile to the camera, and I rolled my eyes. Please.

"I really feel like we could be something. Wanna take a chance on us?"

Having had enough, and needing to put a stop to it, I pressed on the microphone. "I think you have the wrong house, dude."

I smiled as I watched his face drop.

"She's the door behind you."

Brett slowly turned until he was facing my door. I ripped off my comforter and headed over to my dresser, ignoring the wave of nausea.

"What? Really?" he asked, turning to face the doorbell again.

I had my sweatpants halfway up and was trying to hold my phone and tug on my hoodie. "I honestly wouldn't say any of that to her," I said.

With my sweatpants pulled up and my hoodie on, I pulled the hood up over my head as I made my way to the front door.

"You don't think so?" he asked, looking sheepish.

"You're probably wasting your time with this girl," I said as I shoved my feet into my shoes. "She's got guys coming in and out of her place." I slowly unlocked my deadbolt so he couldn't hear it.

I glanced at the camera to see him rub his eyes with his thumb and forefinger. I took that moment to shove my phone into the front pocket of my hoodie, tug the hood further down my face, and pull open the door. I didn't look to see if he noticed. Instead, I headed straight out of my apartment, shut the door behind me, and bounded down the stairs like a guy who just got laid.

I didn't stop until I got to the parking lot. I hurried to hide behind the building while I pulled out my phone to see what Brett was doing. I smiled as I saw him staring at my door and then back to Emerson's place.

"Good luck, bro," I said.

He sighed and nodded. "Well..." Then he shook his head. "Thanks for the heads-up."

"No problem."

He pushed his hands through his hair and turned. I watched him walk down the stairs until he disappeared from view. I stood there, in the morning air, waiting for his car to drive by. Thankfully, it only took a few minutes before his red Toyota Corolla passed me. I rolled my eyes as I headed back to the apartment stairs. Once I got into my apartment and shut the door, I kicked off my shoes.

I wanted to collapse back into bed, but I needed to get ready and out the door if I was going to make it to practice on time.

I took the max number of pain meds I could for my headache and stood in an ice-cold shower to sober up. After throwing on my gym shorts and a t-shirt, I was out the door in ten minutes, and as I stood in front of the elevator, I smiled over at Emerson's door.

My work here was done.

Brett is gone, which meant it was going to be a glorious day.

15

EMERSON

I startled awake.

Confused, I glanced around, trying to get my bearings on where I was. Tilly moaned next to me. I pulled back to see her makeup-smudged cheeks as she lifted her head off the mattress and slowly opened her eyes.

"Why are you up so early?" she asked before dropping her head back into her pillow.

One look at the sun streaming in through her bedroom window and I knew I was going to be late to work. "Get up," I said as I shoved her shoulder and swung my legs off the bed at the same time.

"You're the devil," she murmured, her voice half muffled by the fluff in her pillow.

"We're going to be late for work," I called over my shoulder as I shuffled into her bathroom and turned on the light.

I stared at my reflection, wincing at the state of my face. My hair was matted. My makeup was smudged. I could taste my own breath.

We stayed at the bar way too late last night. A producer for Lucky Records bought all the musicians drinks last, and Tilly insisted that we accept. Even though the guy spent the whole night talking to the band who performed two spots before us, Tilly assured me that the producer saw me, and that was the first step in becoming famous.

Brett texted me and asked me where I was. I mindlessly responded because I was too focused on what wasn't happening between the producer and me. By the time he got there, I was three drinks in, and my inhibitions had been thrown out the window. The rest of the night was a blur, although I do remember Brett asking me to go back to his place. Thankfully, Tilly wouldn't let me go. We ended up at her place, where we crashed in her bed.

I turned away from the mirror and flipped on the shower. I quickly undressed and slipped under the hot water. Thankfully, this wasn't the first time that I'd passed out at her apartment, so I kept a spare change of clothes in her closet.

I sudsed up and rinsed off as fast as I could. Once I was clean, I turned off the water, wrapped my hair and my body in a towel, and stepped out. Tilly was waiting, and as soon as I passed her, she jumped in the shower.

I dressed in the green polo and khakis I'd stashed here and waited for Tilly to finish so I could use the mirror without steam covering it. She yawned as she shuffled out of her bathroom in her fluffy robe.

I hurried in and wiped the mirror down and got started on my makeup. Tilly joined me a few minutes later wearing a pair of bike shorts and an oversized tank.

"Last night was crazy," she said as she stretched. Then she paused, brought her hand up in front of her mouth and blew out a breath. She wrinkled her nose and pulled open the nearby drawer to fish out her toothbrush and toothpaste.

"I wish it had been more fruitful," I said as I grabbed a beauty blender to smooth out my foundation. The producer had left without us knowing it. As soon as I found out, I withdrew from Brett. He seemed heartbroken, but I really wasn't interested in talking to him anymore.

I was getting tired of all the disappointment. I just wanted one bite. That was it. But it was beginning to feel like it was never going to happen. I'd already received three lucky charms from some caring stranger. My luck must have been really bad if I needed more than that to get my career off the ground.

I grabbed my mascara and began to swipe it on my eyelashes.

"You don't know what last night might bring," Tilly said as she opened her face lotion and scooped it out with her pointer finger.

"Tilly, maybe it's just too hard. Maybe it's just not going to happen." I was tired of hoping.

"What are you talking about? If all else fails, we have

Stone in our back pocket." She gave me a pointed look before she pulled her foundation out of her drawer.

I hated that her whole plan to make me famous hinged on Stone. I would never admit it to her—or anyone for that matter—but my willingness to drink last night may have had something to do with running into Stone and the most beautiful woman I'd ever seen.

It wasn't like she was his cousin or something. No, that woman was hanging on him like she owned him. And she wanted me to know that he was hers. I let it get to me. Sure, I said things I shouldn't have, but I didn't regret them. I couldn't believe Stone would tell me off about Brett only to turn around and go out with some other girl that night.

"Hypocrite," I muttered under my breath.

"Excuse me?" Tilly was staring at me with her eyebrows raised.

I sheepishly smiled at her. "Nothing."

She frowned before she turned back to the mirror. "What was with that guy last night. Brett?" She side-eyed me. "He was *all* over you."

"He's nice," I said—and he was. But he wasn't Stone. And that seemed to be bothering me more and more lately. I didn't want to, but for some reason, I kept measuring every guy I came across to Stone. There must be some diagnosis for this in the DSM, because it couldn't be normal.

"Emerson." Tilly emphasized my name as she stared at me. "This is not the time to start a new relationship with some *nice* guy. You need to be all about Stone."

"I'm not dating Stone," I murmured as I turned to swipe some eyeshadow over my lids.

"I know you're not dating-*dating* Stone. But if this is going to work, you can't have loose ends. Some other guy pining for you is a loose end." She pointed her eyebrow pencil in my direction.

"I know," I whispered. I turned my focus back to the mirror. I meant what I said to Stone. There was no way I was going to turn away suitors just because I'd agreed to this fake relationship with Stone. I knew what was going to eventually happen. He was going to leave, and I wouldn't be able to face that again.

"So...what do you need to do?" She looked expectantly over at me.

I studied my reflection in the mirror. "Become polyamorous?"

"Ha." She frowned. "No." She stood and walked out of the bathroom. A few seconds later, she returned with my phone in her hand. "You need to break things off with Brett."

I stared at my phone in her outstretched hand. "What?"

"You need to tell him that you can't date him."

"That feels presumptuous. We've never said we were dating."

"Girl, from the way he was staring at you last night, he wants to do more than date you."

My cheeks flushed as I picked up my phone. I stared at

the black screen before I pressed the side button to wake it up. "Can't I just—"

"Tell him no. It's not fair to him either. Leading him on. What's going to happen when he sees you out with Stone?"

True. I didn't want to hurt Brett. "Fine," I said as I opened my contacts and searched for his name. I put it on speaker and it rang five times before he picked up. I almost thought I was going to have to leave this all in a message.

"Hello." His tone was more curt than I'd anticipated.

"Brett?"

"Yeah."

"Hey, it's Emerson."

Silence. I glanced over at Tilly, who circled her hand in a forward motion. She wanted me to get this over with. I narrowed my eyes at her and turned so I could focus on how I was going to put this.

"Listen, I think you're a great guy. It's just that..." I blew out my breath. "Well, things are a little complicated right now. It's best if we just stay friends." I squeezed my eyes shut. "Do you think we can be friends?"

Silence. I glanced at my screen to make sure I hadn't accidentally hung up on him. The call was still active. "Brett?"

Silence. "I'm here."

I closed my eyes and said a silent hallelujah. I couldn't imagine having to call him back and reiterate what I'd just said. "I'm really sorry. I am. Things are just crazy for me right now, and I don't want to drag you into my mess." I opened my eyes and stared at the vanity counter in front of me. "I really hope you can forgive me."

I waited for his response. He seemed so cold and distant. I hadn't expected him to act like this. It wasn't like I'd ever agreed to be his girlfriend. We'd only flirted a few times. He was acting a little ridiculous for how little we actually knew each other.

He sighed, and it caused me to sit up.

"Listen, I get that we aren't dating, but to give me your wrong address...and then to see a guy coming out of your apartment this morning...I guess I just thought you were different."

I pulled away from the phone, confused. I glanced over at Tilly, who—thankfully—looked just as confused as I did. She mouthed, "What?" and I nodded in response.

"I'm so confused," I whispered. When Brett didn't respond, I focused on what he just said. "When did I give you my address?"

He paused. "Last night. You wrote it down on an old receipt and shoved it into my hand, telling me that I should come over and play Yahtzee sometime."

Tilly laughed and pointed at me. "That sounds like you."

"And I wrote the wrong address?"

"Yeah." He rattled off my address.

I glanced at Tilly. I'd only lived at Poppy's for a week, but that sounded right.

She nodded, "That's right."

"Yeah, that's the right one."

"Oh, 'cause some guy answered the doorbell and said that you were 4A not 4B."

"Umm...what?"

Tilly had abandoned her makeup and was now laser-focused on me. "Some guy?" she whispered. "Maybe someone hacked the doorbell?"

That was weird. I stared at her. "Can people really do that?"

She shrugged and returned to the mirror. "Hackers can do anything these days."

My stomach twisted at the thought of someone being able to hack into something you purchased to make you feel safe. Realizing that I'd ignored Brett for too long, I turned my attention back to the phone. "I am so sorry for earlier. I don't know what happened today, but I wasn't even home. I spent the night at Tilly's."

Brett was quiet for a moment. "So, some guy wasn't leaving your apartment this morning?"

Nerves rushed through my stomach. Did someone else have a key to my apartment? Did Poppy not tell me? "No. But now I'm nervous that there was someone in there without my permission." I paused. "You said someone came out of 4B?"

"4A."

4A. His response echoed in my mind for a moment before relief flooded my body. 4A was Stone. He must have been leaving to go to work this morning. I blew out my breath. "That's just my neighbor."

Brett must not have recognized Stone, which I was grateful for. He'd seen him at my gigs and at the coffee shop yesterday. I wasn't sure how I was going to explain to Brett that the man I dragged into a supply closet just so happened to be the guy living next door to me.

It would make for an awkward conversation.

"Oh, I see." He laughed, and I could tell that he felt sheepish. "I'm so sorry I jumped to conclusions."

I shook my head as I dug around in Tilly's makeup case for some lip gloss. "You didn't jump to conclusions. Some guy lied to you." It was still so weird to me that some hacker would bug my doorbell just to tell a stranger off.

I stopped as I stared at myself in the mirror. "Why did you come over in the first place?" I'd been so focused on the stranger answering my doorbell that I didn't realize he never told me why he was there to begin with.

The silence felt strained. He sputtered for a moment before he said, "I just wanted to make sure you got home safe. Last night, you disappeared on me, and I was worried."

I glanced over at Tilly. She gave me an are-you-for-real look before returning back to the mirror. I thought it was sweet, even if Tilly didn't buy it. What other reason would he have to show up at my place?

"That's sweet," I said as I turned my focus back to Brett. "I'm fine. Tilly took good care of me last night."

"Good. Good."

Silence fell between us once more. Even if Brett wasn't my Prince Charming, he was a nice guy. Maybe once my fake relationship with Stone was over, we could hang out. And maybe from there, we could grow to be something more. "Hey, Brett?"

"Yeah?"

"When my life finally settles, and all my complications are, er, no longer complicated, can we hang out?"

He paused. "Sure, Emerson. I'd like that."

I smiled. At least I wasn't burning a bridge. In a town as big as Nashville, it was good to have a few allies around. I was a small fish in a big pond. It would behoove me to make some new friends.

"Thanks."

We said our goodbyes, and I hung up. After I set my phone down on the vanity, I stared at it, trying to piece together my thoughts. Then I glanced over at Tilly. She saw my confusion and matched it. "That was weird," she said.

"Right?" I paused. "Some guy hacked my doorbell."

Tilly shrugged. "Or maybe Poppy gave access to someone and they thought it would be a funny joke to scare Brett off."

Realization passed over me. "That's it! Someone must have thought Brett was there for Poppy and told them those weird lies to scare him away." I turned so I could face her fully. "Text Poppy. Ask her if she's given anyone access to her doorbell."

Tilly sighed as she set down her blush brush. "Okay,"

she said, picking up her phone. After the text was sent, she returned to her makeup.

It only took a minute or two to get a response, but it felt like an eternity. When her phone finally chimed, I cheered and leaned forward, waiting for an answer that wouldn't have me packing my bags because some strange man had access to the apartment.

"Huh," Tilly said as her gaze remained glued to her screen.

"What?" This wasn't a fun game. My heart was pounding a mile a minute. Was I going to have to find a new place? I didn't have the time, and I doubted that I could find something as perfect as Poppy's—even if I was living next to Stone.

Tilly pinched her lips as she set her phone—screen-side down—on the vanity. She didn't look at me as she turned her attention to the mirror.

"Tilly Jenkins. Tell me what she said right now." I leaned forward to grab her phone, but she beat me to it.

She was fast as she scrambled out of her seat with her hand held high in the air to keep the phone out of my reach. I was not going to let her get away with that, so I lunged after her. She must not have expected my momentum because I managed to knock her onto the ground. Her phone flung out of her hand, and we were both scrambling to pick it up.

Finally, I felt the cool plastic of her phone case, and my fingers wrapped around it before she could get it from me. I held it to my chest and scooted away across her bathroom floor.

"Tell me, Tilly," I demanded. I pulled the phone away from my chest and glanced down at the screen. It was locked, of course. "You know your phone will lock you out if I try to guess your password too many times."

"Emerson," she whined. "I don't want it to change your commitment." Her eyes were wide, like she was begging me to promise her something.

"My commitment..." I repeated, trying to piece together what she was getting at. "My commitment..." I whispered.

Stone.

"No." I shook my head as I tossed Tilly's phone into her lap. "No. Nope." Stone had *lied* to Brett? And then he had the audacity to tell Brett that *I* had guys coming out of my apartment all the time when *he* was the one with some girl on his arm last night? After he chewed me out for talking to Brett?

"You better tell me right now if she said Stone, or we are no longer friends." I narrowed my eyes at Tilly, so she knew I meant business.

Tilly was biting her lips as she stared at me. Finally, she sighed and nodded. "She said Stone."

Fury built up in my stomach. My skin was hot, and all I could see was red.

What a selfish, hypocritical asshole.

He could date, and I couldn't? And not only was I forbidden from talking to Brett, but he was actively trying to scare the guy off even though I told him I wanted to keep my options open.

I shook my head. If I wasn't going to be late for work, I would march over there right now and give him a piece of my mind. But I needed my job, and he probably wasn't even home.

No. I was going to go to work with these festering feelings, but as soon as I got home, I was going to tell him off.

He deserved it.

16

EMERSON

I was still mad as I climbed up the stairs to my apartment. My thoughts were rolling around in my mind like storm clouds rolling in. I was ready to tell Stone off. I'd had the entire day to get my thoughts right, and there was no way I was going to hold back.

He was going to know how mad I was.

As soon as I got to our landing, I turned to his apartment and raised my hand to knock on his door but then shook my head. I was sweaty and gross from work. If I was going to yell at him, I was going to look good doing it.

I hurried into my apartment and peeled off my work uniform. I pulled my hair from my ponytail and ran a curling iron through it. I washed my face and redid my makeup. I picked a black top with a plunging neckline and a pair of jeans that made my rear look amazing. I studied my reflection as I put on some big hoop earrings and a few chunky necklaces.

Once I was ready, I slipped on a pair of white cowboy boots and pulled open my front door. I stomped over to his apartment and pounded on the door. I waited, my breath in my throat, for him to open the door.

Worry that he wasn't even home rushed through me, but I shook my head. He was home. I pounded on his door again, and the second time my fist landed, the door was pulled open. Stone's eyes widened when his gaze met mine.

"Emerson?"

I swallowed, not expecting the emotions that rushed through me as I stared at Stone with his stormy blue eyes, his brown tousled hair, and his bare chest. He had a pair of swim trunks on, and he was carrying a bucket of ice.

"What the hell..." He glanced behind me. "Is your apartment on fire?"

"Wh-what?" I stammered and scoffed. "My apartment is not on fire."

He brought his gaze back to mine before he took a step forward, bringing him within inches of me. "Then why are you pounding on my door like someone is dying?"

I stared at him, my brain struggling to keep up. Why was he chastising me? I'd come over to give him a piece of my mind, not face his frustration.

"I wouldn't come over here, banging on your door, if you'd just mind your own damn business." I finally found my footing, and I wasn't going to let him rattle me again.

"What the..." When his eyes widened and his ridiculous half smile spread across his lips, I wanted to deck him. He knew exactly what I was talking about. He not only knew, but he was pleased with himself. "Brett." He leaned against the doorframe, his smile never wavering.

"Yes, Brett," I said, my frustration reaching an all-time peak. I don't know why I thought he would feel bad about what he did. That had obviously been a miscalculation on my end.

And call me crazy, but it seemed like my anger only made him more pleased with himself. Like this was some show and he was enjoying the entertainment.

I crossed my arms and stared at him. "What do you have to say for yourself?" I widened my eyes in an effort to intimidate him.

He didn't look phased as he glanced to the side and then back over to me. "Nothing. I did the right thing." He shrugged.

I let out an exasperated sigh. "You did? How?"

"He's not right for you." Stone shifted the ice bucket to his other hand.

"He's not right for me?" I repeated in an effort to make it make sense. "What do you know about what's right for me? When have you ever cared what's right for me?"

He was acting like my protective older brother. Which I didn't need. I already had a brother—and a family, which was in shambles because of him. If he cared so much about what was right for me, maybe he should have started with what happened Cayden's senior year.

My meaning wasn't lost on him. His eyes widened. Then he straightened, bringing himself to his full height as he stared down at me.

"I don't care what you think I tried to do. Brett isn't right for you, Emerson. You have to trust me on that."

I glared at him. Frustrated, I dropped my gaze to his chest, which was now a mere foot in front of me. My mind was racing, but everything seemed to fade away when I noticed that he had a tattoo on his left pec. It looked like a four-leaf clover keychain. Exactly like the one I'd given him years ago.

I stared at it, wondering if I was seeing things. I frowned and dropped my gaze, trying to clear my mind before I glanced back up at the tattoo—it was still there. I wasn't losing my mind. Stone had a tattoo of my lucky charm on his chest.

Why?

I shook my head. This wasn't what I was here for. "Just, leave me alone, Stone," I finally managed. I shoved the fact that he had a tattoo of something that meant so much to me into the far corner of my mind, where it belonged. "I agreed to fake date you, but that's it. It's fake. It's not real. I need you to stop chasing away people that have the potential to be real for me." I brought my gaze back up to his only to find him staring down at me.

His eyes were a dark blue now. His emotions were

storming inside of him; I could see them. Feel them. I'd made him mad.

"You just have to understand the boundaries." I forced a smile. "Then you and I can coexist."

His jaw muscles were twitching. I wondered what he was thinking but shook my head. I didn't want to know, nor did I need to know. Opening up emotionally would lead to a closeness that I couldn't bring myself to have with him. I thought I meant something to him back in high school, but his actions had quickly told me I'd been a fool to think so.

I needed to keep my distance, so I could keep my sanity.

To say I was worked up would be an understatement. I knew if I went back into my apartment, I would spend the next thirty minutes pacing back and forth. I needed to go on a walk.

Unable to say anything else to Stone, I turned and started to make my way down the stairs. I needed some fresh air and to walk off my nerves.

"Where are you going?" Stone asked. His voice drew nearer, so I could only assume that he'd stepped out of his apartment and onto the landing.

"Wherever I want to go," I called over my shoulder.

The sound of his door shutting startled me, but I just waved him off. I wasn't his to protect. I could take care of myself.

I continued down the stairs, and I'd almost made it to the upper parking lot, when I heard footsteps behind me. I turned to see Stone, wearing a sweatshirt and sandals, coming down after me. "I don't need you to babysit me," I called over my shoulder.

"I'm not babysitting you," he said as he kept a few feet behind me. I glared at him, but he just pulled his hoodie over his head and stared straight ahead.

"Where are you going?"

He flicked his gaze over to me. "I have somewhere I need to be."

I rolled my eyes as I crossed the apartment complex's yard and got onto the sidewalk. "Sure."

He laughed and rolled his eyes. "Not everything is about you, Emerson."

I glanced over at him. "What does that mean?"

He shoved his hands into the front pocket of his hoodie. He was quiet for a moment before he shrugged. "I don't know." His voice was quiet, like he was accepting defeat or something.

"It's just rich of you," I said, my anger still peaking. "You tell me not to date anyone so we can create this facade, but when I came home last night, *you* were leaving with someone else." I glared at him, daring him to respond.

He glanced over at me and then returned his attention ahead of us. "Priscilla is just a work colleague."

"Ha!" I glared at him. "I've never seen her on the field before."

"She's not with the Tigers. She's a sports reporter."

I rolled my eyes. "That's not a colleague."

He shrugged. "Well, that's how I see her."

"That's not how she sees you," I muttered, recalling how she basically claimed him last night when I talked to her.

"Does it matter?"

Stone's question threw me off guard. "Does what matter?"

"If she sees me as something more. Does it matter?"

I turned my attention to my feet as I walked down the sidewalk. Most of the spots were smooth so there was no chance I would trip. But every so often, a tree root or shift in the ground had caused the concrete to jut up. The last thing I needed was for Stone to come to my rescue again.

"Well, no," I finally said, glancing over at him. Then I frowned. "Why don't you see her as something more? I mean, she's beautiful, elegant. And if she's a reporter, she's got a good job." The more qualities I listed off, the more confused I got. "She's perfect," I whispered, feeling completely incompetent next to her.

Stone frowned. "She's not perfect."

"But she's beautiful."

He studied me. "Sure, okay. Objectively, she's attractive."

"And..."

He drew his eyebrows together. "And...I'm not here for just *attractive*."

My mind started whirling. He'd mentioned to me at one point that he was known as the MEP of the NFL. Which meant he didn't date. If he didn't like Priscilla like that...then who did he like? What was he waiting for if he wasn't waiting for a girl who looked amazing in anything she wore, had hair that looked like it was created by the gods, and skin that would make roses envious.

"So, you're just waiting for a goddess, then?" I said. I tried to think of another way to describe someone better than Priscilla, and that was the one word I could come up with.

"A goddess?" Stone wrinkled his nose. "Where did you get that from?"

I stared at him, hoping he would understand how flabbergasted I was. "You're saying no to Priscilla. Who is better than that?"

He shook his head. "It's not all about looks, Em. She may be pretty, but that's not enough."

I understood that. There were plenty of guys that swept me away with their good looks only to drop me back down to reality with their behavior. "So, you've never met a girl that is enough?" I raised my eyebrows. I wasn't sure I wanted to hear the answer, but I was intrigued enough to ask anyway.

He paused before he glanced over at me. I could tell that he was chewing on my words as if he were weighing how much he wanted to say. Suddenly, I didn't want to hear whatever he was struggling to get out.

I didn't want to hear about the one who got away. She had to be amazing if he was holding on for this long. If Priscilla wasn't good enough, I couldn't even fathom who this "enough" girl was.

"You know, you don't have to tell me," I said, laughing

uncomfortably and turning to head back to our apartment complex. This whole night had been a giant mistake. I'd been mad, and I hadn't really thought through the kind of conversation we were going to ultimately have.

I should have just kept my mouth shut and moved forward.

We walked in silence—Stone a foot or two behind me. It was almost as if he were chaperoning me instead of joining me on a walk. I thought about pointing this out but decided against it. If he was walking next to me, I would feel the need to talk—and when I talked, I said stupid things.

It was best if I kept my mouth shut.

He followed behind me as I climbed the stairs to the fourth floor. I wanted to say something, but I wasn't sure what. The last time I allowed myself to freehand our conversation, I took us into some strange territories. But I also didn't want to leave the night on a strange note.

I was halfway to my door, in an effort to run and hide from Stone, when I changed my mind. I could clear this up. I could say something to clear the air.

I whipped around, but when I was met with Stone's broad chest, I stumbled backwards. I'd figured he'd head to his apartment—not follow me to mine.

But here we were, standing face-to-face on the landing, him staring down at me as I stared up at him. His gaze locked with mine. My body warmed from the intensity in his eyes. He studied me like he was looking for an answer, but I didn't know what question he was asking.

And then, ever so slowly, his gaze drifted down to my lips. I swear he took a step forward, but I was too locked in on his lingering gaze to check. He brought his gaze back up to meet mine. For a moment, I wondered if he was going to kiss me. Because I wanted him to.

I wanted him to so damn bad.

"Emerson," he said, his voice low and gruff.

My heart pounded from the sound. "Yes?" I whispered.

He glanced to the side before he brought his gaze back up to lock with mine. "Make me a promise?"

I pulled back slightly. I hadn't expected that. "Sure."

"Don't go walking around at night by yourself."

I frowned. "Okay."

He studied me again before he nodded and stepped back. It was like ripping a warm blanket off in the middle of the night. I felt cold without his body warmth surrounding me.

"Good night," he said as he pushed his hand through his hair.

I blinked, reality crashing down around me. I watched as he nodded to me and turned to head into his apartment. The sound of his door engaging filled the air, marking his departure.

He was gone.

That man left me like that.

I glared at his door before I turned and headed to my apartment. When I got inside, I kicked off my shoes, grabbed a bottle of wine from the fridge, and padded into my bathroom.

I turned on the tub faucet, and while the water flowed, I pulled my hair up into a bun on the top of my head. I was so confused and discombobulated by what had just happened. I'd wanted Stone Walker to kiss me. I'd wanted him to touch me.

I'd wanted him to tell me that I was the girl he couldn't seem to forget.

And the fact that I wanted that scared me. Because one thing was for sure, a King should never want a Walker.

Ever.

17

STONE

I had to blow off Isaac after practice. He was telling me all about the Saturday night party tomorrow, like he expected me not to have plans. Which, in all fairness, would have been correct in the past. But tomorrow was different. Tomorrow I had plans.

Emerson and I were going to make our relationship public.

After our impromptu walk through downtown Nashville, where I almost did the stupidest thing and kissed her, I spent the rest of the week avoiding her. Sure, I smiled at her when we met on the landing on our way out the door. And I had Hayden deliver an easter egg and a cornicello to her for the gigs she picked up. But that was all the interaction I had with Emerson.

I'd needed a break from her, or I feared what I would do

once I had the green light to touch her. To kiss her. To show her what it felt like to be loved by a man.

And that desire was eating me alive.

I spent Friday night on the couch with Oscar in my lap, eating Chinese food and watching football. Emerson texted me at ten, reminding me to come over tomorrow around three to go over the game plan. She was acting like I was going to forget. If she only knew.

I passed out in my bed after I sent her a thumbs-up emoji, but as the sun started peeking through Gran's drapes, all I could do was toss and turn until I finally got out of bed and went for a run.

I finished with a thirty-minute jump rope session on the landing. I must have been making some noise, because at minute fifteen, Emerson peeked out of her door. Her gaze landed on me, and she shook her head as she disappeared back into her apartment.

By the time I showered and dressed in a white t-shirt and dark jeans, Hayden had sent me a text to say she'd secured the pig charm and was sending it to Night Spirits.

I'd talked to Troy earlier this week to see if he could squeeze Emerson in tonight. He was hesitant but had agreed. After eating lunch and lounging around on my couch, trying to read a book, it was finally three. I grabbed my wallet and keys and pulled open my door. I crossed the landing and knocked.

Seconds ticked by before the door opened. Emerson stood there in a satin robe. Her hair was pulled up into curlers, and her eyes were wide as she stared at me. I had to use all my self-control to keep my gaze trained on her face and not the way her body looked in the satin material.

"Wow, you're right on time," she said as she leaned back to glance into the kitchen.

I shrugged. "When you're always running by network time, you learn to be punctual."

She glanced over at me and nodded before stepping back so I could come in. "Well, I am on musician time, so I'm always running behind."

"Noted." I waited as she shut the door and then turned to face me.

"Well, I'm going to go finish getting ready. You can make yourself at home." She waved toward the living room.

"Great," I said as I stepped further inside.

She passed by me, and my gaze drifted down her back. Her hips were swishing, and her bottom...

"Stone?"

"Yep," I said as I ripped my gaze away from her body. My entire body felt as if it were going to catch on fire, but I hoped she didn't notice. I prayed she didn't notice.

"I wrote out some rules." She pointed toward the coffee table, where a piece of paper sat.

"Rules?" I asked, frowning.

"Yes." She leaned forward. "You know, for the fake dating."

"Ah."

"Yeah, so if you could go over them, that would be

great." She smiled, but it felt forced. "So that we are both on the same page and know what to expect from the other person."

I studied the piece of paper from where I was standing, trying to determine if I really wanted to go over there and read it. By the time I turned to talk to Emerson again, she'd left.

Now alone, I sucked in my breath and closed the space between me and that blasted piece of paper. Might as well get it over with. I dropped down onto the couch and leaned forward to pick up the paper.

The first rule stuck out like a sore thumb.

Rule #1: No kissing

Ha. Fat chance. There was no way the public would believe that we were dating when we didn't kiss.

Rule number two was just as insane: *No touching*.

"They won't believe us," I called back toward Emerson's room.

"What?"

"They won't—" I cut off. There was no point trying to shout at her from across the apartment, so I stood and made my way into the bedroom. Emerson was sitting at the vanity in her bathroom, her gaze snapping to mine in the mirror.

She looked beautiful, sitting there with the lights all around her. The desire to tell her that rushed through me, but I hadn't gotten through all the rules. I was certain that if kissing and touching were at the top of the list, compliments had to be further down.

I leaned one shoulder against the doorframe as I held up her list of rules. "The public won't believe that we are in love if we're not all over each other." I cocked an eyebrow just so she knew that I was serious.

Her cheeks flushed, and I inwardly smiled. I loved that I had this effect on her. It was vindicating since my insides always twisted into knots when she was around.

"I think they will be fine," she said as she returned to rubbing a brush around on her face.

"It's fine with me if you want to go through all of this work only to not have the public buy it. But if no one buys it, no one will be talking about it. Which means no scout will see you, and no contract will be signed." I shrugged as I turned my attention to the list. "After all, normal couples call each other pet names. If you don't want to be a normal couple..."

I could feel Emerson's stare on me, but I didn't look up. This whole fake-relationship thing was more for her benefit than for mine. Sure, if she did get discovered, we had the potential to pack the stadium with fans interested in our relationship. An NFL player and a singer would make for great content. It was well known that a player who packed the stadium got preferential treatment every time.

All of that hinged on if we could get people to believe that we were in love. If we stood next to each other like cousins, no one was going to believe our lie.

I watched as the uncertainty my words bred raged in

Emerson's gaze. I could tell that her first instinct was to say no. But she knew that I was right, and it was eating her alive.

"Are you worried that if you kiss me, you'll like it?" I made sure my voice was innocent, even though I knew exactly what I was doing.

She sputtered and pulled her gaze away. "Yeah, right." Her cheeks were flushed as she stared at herself in the mirror. Then she flicked her gaze up at me. "I'm worried that if you kiss me, you'll never be satisfied with another woman again." She glared at me like she was daring me to respond.

What she didn't know was I already wanted to kiss her. Daring me to kiss her only made me want to do it more. I knew kissing her would change things for me. But I was already tortured every moment of every day by this girl. Adding a little more to the pot wasn't going to make a difference.

I shrugged. "I doubt that." I widened my smile. I may be miserable, but I was content with being alone in my misery. No need to have her suspect anything.

Emerson's lips parted. I could see the fury in her gaze. It was taking every ounce of her control to not march over to me. I wanted to keep pushing her, but this wasn't how I wanted our first kiss to go. I wanted her to *want* to kiss me. Not to feel goaded into doing it.

I sighed. "I think we should do what comes naturally. We're both adults. We can handle a little kissing or hand holding." I held up the paper. "I promise not to take advantage of it if you do the same."

Her gaze drifted to the paper before landing back on me. She was chewing her bottom lip now, and it was taking all of my control to stand my ground and feign a platonic relationship with her.

"Okay," she whispered.

"Okay?"

She nodded. "The rules stay but can be broken occasionally with purpose." She swung her legs out from under the vanity and walked over to me with her hand extended. "Deal?"

I eyed her slender fingers and soft skin. I didn't want to touch her. Not because I didn't want to, but because I knew that as soon as I did, the memory would haunt me forever.

She looked expectant, so I slipped her hand into mine and gave it two exaggerated shakes up and down, before I dropped it and shoved my hands into my front pockets.

"I'm glad we got that out of the way." Then she glanced around. "I'm gonna get dressed, so if you want to..." She nodded toward the door.

"Oh, yep," I said as I turned and headed back out to the living room.

I tried to keep my mind blank as I sat on the couch. I didn't need to think about kissing her or the fact that she was changing on the other side of the wall.

I forgot to breathe when she walked out of her room. She was wearing a brown off-the-shoulder dress that hugged all of her curves. She'd put a cropped denim vest over it. Her hair fell past her shoulders in soft waves. When I stood, her strappy heels made her only a few inches shorter than me. I wanted to tell her that she looked amazing, but I bit back the compliment. Instead, I just smiled at her, and when she moved to pick up her guitar, I beat her to it.

"I can carry it," I said, hating that when she moved, I was surrounded by the smell of her perfume. It made my heart pound harder.

She glanced over at me, her entire body tensing from my proximity. I hated that she still reacted this way. I wanted her to feel comfortable around me. Why did she always act like being near me hurt her?

"Okay." She straightened and then glanced at the clock on the wall. "Ooo, we're going to be late," she said as she crossed the room and slipped on her purse.

"Wanna ride on my motorcycle?" I asked as I followed her.

She gave me a pointed look. "I don't think I can get on in this getup." Her dress was tight against her legs and went down past her knees. "Plus, it's not that far."

We could make it work with my motorcycle, but with the way I was feeling, it was probably best for me to keep my hands to myself. I just nodded and walked out onto the landing when she opened the door. I waited for her to lock up before we started down the stairs.

We walked in silence for a few minutes as we made our

way to the sidewalk. I glanced over at her, wanting to ask her so many questions, but knowing I wasn't allowed to do so.

Finally, the silence felt like it was going to kill me, so I glanced over at her. "Are you nervous?"

She paused before meeting my gaze for a moment. "Kind of."

"Do you normally get nervous?"

She nodded. "Every time. But, once I get onstage and I start playing, all my nerves fade away. I know I just need to get out there."

I laughed, and she looked over at me with a confused expression. I raised my hand. "I'm not laughing at you," I said quickly.

"Really? 'Cause it kind of feels that way."

I shook my head. "It's just that I can relate." I sighed as I pushed my hand through my hair. "It's the same for me. I always get so nervous before a game that I want to throw up. But as soon as I get onto the field and I feel the turf beneath my cleats and the roar of the crowd... My nerves fade away, and all that's left is me and the ball." When I glanced up at Emerson, her eyes were wide as she stared at me.

"It's just me, my guitar, and the song," she whispered.

"That's all that matters."

She smiled softly as she nodded. "It's a sensation that most people don't understand."

"I agree."

The awkward tension between us seemed to fade away.

Even though we were walking in silence, the air felt clearer. There was a bond between us that hadn't been there before. And I loved it.

When we got to Night Spirits, Billy was standing outside. He nodded at me, and out of instinct, I placed my hand on Emerson's lower back to allow her to go first. I felt her back muscles twitch under my hand. My first instinct was to pull back, fearing that I'd overstepped, but Emerson didn't glance back at me as if to ask what I was doing. She didn't skip a beat. She just walked ahead, nodding at Billy as she passed by.

"No hat today?" Billy asked. I glanced to the side. The crowd that was waiting to get in was starting to whisper.

Normally, I'd pull my cap further down on my face but not tonight. Tonight, I was Stone Walker supporting his girlfriend. I really hoped that this was going to work. I wanted the world for Emerson. She deserved to have all the luck she wanted.

"Not tonight," I said as I clapped Billy on the shoulder, waved at the crowd, and then moved to open the door for Emerson.

She glanced at me when she passed by. "Ready for this?" she whispered.

I studied her before a smile spread across my lips. "As ready as I'll ever be."

Once inside, I let her lead me. Tilly joined us near the back door that Billy had snuck me out of last time I was here. I could hear the murmur of the crowd as I walked by. I quickened my pace and slipped Emerson's hand into mine. It felt amazing to claim her as mine.

Emerson's eyes widened as she glanced over at me, and I ignored her as I nodded toward a table of middle-aged women who were staring at us.

"Ladies," I said as I pulled Emerson a bit closer to me.

"What are you doing?" Emerson hissed.

I released her hand and wrapped my arm around her shoulder. I leaned in close, my lips millimeters from her ear. "You're supposed to be in love with me, remember?" The feel of her body and the smell of her shampoo had my senses going haywire. It was both pure bliss and torture at the same time.

Even though I knew at the end of this I was going to be left with a broken heart, I didn't care. I was going to enjoy every moment with her until I wasn't allowed to touch her anymore.

She pulled away from me once we got backstage. Tilly led us to the dressing room. She kept grinning at me and telling me that the performance had been perfect. I wanted to tell her that it wasn't performative for me, but that would negate the fake-relationship deal, so I just smiled and nodded.

I sat down on the far chair and watched as Tilly and Emerson interacted. Tilly walked over to the vanity and picked up an envelope. I recognized Hayden's handwriting, and I waited to see what they were going to say about it.

"Another lucky charm," Tilly said as she ripped open the envelope and handed it to Emerson.

Emerson flicked her gaze over at me like she was unsure if she should open it before she turned her attention back to the envelope. "Oh, that's so sweet," she said as she pulled it open and peeked inside. "It's a pig." A smile spread across her lips.

"What is that?" I asked as I leaned forward, so I could get a better look at what Hayden had bought.

"Somebody is sending Emerson lucky charms," Tilly said as she moved to unclasp Emerson's guitar case and flipped it open. After she pulled out Emerson's guitar, she waved toward the charms at the bottom. "I think the dream catcher is my favorite." Tilly pulled it out and let it hang from her fingertips.

I stood and walked over to the case to glance inside. "You really don't know who is sending these?" I asked as I picked up the easter egg and studied it.

"No," Emerson said, taking the egg from me and setting it back in her case.

Her fingertips brushed my palm, sending shivers up my arm. I glanced up to see her studying me like she wanted to ask me a question. I wondered for a moment if she suspected that I was the one sending her charms. But I didn't know Emerson to skirt around an issue. If she thought I was sending them, she would just ask me.

Instead, she dropped her gaze to the envelope and shook the pig out into her hand. After she pulled out the card, she read the note that Hayden had written. "The pig is a lucky charm in Germany. It signifies wealth and fertility."

"Ooo," Tilly said as she bumped Emerson with her shoulder. "Fertility."

Emerson's cheeks flushed as she shot Tilly an annoyed look. Then she tucked the card back into the envelope and set the pig down in her case. My heart swelled at the sight. It was as if she were carrying a piece of me everywhere she went, and I loved that.

Even if she didn't know that I had sent them in the first place.

There was a soft knock on the dressing room door, and a woman with a clipboard told Emerson that she had five minutes to go. Emerson nodded, and I could tell her nerves were getting the better of her. She wasn't making eye contact, and her hands were shaking. I wanted to pull her into my arms until she calmed down, but there was no one around. I couldn't use our fake relationship as an excuse.

Instead, I just stood there, watching her.

Once it was time for her to go out onstage, she led Tilly and me out of the room. I followed behind the two of them as they waited on the side of the stage to be introduced.

Henry rattled off her name and then extended his hand in her direction as the signal for her to step onstage. She smiled as she turned to the crowd and waved.

She greeted the audience, got adjusted, and strummed a few chords.

I could see her nerves melt away as she started singing.

It was mesmerizing to watch her as she closed her eyes and felt the music she was playing. I wasn't really paying attention to the words because my mind was so clouded with how beautiful she looked that I couldn't concentrate on anything else.

I don't know how long I stood there in a trance, but the sound of Tilly clearing her throat startled me. I glanced down at her to see her smiling as she stared at Emerson.

"You're good," she said, not bothering to look up at me.

"Excuse me?"

She gave me a look that said, *don't play with me.* I wanted to reject her hypothesis that there was anything real going on between Emerson and me, but what was the point? It would be a lie, and from the hint of teasing in her gaze, I could tell she would see right through it.

"Don't tell Emerson," I whispered.

She pretended to lock her lips. "Your secret is safe with me." She rocked a few times on her feet. "Just make sure you don't hurt her."

I shook my head. "I wouldn't dream of it."

She glanced over at me, holding my gaze as if she were sizing me up. Then she reached down and grabbed a dozen roses from her purse. "After her set, bring these onto the stage for her."

I took the flowers. "Okay," I said.

She studied me. "Make the crowd believe that you two are together." Her voice had turned commanding, and I had half a mind to salute her.

Instead, I just smiled. "I can do this," I assured her.

Emerson played the last few notes of her song, and the crowd erupted into cheers. I wasn't sure if I should head out onto the stage or if she was going to play another song. Thankfully, Tilly pushed at my back and demanded that I get going. I stepped out onto the stage. Emerson hadn't noticed me as she thanked the crowd and turned to leave. When her gaze locked with mine, my heart was pounding so hard I could hear it in my ears.

Thankfully, I had enough experience faking confidence that I smiled as I zeroed in on her. We met halfway. I pulled the flowers out from behind my back and handed them to her. Her eyes widened as she took them.

"What are you doing?" Emerson whispered, glancing up at me.

I slid my hand around her waist and tugged her to my chest. I cradled her cheek with my other hand and stared deep into her green eyes. The hushed whispers of the crowd faded into the background. All that existed was me and Emerson. I leaned closer, my gaze drifting to her lips.

If she didn't want this, this was her time to pull away. Otherwise, I was going to claim her lips as mine.

"I'm kissing you," I whispered.

I closed the space between us, my lips finding hers. The moment our lips touched, the dam inside of me broke. My hand slid from her cheek, and I tangled my fingers in her hair. I waited to see what she was going to do before I deepened the kiss.

For a moment, I wondered if I'd done something wrong. She wasn't reacting, she was just standing there like a statue. I moved to pull back—there was no way I wanted to force her to kiss me if she didn't want to—but the feeling of her arms around my chest told me that she didn't want me to leave.

That was all I needed. I teased her lips with my tongue, and she let me in. I got lost in the feeling of her body against mine, my hand in her hair, and her lips on mine. We fell into a dance as our lips moved in sync.

The roar of the crowd around us finally broke through the fog that blanketed my thoughts whenever I was around Emerson. Realizing that this was supposed to be fake, I pulled away. I was the fool that got carried away. I was the fool that wanted this to be real.

Emerson was just along for the ride.

Her lips looked puffy and her gaze glassy as she stared up at me. I grinned down at her as I turned to face the crowd, slipping my arm around her waist and dipping down to whisper, "I think they bought it," in her ear.

She studied me before she glanced to the crowd. The flash of camera lights pinged around us. When she looked back up at me, she nodded. "I think you're right."

18

EMERSON

S leep wasn't coming to me.

I wanted to say that it was because of the adrenaline I normally felt after a gig—but I couldn't lie to myself. I was up, tossing and turning, in the middle of the night because I couldn't forget that kiss.

I could still feel the way his hands tangled in my hair. I brought my fingertips up to my lips. I could still feel the way his lips took mine. I hated how perfectly my body fit against his. I could still feel his broad chest and his heart as it beat in time with mine.

I groaned and grabbed the pillow next to me, covering my face with it.

This whole fake-relationship thing was a bad idea. I should have known that when I agreed to it. But Tilly was persuasive. If I hadn't given in, she would've never let me live it down.

Now I was worried that it had changed me forever. I could never go back to the Emerson who was apathetic to Stone Walker.

That person had died, and the girl who couldn't stop thinking about him had been born.

"Stop thinking about him," I whispered to myself as I pulled the pillow from my face and blew out my breath. I stared up at the dark ceiling above me. Was this now my life? Was I going to spend the rest of eternity thinking about Stone?

He'd made it pretty clear after the kiss that it had all been for show. I don't think I'll ever forget his cocky, wide smile as he pulled me to his side and waved his hand at the audience. To him, this was just a facade. For me, it meant so much more.

And I hated that it meant so much more.

Realizing that there was no way I could fall asleep with my mind racing, I turned to my side and clicked on my lamp. I fluffed the pillows behind my back and grabbed my phone. The screen's light illuminated around me as I opened a social media app and started scrolling.

News about friends getting married and having babies, and random pics of their food filled my feed. I was in the middle of reading about one of my high school best friend's trip to China, when a message popped up on my screen.

I glanced over at it, ready to swipe it away, when I paused. It looked like a picture of Stone.

We were friends on this app, but we'd never talked to

each other. Why was he talking to me now? I hesitated, wondering if I should click on it. But then I shook my head, told myself I was being ridiculous, and opened it.

Stone: Can't sleep?

I glanced in the direction of Stone's apartment. Why was he up? Was sleep evading him like it was evading me? Was it the kiss? Or just nerves for the game tomorrow?

I closed my eyes and shook my head. I needed to stop thinking so much.

Me: Adrenaline. Hasn't worn off yet.

Good. That was good. Vague and understandable. Three dots danced on the screen as I waited for his response.

Stone: You should go to bed. It'll be a busy day tomorrow.

Me: I could say the same to you.

Three dots danced once more only to stop with no message. I waited, staring at the screen for his response.

Stone: Touche.

Stone: I'm watching film for tomorrow's game.

I nodded.

Me: Smart.

I paused, tapping my foot. Did I come clean to Stone? Should I tell him that I knew very little about the rules of football? Sure, I grew up with a football-obsessed brother, but I never really took that much of an interest. I think it was because it was my family's life—and that always rubbed me the wrong way. So, I did what I could to avoid it in high school.

Me: Stone?

Stone: Yeah?

I wiggled my fingers as I tried to think of the right way to say it.

Me: How much does a fake girlfriend of an NFL player need to know about the rules of the game?

Stone: Probably just as much as an NFL player needs to know about writing songs and playing the guitar.

I frowned.

Me: But shouldn't I know at least a little bit? Won't it look weird when I'm there, looking like I have no idea what's happening?

The three dots appeared and disappeared so many times that I wanted to explode. Was he disappointed? Should I have confessed this when we were agreeing to this fake relationship?

Finally, his message appeared, and I sucked in my breath when I read it.

Stone: Wanna come over?

I stared at those three little words. My mind was swirling with all sorts of reasons why I shouldn't get out of bed, get dressed, and head over to Stone's apartment. But those reasons didn't seem to matter. Suddenly, my fingers had a mind of their own, and I texted back, "Sure.".

Then my body went into autopilot as I pulled off my covers and padded into my closet to put on a white shirt and a dark-blue cotton romper. I pulled my hair up into a messy bun, grabbed my glasses, made sure I didn't look like death, and headed over to Stone's place.

I stood outside his door with my hand raised for a solid minute. Finally, I shook my head, cursed myself for being so ridiculous, and knocked.

The door opened shortly. Stone was standing there in a faded Tennessee Tigers t-shirt and a pair of grey sweatpants. He had a pencil tucked behind his ear, and his hair looked freshly washed and fluffy—totally run-my-fingers-through-it.

Blast.

"Hey," he said, his voice soft. He punctuated his greeting with his ridiculous half-smile. The one he gave to all the cameras. Except this one didn't feel fake—it felt genuine, and it was confusing me.

"Hey," I said as I adjusted my glasses.

He paused and then moved to wave me in. "Come on in."

"Thanks," I said.

I kicked off my slippers and stood in the entrance of his apartment, waiting for him to tell me where to go. He shut the door and then stepped past me. The smell of his soap mixed with his laundry detergent washed over me.

"I'm watching on the couch," he said.

"Great." I followed him to the couch, where there were some throw pillows and blankets strewn around.

He quickly picked them up, folding his arms around them. "Sorry."

I shook my head. "Can I actually have a blanket?"

He glanced up at me and nodded. "Sure."

I picked the Tennessee Tiger one that was faded but still soft. I settled down on the couch, propping my feet up on the coffee table and tucking the blanket around my body and legs.

Stone sat down next to me. His sudden weight pitched me toward him. I slid a little to the right, trying to create space between us and cursing my body for tingling from the touch of his skin against mine.

If Stone noticed, he didn't say anything. Instead, he reached forward and grabbed the bowl of popcorn and the remote on the table. He settled back, his arm brushing mine for a moment. Warmth emanated throughout my body from the innocent touch, and I was beginning to think that coming over here had been a mistake.

I was sure I'd be okay being the oblivious football girlfriend. Someone had to be that person, maybe it was what I was destined to be.

"Want some popcorn?" he asked, tipping the bowl toward me.

Realizing that there was no rational way I was going to be able to get out of this evening without either looking crazy or confessing to him, I nodded and took a handful of popcorn.

Stone's gaze was glued to the TV as he pressed play.

We spent the next half hour watching plays. Stone took his time pausing the TV and explaining to me what was going on. I tried really hard to pay attention, but it was a lot. The only thing I seemed to be able to retain is that a touchdown is worth six points and there's something called a first down. If they didn't move the ball past the marker, then they were in danger of losing the ball.

Everything else went over my head.

Thankfully, Oscar came to join me on the couch. He curled up into my lap. His purr was loud as I petted him over and over. The warmth of his body on my lap plus the blanket plus Stone talking in the background made me sleepy, and suddenly, my eyes began to drift closed.

My head felt heavy as I tipped to the side, and as soon as something caught me, I snuggled into it. My body began to relax as I fell deeper and deeper to sleep.

"Emerson."

Stone's voice jolted me awake. I moved to sit up, glancing around, worried that I'd slept here the whole night.

"I'm so sorry, Stone," I whispered as I rubbed my eyes under my glasses to get them to focus. "I think I fell asleep." I turned to the side to see that I hadn't laid my head on the couch. I'd fallen asleep on Stone's shoulder. My entire body warmed from embarrassment.

Stone was just smiling at me. "It's okay. You were only asleep for twenty minutes." He yawned. "I finished watching the footage without you."

"I'm sorry."

He shook his head. "No harm done." He shifted his weight, so he was sitting on the edge of the couch. He hesitated before he glanced over at me. "Will you do something for me?"

I yawned and stretched my arms out in front of me. I was in that groggy and yet wakeful state that you get when you've taken the edge off, but you still want to crawl back into bed. "Sure."

He nodded before he stood and disappeared into his bedroom. I curled up to the side, scratching Oscar under the chin. He stretched his little arm out before settling his chin down on it. Movement by Stone's door caught my attention. He was standing in the doorway, staring down at an orange-and-black piece of fabric.

"What's that?" I asked.

He glanced up at me as he shifted the item between his hands. "So, it's customary for a girlfriend to wear her boyfriend's jersey on game day." He held onto the shoulders as he shook the jersey out. His number, 41, and last name was affixed to the back. He glanced down at the jersey before he slowly brought his gaze up to meet mine. "Will you wear it?"

My entire body warmed as I stared at his jersey. Of course, I was going to wear it. I was going to wear it and pretend that it meant nothing more than just a fake boyfriend asking his fake girlfriend to wear something of his. It would look great for the cameras to have me show up in an article of his clothing. It would sell our relationship, for sure.

But to me it meant so much more.

"Sure," I whispered.

He smiled over at me. "Yeah?"

I nodded. "Of course. We're faking a relationship, right?" I slipped Oscar off my lap and stood. I stretched before I made my way across the living room with my hand extended. "If that's what girlfriends are supposed to do, then I will be the dutiful girlfriend." I shook it out before holding it against my body.

When I glanced up, Stone was staring at me. There was something in his gaze that had my heart pounding. I swallowed, trying to calm my nerves as I studied him. Did he *want* me to wear this? More than just to sell the lie?

I hushed my mind. That was a stupid question. Of course, he didn't want that. He was just helping me out. As a friend. Right?

"I should get some sleep," I said as I folded the jersey and hung it over my arm.

Stone blinked as if he'd just snapped out of a trance and nodded. "For sure." He glanced around like he was looking for something. Then he pushed his hand through his hair before he motioned toward the door. "I'll walk you home."

I shook my head. "Not necessary." I leaned forward. "It's just next door."

Stone sucked his breath between his teeth. "Sorry. Chivalry is not dead. I'll walk you to your door."

I was ready to get away from him, his gaze, and the confusing feelings that being around him stirred up. But I also didn't know how to tell him that without hinting that I cared if he came, so I shrugged. "Suit yourself."

He waited for me to slip my feet into my slippers before he opened the door. We walked side by side across the landing and paused in front of my door. I stood there, fiddling with my keys, not sure what I should say, but not wanting him to leave.

"Good—"

"I just—"

We both pinched our lips shut and smiled awkwardly at each other. Stone leaned forward. "You first."

My body flushed with heat. "I was just going to say, good luck tomorrow."

He studied me before he nodded. "Thanks."

I gave him a soft smile and pulled out my house key. I turned the handle and pushed open my door. "Good night, Stone," I said as I glanced over at him.

His gaze was dark and cloudy. It sent shivers across my skin. Not wanting to stand here any longer, longing for our relationship to be real, I nodded and took a step toward the door. Then I paused.

"What were you going to say?" I asked as I turned to face him fully.

I could see the turmoil in his gaze. Then he took a step closer to me. I took a step back, my body bumping into the doorframe. Stone's arm came up to rest on the trim around my door.

"I just wanted to say..." His voice drifted off as his other hand came up. His finger hooked my glasses and gently lifted them off my face. His gaze intensified as he stared at me. He was so close that I feared he could hear my pounding heart.

"What did you want to say?" I breathed out, barely able to make my voice work.

His gaze dropped to my lips before making its way back up to meet mine. "The kiss earlier?"

My body flushed as I nodded. "Yeah?"

He scoffed and glanced up, his lips breaking out into a smile. Then he glanced to the side. "I can do better. I think the cameras messed up my game."

My eyes widened. His kiss had been amazing, I couldn't imagine what 'better' would look like. I chewed my bottom lip as I nodded. "Okay."

I thought about daring him to show me. I wanted his lips on mine. His hands on my body. If that wasn't his best, what did his best feel like? He studied me, a sort of turmoil coursing through his gaze. I could feel that he was conflicted. It matched my own confusion.

In one swift movement, he pushed off the doorframe and took a step back. He scrubbed his face with his hand before pushing it through his hair. "'Night, Em."

I wanted to grab him and pull him back to me. I wanted to feel his warmth. I wanted him to touch me in a way a fake boyfriend should *not* touch his fake girlfriend. But instead, I just nodded.

"Good night, Stone." I entered my apartment, pausing at the door so I could turn to face him. He was still standing there, watching me. I gave him a soft smile and slowly shut the door.

Once I locked my dead bolt, I leaned against the door and slowly let my breath out. That was intense. There were feelings coursing between us that I hadn't expected. I brought my hand up to my heart. I wanted to turn to check the peephole. I wanted to see if he was still there.

But I knew if I saw him, I wouldn't have the strength not to open the door and leap into his arms. And if I did that, it would ruin everything. Our past was complicated. My feelings now didn't erase what had happened between him and my family. It didn't erase the fact that he'd left when things got hard.

I needed to remember that we weren't just some singer falling for an NFL player. Our past was a confusing tapestry that wouldn't end in us falling in love and living happily ever after. I couldn't just sweep what happened with Cayden under the rug.

Sure, my relationship with my family was strained, but showing up with enemy number one on my arm was a sure-fire way of severing any bonds we still had.

Plus, I wasn't sure if Stone even wanted me like that. For all I knew, I was just a project for him. A way for him to assuage his guilt over what he did to my brother.

I didn't want to allow myself to fall for him if there wasn't a chance he would fall for me.

I pushed myself off the door, slipped off my slippers, and padded into my room. No, the best thing for me to do was focus on this fake relationship, play each gig to the best of my ability, and pray that all of this would result in a contract with a record label.

That would be my only focus.

It had to be.

19

STONE

I needed to leave for the game early today since it was an afternoon game. Instead of having Emerson come with me and hang out by herself in the dedicated family room, I told her to head over an hour before the game started. Hayden dropped the tickets off, so I could bring them over to her before I left.

With my helmet in hand and my leather jacket on, I headed out the door. I crossed the landing and knocked. It took all my strength not to think about last night and how I almost kissed Emerson for real.

The memory of her pressed against the doorframe, her wide green eyes staring up at me. Her pillowy lips begging for me to kiss them. It haunted me all night. Finally, I'd gotten up and taken some cold medicine to knock me out.

That seemed to do the trick. I woke up mostly rested. I

was tired, but I knew as soon as I got out on the field, that would all go away.

I lifted my hand and knocked. I waited, rocking back and forth on my toes. Finally, the door opened, and Emerson was standing there. She looked groggy.

"What's up?" she asked, pulling the door open more. She was wearing a skimpy satin pajama set, and it ignited an inferno in my stomach.

I forced myself to stay calm as I reached into my back pocket and pulled out the tickets. "Just dropping these off. Hayden scored you front-row seats, so we can make a show of this." I winked as I handed the tickets over.

Emerson took them. "Thanks," she said.

"There's two, so you can bring Tilly. I'm sure she'll want to come."

Emerson yawned as she leaned against the doorframe. "I'm sure she will."

"Great." Not sure what to do, I just nodded and then turned to head down the stairs. Then I paused. "Bring something nice to change into afterward. We're going out for dinner."

She looked surprised. "Really?"

I winked as I cocked my head to the side. "We gotta sell this romance. I'm going to give you the Stone special."

She rolled her eyes. "Okay."

I shrugged and just as I got to the top step, her voice caused me to pause.

"Stone?"

I closed my eyes. Why did I love the sound of my name on her lips so much? I really was a glutton for punishment. "Yeah?" I called over my shoulder.

"Break a leg."

I met her gaze and held it for a moment before I nodded and made my way down the stairs. Once I got to my bike, I shoved my helmet on and then swung my leg over the bike. The roar of the muffler filled the garage as I pulled out of my parking spot and waited for the garage door so I could get through.

I parked in my reserved spot once I got to the stadium. I threw my keys up into the air as I made my way to the door to punch in my code. As soon as I walked through the door of the locker room, a cheer erupted. The guys were whooping and hollering as they all surrounded me.

"You did it, man!" Isaac said as he clapped me on the back.

"I'm so glad you locked that down," Colt said.

It took me a moment to realize what they were talking about. Emerson. The kiss from last night must have made it to social media. Which was good. It meant our plan was working.

Instead of telling them the truth, I decided to just go along with it. It felt nice to have my friends this excited for me. No longer were they trying to set me up with their sister or their cousin. I was no longer the single guy, and it felt good.

Plus, I wanted my relationship with Emerson to be real, so with my team, I was going to allow it to be.

"Yep. She finally saddled herself with yours truly," I said as I shrugged.

"I'm happy for you." Isaac beamed as he squeezed my shoulder and then returned to his locker.

The rest of the guys murmured something congratulatory before they returned to what they were doing. I knew I shouldn't be smiling as hard as I was, but I couldn't help it. I wanted Emerson to be mine, and in this moment, she was.

I was on cloud nine during Coach's talk to us. I was still grinning when I dressed and made my way to the field to warm up and get my uniform checked. George and I started practicing. I wasn't fully paying attention. It was getting close to when Emerson was going to show up.

George noticed my distraction and called me on it, telling me that I needed to get my head in the game. I agreed with him and forced my focus to be on George and his throws instead of the stadium seat I'd reserved for her behind me.

Thankfully, I got into the zone. George and I were on point, him throwing me the ball and me catching. I was confused when Issac ran up to me.

"Hey, man. I think your biggest fan just showed up." He nodded toward the seats behind me.

My heart started pounding in my chest when I turned to see Emerson and Tilly standing in the stadium. Emerson's hair was pulled up into pigtail buns on top of her head. Her cheeks were painted with a Tennessee Tiger. And she was wearing my jersey.

Tilly was holding a sign that said, "Learn to take the heat because you're about to be beat!" with a 41 dotted all over the posterboard. She was screaming and shaking the sign, drawing the curious attention of everyone around her.

Emerson shushed her. Tilly was a lot, but I didn't even care. Emerson was in my jersey, at my game. She was mine. My heart swelled with pride. I held up my hand to George to let him know I needed a second as I jogged over to where Emerson and Tilly were.

Right now, fake relationship or no fake relationship, Emerson was mine.

"Hey, ladies," I said once I neared the padded wall. I grinned at Emerson, not wanting to hide the fact that I was happy she was here. "That jersey looks nice on you." I gave her a wink.

Her eyes widened, and her face flushed as she looked down. "Thanks," she whispered.

Even though she thought that these compliments were contrived, I didn't care. I was going to be me. I was going to do all the things that I'd wanted to do for her. I was letting it all out.

"And me?" Tilly asked as she framed her chin with the back of her hand and pursed her lips.

"You look amazing," I said, keeping my gaze trained on Emerson. She kept glancing away and looking back at me. I was enjoying how shy she seemed. It was a side of her that I'd never seen before.

"Are you nervous?" she asked when her gaze finally settled on mine.

I shrugged. "Just normal nerves. Nothing I can't handle." I smiled at her, open and unabashed.

"Ooo!" Tilly grabbed onto Emerson's arm and shook it. "Number 73 is pointing at us while he's talking to a reporter."

73? That was Isaac. I turned to see that his gaze was trained on me as he spoke to Jacob, one of the reporters on the field. Jacob was glancing between me and Isaac as if he were trying to follow what Isaac was telling him.

Suddenly, the cameraman turned his camera to face us. I knew that they were getting pregame footage like they always did, and this was going to be our chance of putting Emerson in the public's eyes.

"Kiss her," Tilly hissed in my direction, but I was already closing the gap.

Thankfully, she didn't have to be convinced. As soon as I got to the wall, Emerson bent down. I slipped my hand through her hair and pulled her ever so gently to me. I pressed my lips to hers, loving the sensation that ran through me. It was the good kind of electricity. The kind you wanted to experience over and over again.

I moved my lips over hers, deepening the kiss. I wanted so badly to kiss her for real. Without cameras. Without crowds. I wanted her. All of her. She was mine to enjoy.

Mine to worship. I just hoped that someday she'd trust me enough to let me in.

I knew this kiss had to end even if I didn't want it to. I had a game to play, and Emerson didn't feel for me like I felt for her. She thought this was fake. I wanted it to be real. I wanted it to be real so damn bad.

I pulled back, but I lingered close enough so I could look her in the eyes. I wanted her to see how I felt for her. Her breathing matched mine. I couldn't quite tell what she was thinking. Was she mad? Should I have stopped the kiss earlier?

Her gaze was locked with mine. I knew I needed to pull back, but I wasn't ready. And she didn't seem in a hurry either.

These intense feelings coursing through my body would be the death of me. If I didn't back away right now, I was going to fall harder and farther than I'd ever fallen before. And I couldn't let myself do that. Not when I knew, at the end of all of this, she was going to dance off into the sunset with *Brett*. The truth was over. Now I was back to playing the game.

"I think that gave them some good footage," I whispered as I broke out into a smile.

She blinked a few times before we both glanced over at the sports reporters who'd gathered a few feet away from us. I shot them all a big smile followed by a wink. I pulled back and grabbed her hand.

"I want to introduce you all to Emerson King. She is the

most talented singer, and lucky for me, my girlfriend." I dropped a kiss on her hand before I smiled over at her.

Emerson gave the camera a small wave. I said goodbye before I dropped her hand. When I was a few feet away, I turned and blew her a kiss. She smiled, pretended to catch it, and tucked it into her pocket.

"Ugh, you two are so cute it makes me sick," Isaac said when he came up to join me after I jogged back to the team.

I just smiled and shrugged. Even though I could pretend that Emerson was mine when I was with my teammates, it didn't make it true. In reality, this was all a facade. One with an expiration date. I needed to accept that.

"Let's play some ball," I growled. I had so much adrenaline and anxiety coursing through me, and I needed to do something to get it out.

We jogged off the field and back into the tunnel to wait for the announcer to introduce us. Coach gave us a few more pointers, and Colt led us in a quick prayer. As soon as our team was announced, we ran through the banner the cheerleaders had put up and out onto the field.

George was the one to represent us in the coin toss, and we won. We chose to receive, and the game started.

I was worried that having Emerson there was going to distract me, but as soon as the ball was snapped and I was running to get open, the stadium faded away and all I could see was the play. My muscles burned and stretched as I leapt to catch the throws that George sent my direction.

Ten minutes into quarter one, we scored a touchdown. I

threw the ball onto the ground in the end zone and started to dance. I looked over to see Emerson and Tilly cheering and dancing right along with me.

They suddenly stopped and were pointing at the mega screens around the stadium. I looked over to see that they had split the screen. One side was me and the other side was Emerson.

There was a heart overlay, and everyone started looking around to get a look at who Emerson was. Her cheeks flushed as she smiled and waved at the camera before turning her attention to me and blowing a kiss.

By halftime, the Florida Stingrays were up one touchdown. The locker room was quiet as we sat around, listening to Coach yell at us in a way he knew would motivate us to go out there and kick butt.

We ran back out for the second half. I paced the sidelines when defense was up. I was nervous we might not win this game. I was handed a water bottle, and I tipped my head back and sprayed a stream into my mouth.

And then, even though I knew I shouldn't, I let my gaze drift over to Emerson. She was standing in front of her seat with her hands covering her mouth as she watched the play. For someone who knew so little about the sport, she was invested. I smiled as I watched her shout at the refs.

An arm falling hard on my shoulders snapped me out of my trance. I looked over to see Jayden standing right next to me.

"Coach is going to be pissed that your head isn't in the

game," he said as he looked straight ahead and slowly turned to face me.

"What are you talking about? It's in the game."

He shook his head and pointed to the mega screens. They were playing my smile as I stared up at Emerson on repeat. They even emphasized it with a pounding heart that was growing bigger and bigger.

I cursed under my breath and swore to myself that I wasn't going to look in her direction until the game was finished. Thankfully I kept that promise, and we managed a close victory of 13 to 12. We cheered as we met together in the center of the field. After celebrating, I ran over to Emerson, who had remained in her seat.

"Hayden is going to come get you. She'll take you to the family room to get some food." I pointed my finger at her. "Don't eat a lot. We have another public appearance to go to."

Emerson nodded. Tilly popped into my line of sight to congratulate me. I nodded at her, glanced one more time at Emerson, and rejoined the team as we ran off the field.

I showered and got ready in record time. Coach wanted me to stop in the press room before I left. I nodded as I walked out. After my interviews, I made my way to the family room in search of Emerson.

I pushed through the claps on the back and the congratulations. I tried not to seem rude, but I was ready to find Emerson and leave. The crowd parted, and I found her standing along the far wall. She was leaning toward Tilly and whispering.

She hadn't noticed me, so I took my time taking her in. She was wearing a strapless black jumpsuit with lots of jewelry hanging from her neck and ears. She tucked her hair behind her ear as she glanced around. Her gaze found mine, and she paused before she smiled.

My heart surged as I crossed the space between us. "Hey, ladies," I said. I glanced down at Emerson and smiled. She was watching me, holding my gaze like she didn't want to let it go. I was trying hard not to read into our interaction, but I wanted this to be real so bad.

"You clean up nice," Tilly said as she motioned to my black suit and white button-down shirt.

"Thanks." I glanced back over to Emerson. "Ready?"

She nodded as she pushed the strap of her blue purse further up her shoulder. "Sure."

I reached out my hand and gestured the direction we needed to go. I kept my hand centimeters from her lower back. I wanted to touch her, but I didn't want to make her feel uncomfortable. As soon as we exited the family room and entered the tunnels, I dropped my hand to my side.

"Be prepared," I said as we neared the press tunnel, where I knew people were going to snap pictures of us.

Emerson glanced over at me. "For what?"

I slid my hand into hers and squeezed. She glanced over at me, her eyes wide. "For the cameras," I whispered as I leaned into her.

Just then, flashes from the press sparkled around us. I nodded in their direction as I ushered Emerson through the tunnel toward the parking lot.

As soon as we were away from the cameras, she dropped my hand. "Is it always like that?" she asked as she blinked a few times.

I shook my head. "Not that intense." I shrugged. "I think word is getting around. Most of the team congratulated me when I walked into the locker room this morning."

Emerson's eyes widened. "Wow. That's fast."

"It's a good thing."

She frowned as she studied me. "Why do you say that?"

I quickened my pace so I would reach the door before her. I pressed on the release and it swung out. "It means you'll get discovered quicker." I paused, not wanting to say the words but needing to. I didn't want her to feel pressured to stay in this fake relationship longer than she wanted. "And the quicker we can stop fake dating."

Emerson snapped her gaze to mine. She held it for a moment before she looked away and nodded. "You're right. The sooner we get the desired result, the better."

We walked in silence through the parking garage until we got to my motorcycle. Thankfully, I didn't have to convince her to get on this time. She swung her leg over before extending her expectant hand. I handed her my helmet and leather jacket before climbing on in front of her.

It was torture, feeling her body pressed against mine as I started the engine and took off through the parking lot. But it was a kind of torture that I never wanted to end. She belonged on my bike.

The thought of her like this with another man was enough to make me see red. I needed to convince her that she needed to fake date me forever. I was certain, with our history, she could never fall for me for real. Why would she?

Her family had probably poisoned the water. I knew what they thought about me. They'd made it clear when they promised to help me but shoved me out the door as soon as I wouldn't give them what they wanted.

This relationship was going to come to an end; I needed to accept that.

I took in a deep breath and straightened as we idled at a red light. Emerson straightened as well, her hands lingering on her thighs as we waited for the light to turn green. I hated how comfortable I'd gotten with touching her. I hated how this felt real.

I pulled into the valet for Burton Steak and turned off the engine. Emerson climbed off, and I followed after her. I handed the key to the valet driver before turning to see that Emerson had pulled off her helmet. The maître d' was standing at the hostess stand. I walked up and told her the name for the reservation.

She nodded as she offered to take our jackets. Emerson handed her my helmet, and I moved to help her out of my leather jacket. My fingers brushed her skin, and I hated how electricity rushed through my body as a result. I handed the jacket to the expectant maître d', and she disappeared into the coat closet.

When she returned, she waved for us to follow. Our table was in the back corner of the restaurant. As I made my way through the tables, Emerson slipped her hand into mine. My heart surged as I glanced down to see her nodding at a couple that were obviously staring at us.

I squeezed her hand, which made her glance up at me. I held her gaze, hoping she would see just how much this meant to me—even though it wasn't supposed to mean anything.

She just smiled and pressed closer to me. "It's all for the crowd," she whispered before she turned to wave at an older couple who were trying to sneak a photo of us with their phone.

Her words felt like a dagger to my chest. I knew this was fake. I knew this was going to end. She didn't want to be with me like I wanted to be with her.

And she hadn't fallen deeply in love with me like I'd fallen for her. If I didn't stop myself now, I was never going to be able to come back.

Ever.

20

EMERSON

Dinner was lovely. I let Stone order my food. I'd never been to this restaurant before, and he seemed familiar with it, so when the waiter asked us what we wanted, I nodded at Stone and told him to surprise me. I loved the little half smile that emerged as he studied me. Like he enjoyed the fact that I trusted him to choose something for me.

I'd made the right choice, letting him decide. The food that came was impeccable. The meat was tender, and it was paired with a sauce that made each bite melt in your mouth. I let out a soft moan and closed my eyes. When I opened them, Stone was studying me with an intensity that took my breath away. I smiled at him sheepishly, and he dropped his gaze to his plate, cleared his throat, and asked me a question about music.

Our conversation was easy, and I enjoyed it. I told him

about the dreams I had; he told me his plans for the future. We both said we wanted to find the person we were meant to be with and start a family. My heart pounded when Stone studied me as I spoke. There was something in his gaze. A want that I couldn't quite figure out, and I feared I was misreading it.

After some chocolate mousse for dessert, Stone placed his fabric napkin onto the table. I moved to scoot my chair out, but he held up his hand to stop me. I waited as he came over to my chair and helped me pull it out.

When I stood, the movement brought me inches from his chest. I could smell his cologne and feel the warmth of his body. When I peeked up at him, he was staring down at me once more in a way that made me feel like I was going to melt into a puddle.

Stone stayed a few inches behind me. I could barely feel his hand on my lower back as he guided me through the restaurant. He grabbed my hand and changed spots with me when a waiter came by with a tray of food propped up on his shoulder. Stone protectively reached out his hand in front of me as he shielded me from any possible misstep.

My heart was pounding now. Never in my life had Stone Walker touched me as much as he had touched me tonight. Electricity was coursing through my body at every point of contact. I was enjoying this so much, but at the same time, I was frustrated with myself for enjoying it so much.

Stone wasn't mine. He wasn't touching me because he

wanted to. He was doing this for show. Each table we walked by, he nodded at the other patrons and even stopped to sign an autograph for an elderly man. Sure, he was good at playing the doting boyfriend, but it was all an act. And I was the idiot who was buying it hook, line, and sinker.

When we got to the hostess stand, the maître d' disappeared in the coat closet and returned with Stone's helmet and leather jacket. Stone took the jacket before I could. He shook it out before holding it up for me to slip my arms into.

I wanted to yank it from him and tell him that I could do it myself. That if he kept touching me like this all night, I was going to fall for him so hard and fast that I was never going to be able to get out of it.

He was going to ruin me for other men...forever.

But I was a glutton for punishment, so I turned my back to him and slipped my arms in, closing my eyes slightly when his fingers brushed my neck as he pulled the jacket up onto my shoulders. Feeling ridiculous for reading into this more than Stone had intended, I centered myself and turned to smile at him.

"Ready?" he asked.

I nodded. When we got to the front doors, I pressed on the door release and held it open for him. I needed to get some control back, or I was going to explode. Stone gave me a look that told me he was not happy with what I'd done, but I just gave him a wide smile and watched him walk outside.

The roar of his motorcycle filled the air as the valet

drove it up to meet us. I slipped on his helmet as he tipped the valet. I swung my leg over his motorcycle. It surprised me how easy this was for me now. I'd never thought of myself as a biker but wrapping my arms around his body and feeling his broad back against my chest—I had been converted.

I slid further up on the seat and waited for Stone to join me. My entire body reacted as he held onto the motorcycle handle and settled in. The first time I rode on his bike, I did everything I could to pull my body away from his. Now, it was taking all of my strength not to sink into him. And watching his hands as he worked the handlebars to speed up and brake had me feeling all sorts of things.

I closed my eyes and allowed him to drive us back to our apartment complex. Even though there were no cameras around, I didn't care. I was going to enjoy this ride. And if Stone asked, I'd just tell him that we never knew when the paparazzi would be watching.

It may have been my imagination, but I swear Stone kept closer to me than he'd ever done before. He leaned back into me when we idled in front of the garage door, waiting for it to open.

He glanced over his shoulder at me and told me to hold tight as he leaned forward and drove in. He pulled into his parking spot and turned the engine off. In one swift movement, he was off the motorcycle. He held out his hand to assist me. Shivers rushed up my arm when I placed my hand in his.

I climbed off the bike and expected Stone to let my hand go as soon as I was up and stable. But he didn't. His fingers lingered with mine. I peeked up at him, wondering if he meant to do that, but then shook my head. That was a silly thought. He was just being a nice guy. A guy could be nice without being in love with you.

"Thanks," I whispered as I pulled my hand away and moved to slide the helmet off.

He lingered close to me as I handed him the helmet. Then we started walking toward the elevator. Once inside, he hit the button for the fourth floor, and we rode in silence. I glanced over at him a few times, wondering what he was thinking.

His jaw was set as he kept his gaze forward. His expression was unreadable. I couldn't tell if he was happy or mad. Or indifferent. Did he not feel these same jolts of electricity every time we touched? Had I just imagined it all?

I was a fool for reading into our fake relationship. To him, this was part of the act. Somewhere along the line, I'd allowed myself to believe that it meant something more.

"Thanks for dinner," I said, breaking the silence between us.

Stone glanced over at me and nodded. "Of course."

The elevator stopped, and the doors slid open. Stone extended his hand, so I exited first. We both stood on the landing, neither of us moving to our respective apartments. I didn't want to be the first to leave. I wanted to be around Stone—even if, to him, our relationship was fake.

I offered him a soft smile. "Congrats on the win. I don't think I said that today."

Stone flicked his gaze down at me before he looked away. "Thanks. And thanks for being there as support. It meant a lot." He pushed his hand through his hair before dropping his gaze to the ground.

"Of course," I whispered. Then I chuckled as I playfully punched his shoulder. "What's a fake girlfriend for, am I right?"

Stone's entire body tensed. I worried I'd said the wrong thing. But a second later, he relaxed as he glanced over at me. "Exactly."

Not wanting to stand out here and make a further fool of myself, I nodded toward my apartment. "Wanna come in for some coffee or tea?"

He glanced over toward my door before looking back at me. "Um, sure."

"Awesome." I shoved my hand into my purse as I walked toward my apartment. I pulled out my keys and unlocked the door. I slipped off my boots and then stepped further in so Stone could join me. He slipped off his shoes and shrugged out of his suit coat. I slipped out of his leather jacket, and he laid it over his helmet which he had set on the floor.

"You can make yourself comfortable. I'll get the coffee pot started."

Stone nodded as he walked into the living room.

I hated that this felt like a date when it shouldn't. If

Stone had been any other guy, then dinner at a fancy restaurant followed by coffee at my place would mean the date was going well, and I was excited to get to know the guy more.

But this wasn't any other guy. This was Stone. The one guy that would shatter my already fragile family if they found out I was dating him. I blew out my breath, hating that I couldn't just have feelings for Stone. I hated that my family was intertwined with my relationship with him. That I couldn't just be free to fall in love with him.

I peeked over my shoulder in his direction. Did he feel that way toward me?

There were signs. If this was a normal situation, I would have figured he was interested. But our relationship was fake. Maybe he was just that good of an actor. I opened the cupboard that held the mugs and took two down.

Maybe I needed to test him. Here, in my apartment, there were no cameras. No one to put a show on for. If I tried to flirt, would he pull back? I squared my shoulders. It was time to find out.

With two mugs of hot coffee in hand, I turned and headed into the living room. Stone was sitting on the couch with both arms draped across the back. He had his eyes closed, and his head tipped back. As soon as I set the mugs down on the coffee table, he glanced over at me.

I gave him a big smile. "Didn't mean to wake you," I whispered as I moved to sit down right next to him. My knee brushed his, and I waited to see what he was going to do. When I glanced up at him, his expression was unreadable.

"I don't know what you like in it, so I just put some of my creamer in." I leaned forward and grabbed his mug. Then I turned and handed it to him. I made sure to touch him more than normal as I transferred the mug into his hands.

I could feel his gaze on me as I turned back to pick up my mug. I took a sip and then turned to face him. "Do you want to watch a movie or play a game?" I set the mug back onto the coffee table. With my hands now free, I rested one on his knee. "Unless you're too tired and just want to call it a night."

I peeked over at him to see his gaze was fixed on my hand. He didn't look mad, but he also didn't look happy. Was I reading this all wrong? I slowly pulled my hand away and moved to fold my arms across my chest. My confidence was quickly waning. Maybe I'd wanted this to be real so bad that I'd imagined things.

Was I that naive?

Stone straightened and then moved to stand. "I'm sore. I'm going to go do an ice bath," he said as he made his way across my apartment to my front door. He had his things collected and his shoes on before I could even process what was going on.

He called a quick "good night" over his shoulder before he opened the door and disappeared. The sound of the door engaging filled the air. I blinked as I glanced around.

What just happened?

I glanced down at the two coffee mugs in front of me. Both still had steam swirling up from the drink's surface. He hadn't even stayed long enough to finish the cup. He agreed to come over only to leave so abruptly minutes later. Sure, I wasn't his real girlfriend, but that didn't mean he could just cast me aside.

Maybe I was a fool. He was always the first to walk away. He'd walked away from me in high school, and now this. When was I going to learn?

Anger filled my chest to the brim, and I paced back and forth in the living room. I was sick and tired of Stone thinking he could just walk all over me. Even if our relationship was fake, there was something called common courtesy. And I was seconds away from storming over there and giving him a piece of my mind.

I'd always been nice to him. I'd always taken care of him. I'd given him the lucky charm from my grandparents, for heaven's sake. And to be treated like this?

This was crap. And I was tired of it.

21

EMERSON

I walked over to my purse and pulled out my phone. I scrolled through my texts until I found my chat with Tilly. I opened it and started typing.

Me: I can't do this

Thankfully it only took a few seconds for her to respond.

Tilly: Do what?

Me: Fake a relationship with Stone. I just can't do it anymore.

Tilly: What happened? What did he do?

I shook my head. It wasn't what he did. It was how I was feeling. I hated misreading his actions toward me. I knew it was all fake, but my heart didn't seem to understand that. And the longer I stayed in this relationship, the harder it would be on me when we had to call it quits.

Me: I just can't, Tilly

Tilly: Oh.

I frowned. What did that mean? I sent her a question mark. When she didn't respond right away, I shook my head. It didn't make a difference if she wanted me to continue doing this or not. My issue ran a lot deeper than a fake relationship. I was over him walking away from me. And I was going to tell him so.

Me: NVM. I'm just going over there to give him a piece of my mind.

I sent that text off, shoved my phone into my pocket, and headed to the front door. I pulled it open and crossed the landing. I pounded on his door. My resolve began to waver as the seconds ticked by and Stone didn't answer.

I'd built myself up so much earlier, that my adrenaline started to slip. I raised my fist and knocked again, vowing that if he didn't answer after this attempt, I would go back into my apartment and hide from the world.

The sound of locks clicking caused me to hold my breath, and suddenly, Stone's door was open, and he was standing on the other side in a pair of swim trunks and nothing else. His eyes were wide as he stared at me.

"What the hell, Em?" he asked.

I glared at him. "Why do you keep doing that?" I wasn't sure what I was going to say. But I knew I wasn't going to hold back. Not this time.

He frowned. "Why do I keep doing what?"

I hadn't realized he was carrying a bucket of ice until he transferred it from one hand to the other.

I waved toward my apartment. "What you did earlier." He had to know what I was talking about.

He glanced toward my apartment door. "Drinking coffee? Sitting on your couch? You're going to have to give me something here, Em."

"Stop doing that." My mind was swirling. I had so much I wanted to say to him, but I couldn't seem to get any of it out. And him using the nickname he'd given me in the past wasn't going to fly.

"Doing what?"

"Calling me Em."

He sighed and glanced behind him. "Why can't I call you Em?"

"Because we don't have that kind of relationship."

He paused. I could see his body tense for a moment before he relaxed. He glanced over at me and nodded. "Okay."

"Okay?" That was all he was going to say?

"Okay. I won't call you Em anymore. Is there anything else?"

My lips were parted, and my head was spinning with thoughts. No, that wasn't the only reason I came over here. I wanted him to tell me that our relationship wasn't fake. That he wasn't going to walk out on me like he always seemed to do. I wanted him to tell me that he cared for me like I cared for him.

Stone sighed. "Listen, Emerson. I understand that our relationship is just transactional. You don't have to worry."

He glanced over to his living room. "If you want to keep yelling at me, you can, but I have an ice bath to take." He held up the bucket and twisted it. The sound of ice hitting the sides echoed in the silence between us.

When I didn't answer, Stone waved toward the door. "I'll leave this open for when you decide what you want to do."

He gave me one last look before he turned and made his way toward the balcony just off his living room. I watched him walk away yet again. I knew I should shut the door and go back to my apartment. I knew that following after him was a big mistake...

But I didn't care.

I was never going to be able to move on until he told me that he would never care for me like I wanted him to. I needed to hear those words.

I walked into his apartment and shut the door behind me. Then I crossed the living room and stepped out onto the balcony. Stone was sitting in the ice bath, and his eyes widened when he saw me.

"Where's my keychain?" I blurted out.

When Stone didn't answer me, I motioned toward his chest, where I'd seen the tattoo earlier. "The one I gave you when we were kids. The one that was so important to me." Tears were pricking at my eyes. "Where is it?"

"Emerson," Stone whispered as he dropped his gaze to the water in front of him. "Go home."

I shook my head. "No. Not until you tell me where it is.

Did you lose it? Throw it away? Sell it?" Was I worth so little to him that he would toss something that meant so much to me?

"Emerson."

Realizing that he wasn't going to tell me, I decided to do something drastic. I lifted my hand behind my back and found the zipper to my jumpsuit. In one swift motion, I tugged it down. The jumpsuit fell to my feet, leaving me standing there in my bra and underwear.

"Emerson, what are you doing?" Stone asked as he straightened in the tub.

"If you're not going to tell me, then I'm getting in there with you." Without thinking things through, I lifted my foot and dipped my toe into the freezing cold water. Before Stone could answer, I plunged my foot in, sucking in my breath as the cold water felt like daggers on my skin.

"Don't do this," Stone said, but I just shook my head. I lifted my other foot and then I sunk down below the surface. My head swam from the panic coursing through my body as it tried to regulate what was happening to it. I felt like I was freezing and on fire at the same time.

"Dammit," Stone's voice grew near, and suddenly, his arms wrapped around me and tugged me to his chest. His breath was warm on my ear as he held me. "Why don't you ever listen?" he whispered.

My hands went up to his arms, and I held onto them like they were my life raft. "Why do you never answer my questions?"

He sighed. I could feel the rise and fall of his chest. "My dad tried to pawn your keychain. When he found out that it wasn't real gold, he threw it away. By the time I found out, it was already gone." He paused. "I didn't know how to tell you."

I closed my eyes as I took deep breaths in through my nose and out through my mouth. My body was adjusting to the cold, but it was taking all my strength not to collapse from the overstimulation.

"Em—er, Emerson?" Stone straightened, and I could feel him lean forward to look at me. "Shit."

He hooked his arms under mine, and stood, lifting us both out of the water. He supported my back with one arm and swept up my knees with the other. I was shivering as he pulled me to his chest and climbed out of the tub. He carried me through his living room and into his bedroom. When we got to the bathroom, he carried me into the shower and set me down. He closed the glass door and flipped the water on to hot. Water started to pour out of his rainfall shower head.

I winced as the hot water cut my skin like knives. Going from ice water to this was shocking my system. Thankfully, my body began to adjust. I glanced over to see Stone standing near the wall, watching me. His brows were furrowed, and he looked...concerned.

"Why didn't you just tell me?" I asked, pushing my soaked hair from my face.

He studied me. "I didn't want you to be disappointed in me. I knew how much it meant to you."

My gaze drifted to his chest, where I could see the tattoo he'd gotten. "Why did you get a tattoo of it?" I asked.

He studied me for a moment before he scoffed and dropped his gaze. "I figured you'd know the reason by now." Then he brought his gaze back up to mine.

My stomach lightened at his words. I stepped forward and lifted my hand. Without thinking, I brushed my fingers against the tattoo.

His body tensed, and a moment later, his hand engulfed mine. "Emerson," he mumbled. "Please don't do that."

I glanced up at him. "Why?"

He stared down at me. His gaze was full of heat. Desire. It made my heart pound.

"I don't think you know what that does to me."

I bit my lower lip, electricity rushing through my body in response to his words and the look in his eyes. "Show me," I dared.

It felt like an eternity passed with him just standing there, staring at me. I started to wonder if I'd made a mistake. I parted my lips to take the words back, but in that moment, he crossed the space between us. His hand cupped the back of my head as he backed me up against the shower wall.

His lips crashed into mine in a hungry and frenzied way. His arm wrapped around my waist, and he pulled my body against his. My hands went from his chest, to his shoulders, and then up to the back of his neck.

I parted my lips, and he parted his. Our lips. Our tongues. Our breath became one. We moved together in unison like we'd done this a million times before. I was born to kiss Stone.

He pulled back from the wall, taking me with him. We were standing fully under the water now. Stone bent down and cupped my rear and pulled me up. I wrapped my legs around his waist, and he supported me underneath.

I was higher than him now. Water flowed down all around me as I kissed him. I wanted him to know what this meant to me. I wanted him to feel what I felt. I wanted this moment to be just about me and him.

Our families. Our pasts. None of that mattered. It was just him and me.

I never wanted this kiss to end, but I knew at some point, it was going to have to. When he lowered me to the ground, I whimpered as my feet felt tile. He pulled back and studied me.

I'm sure I looked like a raccoon. I hadn't taken off my makeup before coming over, and I'd spent the last few minutes under the water. I didn't care. I didn't want to wake back up to reality.

"Emerson," Stone whispered. His voice was hoarse and rough. It sent shivers down my spine. He cupped my cheek as he stared into my eyes.

"Yes?" I asked. I wasn't sure what he was going to tell

me, and I was scared to hear what he was going to say. In here, it was just the two of us. Once we left the safety of his bathroom, the world had a chance of creeping in on us.

Stone turned and flipped off the water. He studied me before he opened the glass door and stepped out onto the bathmat. He opened the nearby cupboard and pulled out two towels.

"Here," he said, handing one to me.

Still confused as to why he stopped the kiss and how he could be so calm, I took the towel from him. The chill from the air outside the shower hit my bare skin, and I shivered as I wrapped the towel around me.

I told myself it was to help me get dry, but the truth was I felt vulnerable, standing there in my wet underwear in front of Stone.

He quickly dried off and wrapped the towel around his waist. Then he motioned toward the door. "I'll get you some clothes to wear."

I stood there, staring at the doorway as if that would make him reappear. I felt so confused. One minute, he was kissing me breathless, and the next, he was walking away from me.

Why did this keep happening?

I shimmied out of my underwear and removed my bra. Then I wrapped the towel around my body, gathered my undergarments, and stepped out of his shower. Not sure what to do with them, I blotted them against my towel with the hopes of getting most of the water out of them.

Stone returned in a pair of sweatpants and a black t-shirt. He was carrying some folded clothes in his hands. He stopped when he walked through the door, his gaze drifting from my neck, to my shoulders, and then down to the underwear in my hand. He swallowed, his jaw muscles tensing as he walked over to the vanity and set the clothes down.

"Some fresh clothes," he said before he turned and walked out of the bathroom, shutting the door behind him.

I stared at the door, still trying to process what just happened. We'd kissed, right? Like, a mind-blowing, life-changing kiss. Had I imagined it? I glanced over at the shower. No. I was there. *Stone* was there. Why was he now pretending that it never happened?

Anger rose up inside of me. Yet again, I'd tried to get close to Stone only to have him walk away from me. This was getting ridiculous.

I pulled on his sweatpants and t-shirt, wrapped my underwear in the towel I'd used to dry off, and pulled open the door. Stone was in the kitchen, standing in front of the microwave. He had his hands resting on the counter in front of him, his head tipped forward.

"I guess I'll head back to my apartment," I said, testing the waters to see what he was going to do.

He tipped his head and glanced over at me. "Okay."

I was shocked. "Okay? That's it?"

He sighed, straightened, and turned to face me. He crossed his arms in front of his chest. "What do you want from me, Emerson?" He held my gaze.

He had to be joking, right? "The truth," I finally whispered.

He dropped my gaze and sighed. "The truth is, we"—he motioned between us—"can't happen."

Tears pricked my eyes. That was what I feared he would say. No matter what happened, Stone was going to leave. Because Stone *always* left.

"Why not?" The words were out before I could stop them. I knew I should walk away. If that was what he wanted, I should accept it and leave. But for some masochistic reason, I needed to hear the words from his lips. I needed him to tell me that he didn't care about me—that he'd never cared about me.

His eyes widened as he stared at me. I could see the turmoil in his gaze. It was moments like this that I felt hope. Like, maybe, I could get through to him.

"Emerson, please..." He scrubbed his face with his hands before pushing them through his damp hair. "Can't you just let this go?"

A tear slid down my cheek. "No," I whispered.

He frowned. "Why?"

I swallowed, choking back my emotions and tears. I wanted to be strong, but I was moments away from losing Stone. I couldn't handle that. I needed him. Even though I'd fought back my feelings for him in high school, and I pretended not to care about him every day I'd lived next to him, the truth was, I'd fallen in love with him.

I wanted to be with him. Morning, noon, and night. I

was made to love him. And I couldn't imagine walking away from him. Not for my family's sake. Not for anyone's sake. I was ready to live for me, and I was ready to live for him.

"Because I've fallen in love with you," I whispered.

His entire body stilled as he stared at me. The storm that was raging in his dark blue eyes settled for just a moment before his gaze turned dark and he shook his head. I knew the words he was going to say before he uttered them.

"You shouldn't have done that." He crossed his arms over his chest. "That wasn't part of our agreement." His expression stilled. "You should go."

I angrily wiped at the tear that had escaped and rolled down my cheek. I wasn't going to cry over him anymore. If that was how he wanted things, then that's what he would get.

"Goodbye, Stone Walker," I said. With that, I turned and marched over to his front door. I pulled it open and closed it behind me.

For some absolutely insane reason, I thought he was going to follow me. I waited, my ears straining for any hint of movement as I crossed the landing between our apartments, but no sound came.

I was alone when I pushed through my front door. He didn't come after me when I pulled off his clothes and slipped into my pajamas. And I was still alone when I crawled into bed and pulled the covers up over my head.

He never came to get me as I cried until I had nothing left and eventually fell asleep.

22

STONE

I never considered myself a wallower. In the past. I never had a reason to mope around my apartment, feeling sorry for myself. Then again, I'd never had someone I loved as much as Emerson confess her love, only for me to tell her off.

I barely pulled myself out of bed the next morning to get ready. Even though we had a win last night, Coach wanted us at the practice facility bright and early the next day. Waking up after breaking Emerson's heart was worse than waking up with a massive hangover. At least with a hangover, I could nurse myself back to health. I had no idea how I was going to fix a pulverized heart.

I took a quick shower, hoping it would help me feel better—it didn't. All I could think about was how good Emerson looked standing under the water last night. I could still feel her lips on mine and her body's response to my touch. It made me ache to hold her once more.

By the time I was clean and flipped the water off, I came to one conclusion—I needed a new shower.

After I dressed and grabbed a protein bar from the kitchen, I grabbed my helmet and leather jacket and headed out of my apartment. Thankfully, everything on Emerson's side seemed quiet, so I was able to sneak away without having to face her.

I never meant for the two of us to get as close as we did. Kissing her had been a mistake. A glorious, but completely selfish mistake. And then to hear her confess her feelings for me—I knew I'd messed up.

Emerson was too good for me. I'd started our fake relationship with one goal in mind: to pay back the luck that she'd so graciously given me all those years ago. I wanted her to use me because I knew she had the talent, and she just needed the visibility. I wanted to be the one to walk away with a broken heart while she got everything she wanted.

I never wanted her to fall for me.

I would never be worthy of a girl like Emerson. She may think she knew me, but the guy she fell in love with had been fake. And I didn't want to be there when she realized that I was exactly who her parents told her I was all those years ago. So many people had walked out on the real me in the past—I couldn't have her leave too.

The only thing that kept me together this morning was the thought that when she woke up, in the cold light of day, she would realize that she didn't love me. That she could never love me. And she would feel relief, leaving the pain of our almost love to be felt only by me from that moment on.

Because that was the future only I should have—not her. One full of pain and regret.

I pulled into my parking spot and turned the engine off. I swung my leg over my bike and took a moment to pull off my helmet. I felt like I was suffocating, and I needed to breathe. No one was around, so I took my time, taking in deep breaths and letting them out slowly as I walked. When I got to the doors, I punched in the code and entered.

I didn't really talk to the guys during practice. They tried to engage me, but I just blew them off. After I sacked Isaac a tad too hard, George asked me what was wrong, but I just ignored him. I didn't have the strength to tell him that Emerson and I were finished. Not after how happy they all were to find out we were dating.

I also didn't have the patience to explain why her loving me was a bad idea. I knew that they would tell me I was being ridiculous, which I wasn't. I was protecting Emerson like I'd promised I would do all those years ago.

Her family hated me, and I could never ask her to choose between me and them. That wasn't fair. It was better for me to walk away. There were plenty of guys out there for her; she just needed to forget about me.

I was standing by my locker after practice, freshly showered, with a towel around my waist. I was putting on deodorant when Colt came up to me.

"Does Emerson have a gig tonight?" he asked. "Katie has been begging me to find out."

I frowned. "Katie?"

A goofy smile spread across his lips. "She's my new girl."

"Nice."

He raised his eyebrows expectantly.

"I'm not sure about Emerson."

"What? Why?" He punched me in the arm before wiggling his eyebrows. "You two seemed pretty close yesterday."

George moved to join our conversation. "I think you made half the stadium jealous of you and the other half jealous of her." He made a face. "It was sickening to watch."

I scoffed. "Don't get your hopes up, guys."

George groaned like he was in pain. I glanced over to see him shaking his head. "What?"

"You didn't, did you?"

I'd never realized until right then, but my friends were annoying. "Did I what?"

"You chased her away."

"I did not." It was hard to chase away someone who was never yours to begin with.

"Dude. Don't be an idiot. Whatever you think is going on, it's not. I'd kill to have a girl look at me like Emerson looked at you yesterday." Colt fanned his face like he was about to faint.

I pushed his words from my mind. If I ever opened the

Emerson door again, there was no way I could ever shut it. "What about Katie?"

He straightened and shrugged. "We're dating, but it's not like we're soulmates."

Soulmates. That word made my entire body react before I shot it down. Sure, Emerson might be my soulmate. But I knew full well I wasn't hers. "We're not soulmates."

"And that's why you're an idiot," Colt said while pointing his finger at me.

"Ah, leave him alone," George said as he moved behind Colt and put him in a headlock. "I like to call it *ignorant in love.*"

I needed this conversation to end. "Why don't you guys worry about your love lives, and I'll worry about mine." I grabbed my clothes and headed toward the bathroom stalls to change just to get away from these guys.

"Ooo! That means you have a love life!" Colt called after me.

I just waved his comment away. Once I was safely behind the stall door, I changed into my jeans and a t-shirt, then threw my towel over my shoulder and walked back to my locker. Thankfully, the guys seemed to have found something better to do, and I was able to finish getting ready by myself. With my leather jacket on, I grabbed my helmet and headed to the parking lot.

Colt's question was still picking at me, so I swiped my phone on and found Hayden's number as I walked. I didn't know if Emerson had a gig tonight or not, but I knew

Hayden would be able to find out. Since I hadn't heard from Tilly today, I could only assume that Emerson told her about last night.

I was most likely blacklisted by both of them.

Hayden was quick to text back that she didn't know but she'd do some digging. I texted her a thumbs-up and slipped my phone into my back pocket.

I stopped by the grocery store on my way home. I grabbed some essentials and rode the rest of the way home. With my bike parked in its spot, I gathered my groceries and headed to the elevator. When it got to the fourth floor and the doors opened, I paused before I leaned forward to see if I was alone.

Thankfully, no one was there, so I stepped out and hurried to my door. I unlocked it and went inside, closing the door quickly behind me. I had resolved to stay away from Emerson, but I had a feeling that resolve would quickly dissolve with one look at her. It was hard enough watching her walk away last night. I wasn't strong enough to let her do it again.

Once I was safely behind the door, I kicked off my shoes and put the groceries away. After feeding Oscar, who was very vocal in letting me know he was not happy I skimped on feeding him this morning, I searched the freezer for some of Gran's famous homemade chicken noodle soup that she'd made me before she left. I was saving each bag for a special occasion, and while this occasion wasn't special, it was needed.

With my bowl of heated soup, I grabbed a spoon and headed into the living room. I set my food down on the coffee table as I pulled open my laptop. I'd missed Gran's last few emails because I'd been so busy with Emerson. I spent the evening reading and eating, laughing at the anecdotes that Gran sent. She was having a blast, and I was so happy for her. I missed having her here—especially right now—but she deserved this.

I kept my response pretty mild. I didn't go into what had happened between me and Emerson. I didn't want her worrying about me.

After my soup was gone and the email sent, Hayden texted me that Emerson had a gig and asked if I wanted to know where it was. I told her that I didn't—I wasn't sure I could stay away if I knew—and told her to send an acorn. They're an English charm that helps people heal.

Hayden sent me a thumbs-up, and I thanked her. I set my phone down and leaned back on the couch. I closed my eyes and took in a few deep breaths. Soon, Emerson would be signed to a label. She would be happy and find her soulmate. She would get everything she deserved in this world.

And me? I was going to stay here until my heart stopped breaking or old age took me. Whichever happened first.

23

EMERSON

I was not in the mood to talk to Tilly Monday morning, but she wouldn't stop trying to call me. I begrudgingly answered the phone after she sent me a scathing text to *PICK UP THE DAMN PHONE.*

"What?" I barked as soon as I brought the phone to my ear.

"Oh, my Lord, Mary, and Joseph," Tilly panted like she'd just finished a long run. "Why the hell haven't you been answering my calls?"

I rolled my eyes as I flipped onto my back and stared up at the ceiling. "I was asleep, like most people," I lied. Truth was, I slept horribly last night. All I could see was Stone's dark blue eyes as he told me to leave. I could hear his words as he told me that I shouldn't have fallen in love with him. I felt the absence of his body as he let me walk away.

It was torture, living with those memories. Move over

waterboarding, give me another dose of rejection from Stone, and I'd be spilling my guts to whoever could keep me from feeling that way ever again.

After a night of tossing and turning, I'd called into work to tell them that I was going to be late and spent the morning watching the sunlight slowly seep through my blinds as the sun rose in the sky.

"Well, next time answer when I call." Tilly sounded a bit more normal now. Hearing her calm down was helping stabilize my emotions as well.

"Sorry," I murmured, feeling bad for making my best friend so frantic. "What did you need?"

"You'll never believe the phone call I got this morning."

My heart started to pound as I moved to sit up. "Who was it?"

She sucked in her breath and paused. I was just about to scold her for yelling at me only to clam up on the most important details, but she spoke before I could.

"Cherry Red Records! They liked what they heard the other night and are coming to The Curfew tonight. They want to talk after your gig!" She was screaming now, but I didn't care, I was screaming right along with her.

"Are you serious?"

"I'm serious!"

I set my phone down on the mattress and pulled my pillow over my face to scream into it. I pushed my covers off, kicking my feet in the air. It was happening. It was *finally* happening!

This was just what I needed to hear today after the shitty night I had. And then reality came crashing down around me. Was this just because of my weekend of fame with Stone? Did they only want me because he was part of the package?

My enthusiasm slowly faded as I pulled the pillow off my face and felt for my phone. "Tilly?" I whispered.

She was still cheering, so she took a moment to respond. "Yeah, girl?"

"Do you think they only want me because of Stone?"

"No. I mean, I'm sure it helped, but your socials have been blowing up all weekend. So many people are watching your video channel. It's crazy!"

"Really?" I put my phone on speaker so I could look. Tilly wasn't wrong. I'd gained hundreds of thousands of followers overnight. "Oh my..."

"See? They wouldn't listen to your music if they didn't think you were good. So, celebrate! You deserve it."

My smile pulled at the edges of my mouth. I wanted to feel happy, but at the same time, I knew that Tilly was only telling a half-truth. Most of these people were following me because Stone and I made a juicy story. I bet as soon as it got out that we weren't dating anymore—or that it had all been fake from the beginning—half of those followers would fade away.

Had I crafted this victory by myself, I'd be happy. Now, it came with the memory of Stone, which hurt every time I thought about it. But there was no way I could go back now, so I might as well take the win. Even if it felt like a half-win.

"Thanks, Till."

She continued on talking about how she couldn't wait until tonight. She was coming over as soon as I got off work to help me prep. I just nodded along with her. My elation finally settling in my body caused me to feel sleepy. I wanted to shower and get ready for the day.

We said our goodbyes, and I set my phone down on my nightstand. I stood and padded to my bathroom, where I took my time showering and shaving. By the time I got to work, I was only a few minutes late. We were busy throughout the whole shift, so I never really had any down-time to sit and wallow in my thoughts about Stone.

I texted Tilly before I left work, and by the time I walked up the stairs, she was nervously pacing in front of my door. I thought about asking if she'd seen Stone but decided against it. I didn't want to know. I didn't need to know, so I just forced a smile and walked up to her.

"I am so freaking excited about tonight," she squealed as I pulled out my keys and opened my apartment.

I glanced back at her. "Me, too," I said as I walked inside and left the door open for her to follow me.

"Hayden called me earlier to ask if you had a gig. I'm guessing she wants to pass the information on to Stone, so he can be there."

I stopped and slowly turned to look at her.

"I thought it was strange 'cause he could just ask you." She shrugged.

"Did you tell her?" I asked, trying not to sound needy.

Tilly flicked her gaze over to me. "Yeah. Why wouldn't I? This would be the perfect time for him to come. Really help seal the deal."

I did not need her to say that. That was not what I needed tonight. I couldn't entertain the thought that my record deal might be compromised because I did something as stupid as confessing my real feelings to my fake boyfriend.

"I'm not sure he's coming," I whispered as I quickly headed to the bathroom to shower.

"What did you say?" Tilly asked, following after me.

"Nothing," I called over my shoulder.

"Emerson King." She dragged out every syllable of my name. "What did you say?"

I closed my eyes and brought my shoulders up in preparation for her freak-out. "I may have kissed Stone for real last night and told him I love him." I paused, waiting for her to start screaming at me. I peeked over and saw her standing there, calm as a cucumber.

"Wh—why aren't you mad?" I asked, relaxing my shoulders and opening my eyes fully.

"I thought you were going to say you broke up with him. Why would I be mad? He's obviously in love with you... Ooo! This is so much better. You two actually being in love!" She clapped her hands and smiled at me.

My face fell. She didn't pick up on it right away, but then she did, and slowly her smile faded away.

"What happened?" she asked gently.

Tears pricked my eyes like they did last night. I didn't want to relive what he said to me, but I couldn't go on having Tilly think that Stone and I were some love story written in the stars. If she knew what happened, she'd know what to avoid when talking to me.

And I needed that. I was only so strong.

So, I told her everything. I told her about dinner, the ride home, him coming over to my apartment. Understanding passed over her face when she connected the timeline with our texts last night. Her eyes widened when I told her about the ice bath and then the shower. She frowned when I recounted how he went from burning hot to ice cold when he got out of the shower and how he blew me off when I confronted him.

She stood there, her eyebrows drawn together, like she was trying to figure out why Stone had pushed me away like that.

"He's a commitment-phobe," she said, shaking her head. "I didn't think he was the type, but your confession scared him off."

I widened my eyes.

"Not that it's your fault. He would have commitment issues no matter what." She shrugged. "It's his loss. I mean, he did a good thing getting you some visibility. But, girl, you can take it from here. You don't need him." She crossed the space between us and pulled me into a hug. "We're going all the way to the top."

I leaned into her hug, letting out the stress that I'd been holding. I was worried she would be upset with me, and it was a relief that she was on my side—and not Stone's. Although a part of me didn't believe her assessment—a guy scared of commitment didn't get a tattoo of the keychain his ex-best friend's little sister gave him—but I didn't want to argue about it.

Instead, I wanted to shower and focus on tonight.

I got out of a hot twenty-minute shower to find that Tilly had pulled out half my wardrobe. Thankfully, she was done, having settled on a white one-shouldered bodysuit with a floral skirt and brown chunky belt. She told me to look dressy without looking *too* dressy.

Not wanting to think about anything I didn't have to, I just nodded and started doing my makeup. While I was in the process of putting on blush, my phone rang. I glanced over at Tilly. She looked at me. We both asked, "Who is calling?" at the same time. Anyone I knew would just text me.

For a split second, I wondered if it was Stone. But then I pushed that thought from my mind. He didn't want to talk to me, be with me, or love me. And he wasn't mean enough to call and remind me almost 24 hours after he'd made that clear.

"It says, *Mom,*" Tilly said as she held up my phone, which she'd just fished out of my purse.

"What?" I asked, dropping my brush and startling when it clattered on the counter.

"It's your mom," she half-whispered, half-mouthed as she held the phone out like it was now diseased.

Butterflies were dive-bombing my stomach as I took the phone from her. It had been months since my mom called. I doubted it was the quarterly check-in she liked to do with me. I had a sinking suspicion that she'd finally received the news about Stone and me. Great.

"Hey, Mom," I said as I pressed the talk button and brought my phone to my face.

"Emerson" was all she said.

I waited, staring at Tilly, who looked like she was about to explode if I didn't let her in on our conversation. I pulled my phone away and pressed the speakerphone button. "How's it going?" I finally asked when I realized that my mother wasn't going to speak first.

"Not good." Yeah. She knew.

"Really? Why?"

She sighed. I could picture it now. Mom, sitting on the couch. Her nose tipped into the air. Her eyes closed as she took in a deep breath through her nose to expel it from her mouth so I would know just how disappointed she was. She was so predictable.

"Imagine my surprise when I'm standing in line at the grocery store, and I see my daughter's face plastered all over a tabloid."

I covered the phone's speaker with my hand and stared

over at Tilly while I mouthed, *"Tabloid?"* She nodded, her eyes just as wide as mine felt. Wow. News traveled fast.

"Not only is my daughter there, but holding her hand is *Stone Walker*. Now, I told myself, that can't be. That's not my daughter. She would never date a man who tore her family apart, would she?"

I waited, wondering if her question was rhetorical or if she wanted me to answer.

"Emerson?"

"O-of course not," I muttered, not really taking a moment to process what she was asking me. I just didn't want to disappoint her yet again.

"So, perhaps you can explain what is going on in Tennessee."

I took in a breath and gathered my thoughts. My first instinct was to tell her that I could date whomever I wanted. They might have been able to control Cayden and his future, but I wasn't interested in them trying to control mine. I did what I could to try to keep the family from breaking apart, but if this was the kind of mothering she thought she could use on me, she was grossly misjudging our relationship.

She and Dad always made it seem like Stone purposely stole Cayden's scholarship. But, like Tilly claiming that Stone had commitment issues, I just didn't see it.

My parents weren't the most honest people in the world. I loved them, but I was starting to wonder if everything they'd told me was the truth. Or if they were so bitter when

Stone got the scholarship over Cayden that they needed everyone to cut Stone out of their lives.

If that were true, that would be horrible. My family had been a safe place for him to land. They'd made him promises that they didn't keep.

But, if I didn't ease my mom's mind right now, in this conversation, she was only going to keep calling me, or worse, head over here to confront me face-to-face.

So, I did something that my family seemed to struggle with: I told her the truth. I told her about Tilly's plan to get me exposure. I told her how Stone was willing to go along with it. How he wanted nothing in return. I made sure she knew that he expected nothing from me. I left out last night's shower and my confession.

She just listened and offered a "mm-hmm" along the way to let me know that she was still on the line.

"That's pretty much the story in a nutshell," I said as I turned back to the vanity to finish dusting blush over my cheeks.

"Well, I'm impressed," Mom said after a few seconds.

"Impressed? With what?"

"That you did the right thing, using that boy like he used your brother to steal his future."

Anger brewed in my stomach as I stared at my reflection. How had my mother grown so calloused? "That's not fair, Mom," I said as I set my makeup brush down. With how I was feeling, anything I did to my face right now would come out disjointed.

"Not fair? Not *fair*?" Mom's voice rose with every word. "What's not fair is us sinking money and time into your brother's career only to have Stone rip it away from him. Do you know how much money your father had to pay to get a scout to come out to our small town? Only to lose it all because of one game. And to that boy!"

I shook my head. I wanted honesty, I guess. I just hadn't realized she would be this honest. "Wait, so you and Dad *bribed* a scout to come out? And then you blamed Stone when he changed his mind?" I paused. "Does Cayden know about this?"

Mom was so upset she was sputtering. There were curse words intermingled with her explanation, but I wasn't listening anymore. I was over the past. I was tired of living in Cayden's shadow. If Mom wanted to talk to someone who would support her conclusions, she should call my dad or Cayden. Not me. Apparently, Cayden knew the whole story but still blamed Stone. My brother was an ass.

My whole family seemed to only want to live in the past but I was ready to focus on my future. And it was waiting for me at The Curfew tonight.

"I'm going to have to let you go, Mom," I said, raising my voice so she could hear me. "I'll talk to you later."

I hung up the phone before she could respond. I set my phone down on the vanity and stared at it as I tried to process what just happened. I knew my family was broken— I just hadn't realized we were shattered beyond repair.

Tilly appeared behind me in the mirror. She looked concerned. "You okay?"

I nodded. I was tired of crying. And I certainly wasn't going to cry over my family. Someday, we'd fix what was broken. But I wasn't going to hold my breath.

It was best for me to just focus on me. I seemed to be the only one who cared. Well, Tilly cared. She always supported me. I smiled at her, and I watched her shoulders visibly relax. "Thanks," I said. "I'll be fine." I picked up my makeup brush. "Let's get ready so we can get down there and start the rest of my life."

Tilly's wide smile was back as she nodded along with my words. "Let's do it."

24

EMERSON

I was grateful that the crowd was supportive even though Stone was nowhere to be found. I think it would have crushed me to have them pack up and leave when it was announced that Stone was unable to make it tonight. Luckily, Tilly kept the reason vague, and everyone seemed to understand.

They stayed in their seats and cheered after every song. I even got a request to play an encore, and this one had me out of the chair, singing and engaging with the crowd.

Tilly had pointed out Mr. Smith with Cherry Red Records as well as Mr. Thomas with Silver Bell Records. Both had come tonight, which was a good sign. It was always better to have two people interested instead of one.

I was smiling and sweating when I made my way off the stage. Tilly pulled me into a hug and jumped up and down

—I'd done such a good job, a proposal had to come from this night.

I grinned as she pulled back, unable to speak. I'd sung with my entire soul, and my throat was tired. She nodded, understanding what I needed without me saying it, and ushered me to the dressing room so I could unload my guitar before saying hi to the two reps.

Tilly was pacing as I pulled my guitar over my head. I set it down next to me and stared into my case. An array of lucky charms was scattered across the bottom of the case. I laughed.

Tilly paused. "What?" she asked.

I glanced over at her. "Who knew that it was the acorn that had all the luck," I said, picking up the small brass acorn that had been left in the dressing room when I first got here. "I mean I got the pig, the dream catcher, the easter egg—"

"That one was weird."

I shot Tilly a look. "An elephant, a Chinese coin, and then..." I tried to remember the Italian charm's name. "The corn—cornicello?" I attempted knowing I was completely butchering it. "But it was the acorn I needed." I moved to set it in my purse.

"What is with you and lucky charms?"

I stared at her. She already knew. I'd told her the story of my grandparents numerous times—mostly when I was drunk and lonely.

"My grandparents met—"

"In Ireland because of a keychain, I know."

I flattened my lips and gave her a deadpan look that said, *then why did you ask?*

She shrugged. "It was more of a rhetorical question."

"Lucky charms mean something to me," I said as I picked up my guitar and set it down in my case. Now, if there was a lucky charm that helped heal a broken heart, I'd buy that in bulk.

With my case now shut, I turned to face her. Before either of us could say anything, there was a knock on the door. The butterflies started dancing in my stomach once more as I stared at Tilly. "Is it time?"

She nodded. "I guess it's time."

She crossed the room and opened the door. I held my breath until she said, "Brett? What are you doing here?"

"Brett?" I asked, stepping toward her to get a look.

Sure enough, Brett was standing there holding a bouquet of flowers. When his gaze caught mine, he stepped past Tilly and extended the flowers to me.

Tilly protested, but Brett didn't seem to notice. "Can we talk?" he asked.

Tilly looked upset, but I just nodded. "It's fine. Why don't you schmooze the reps, and I'll be right out."

Tilly glanced between us before she nodded. "If you're not out in five, I'm coming to get you."

"Sounds good."

She left, closing the door behind her as she went. Brett and I were left alone, so I turned to face him. "What's up?" I asked.

Brett was standing a few feet off and took a step closer to me. "Listen, I know things started off good and then got rocky with your whole neighbor situation. And then I saw you were dating that Stone guy on social media..." He paused as he studied me. "But I can't believe that was real. Was it?"

My heart squeezed at his question. Memories of Stone came crashing back into my mind. I was never going to be able to shake him. Not now that my name was synonymous with his. The truth was, if I wanted any chance at a normal relationship, Brett was it. After all, he'd seen Stone and me before our arrangement, and he didn't seem bothered that he could possibly upset one of the most popular NFL players in the league.

I decided to tell him everything. I told him the arrangement. That we weren't really dating. And that we weren't really fake dating anymore either. Brett listened intently until I was finished. When I was done, he studied me.

"So does that mean I can take you out tonight?"

My eyes widened. "Tonight?"

He nodded and reached forward to take my hand. "I don't want to wait anymore."

I stared down at the way his fingers encircled mine. There were no tingles like the way my body reacted to Stone's touch. Going out seemed a little too soon. Did he mean as girlfriend and boyfriend? Or just as friends? How did I ask him without seeming presumptuous?

I took in a deep breath. Going out for dinner wasn't a

commitment ceremony where we signed our lives away. Plus, if I wanted to move on past Stone, I needed a rebound. Brett could be that rebound.

"I'm having drinks with the music reps who came to see me, but maybe after that we can just go back to my apartment. Would that work?"

He studied me and then nodded, a slow smile spreading across his lips. "That would be perfect."

He offered to put my guitar in his car, and I thanked him. Then I hurried from the dressing room and out to the bar, where I found Tilly talking to Mr. Smith and Mr. Thomas. We had a few drinks, and I talked to them about my music. They both seemed to side-eye each other when it came to talking details, so in the end we scheduled times for me to come into their prospective companies to discuss things further.

I didn't end up with a contract, but they both seemed eager to talk, so I left the bar feeling confident something was going to come of this. If not, at least the ball was rolling. My name was out there, and someone was bound to pick me up.

I was tired, so after I said goodnight to Tilly, I was glad I'd asked Brett to come over to my apartment. I couldn't imagine being anywhere but at home on my couch, relaxing for the rest of the night.

We kept our conversation light as Brett drove me to my apartment. We talked about music and what he did for work...something in finance. Numbers were never really my thing, so when he started talking about them in terms of his job, he quickly lost me.

He pulled into a visitor parking spot, and we both got out. I went to retrieve my guitar, but he beat me to it, his hand grasping the handle just as I leaned in to pick it up.

"Let me," he said as he pulled it out.

It startled me that he would move so quickly to pull it away from me after he saw me basically lean in to get it. But maybe this was his way of being chivalrous, so I just shrugged it off. We walked side by side to the stairs and started up to the fourth floor.

Just as we got to the landing, Brett did a double take. "So, that is your apartment, right?" he asked, pointing to my door.

I nodded. "Yes." I pointed to my door. "Emerson's apartment." Then I pointed to Stone's door. "Not Emerson's apartment."

He chuckled. "It's locked away," he said as he tapped his head.

The sound of the elevator doors opening caused us both to stop and wait. My entire body froze when I saw Stone standing there with his phone in his hand. He had a white bag of Chinese food in his other hand—I recognized it from the night he invited me over. My eyes felt as wide as saucers as my mind raced through all the emergency exits.

Then, realizing that he was a mere second away from seeing us, I just took a deep breath and braced for the inevitable. I took a step closer to Brett, and that movement seemed to draw Stone's attention. He glanced up, first to me, and then to Brett. His body stiffened as he lingered on Brett and then slowly met my gaze.

"Stone," I said, nodding to acknowledge him and then hurrying over to my door to unlock it.

"Stone Walker?" Brett asked. I wasn't sure if the question was directed at me or Stone. But the sound of Stone's door shutting answered that question. I turned to see Brett standing behind me, but his attention was on Stone's apartment. "Stone Walker is your neighbor?"

I felt the lock release, so I pulled my key out of the handle and shoved them into my purse as I pushed open the door. "Yeah, he is."

"You're not-real boyfriend, who is also an NFL player, is your neighbor?"

I nodded as I held the door open for him, praying that Brett would get the picture and join me before I just slammed the door on his face. I was not prepared to see Stone again, and I was most certainly not prepared to see him again with *Brett*.

This evening was a mess, and I was ready for it to be over with.

Thankfully, Brett saw me start to shut the door, so he scooted his way into my apartment. "Should I be worried?" he asked, as I shut the door.

I shook my head. "Nope." And that was the truth. Sure, I was still in love with Stone. My pounding heart from seeing him was proof of that. But Stone had no interest in me—fake or otherwise. Brett had *nothing* to worry about.

"I need alcohol," I said as I turned and made my way into the kitchen. I pulled open the fridge and grabbed out a bottle of wine. I turned to get the glasses, only to run into Brett.

"This is a nice apartment," he said, glancing around.

I sidestepped him and opened the cupboard. "Thanks." I pulled two wine glasses down, and they made clinking noises on the countertop.

He made himself busy, walking around and opening cupboards and looking in my pantry. Then he moved to the living room, where I heard the sound of the closet door opening and closing.

I poured the wine while watching him inspect my apartment. It was strange to the point where it made me feel uncomfortable. "Are you looking for the bathroom?" I asked as I grabbed the glasses of wine and walked toward him.

"Hmm?" he asked as he took a glass from me. "Oh, no. I'm just looking around."

I studied him, not sure if I should say something. Maybe this was a weird quirk of his. I just wanted to relax and get a little tipsy, so I took a sip of my wine. "Wanna join me on the couch?" I asked. The next room for him to inspect was my bedroom, and there was no way I wanted him in there.

"Um, sure," he said, glancing over at my shut bedroom door. But, thankfully, he followed me to the couch.

We sat down next to each other, our knees touching. I

cradled my glass in my hand while Brett set his down on the coffee table in front of us and leaned back. He rested his arm on the couch behind me as he leaned in.

Maybe this had been a mistake. Maybe I shouldn't have invited him up here. Sure, we'd spoken a few times, but did I really know this guy? Like, *know him*, know him?

"What are you thinking?" Brett asked, leaning a little closer to me. He rested his other hand on the couch cushion, inches from my knee.

I flicked my gaze down at his hand and then back to my wine. I took a sip. "Cataracts," I said, trying to think of the most boring topic we could discuss.

"Cataracts?" He frowned. "Why?"

I shrugged. "They are fascinating." I turned to face him, which put me further away from him and his hands. "Wanna know why?"

He shook his head as he scooted closer to me. "No."

My back was now pressed into the couch's armrest, and I had nowhere else to retreat to. "But they are really interesting," I said, wishing I hadn't left the pepper spray in my purse on the other side of the room.

"Wanna know what I'm thinking about?" Brett asked, his arms now pinning me between his body and the couch.

"No," I whispered.

He leaned closer. "Debt."

I stopped. I had not expected him to say that. "Debt?" I asked.

He nodded, and suddenly, I felt his warm, sweaty palm

on my knee. "How you owe me a debt, and I'm ready to collect."

"I owe you a debt?" I asked.

He smiled. It was wicked and sent shivers down my back. "You have this apartment, don't you?"

An icy shiver rushed down my spine. I blinked a few times, trying to process what he'd just said. "You're—you're the one who wanted to help me with my future?" I asked as I internally screamed at Tilly. She promised me it had come from someone good. Not a creeper. And then I realized *he* was the one who had sent me all those good luck charms.

I felt violated. He'd really done his research.

"Yes. It looks like you've done well for yourself." He glanced around. "You do like it, don't you?"

"Yes," I whispered.

"Now you owe me...right?" He slid his hand further up my leg.

Out of instinct, my hand flew down to stop him. "Please, don't," I whispered.

"It's only fair. You have what you want, now I get what I want." He leaned closer, his breath was hot on my skin.

Three solid knocks on the door reverberated through my body. My gaze whipped to the front door.

"Just ignore it."

"It's my neighbor. He checks on me every night."

Brett frowned. "You said you weren't really dating."

"Doesn't matter. He will break this door down if I don't answer."

"Really?"

I shrugged, trying to come across as nonchalant. "We can wait and see."

Brett stared at me and then the door. Finally, he sighed and sat back. "Fine. Tell him everything is good and he can go."

"Okay," I said as I stood and straightened my skirt. I really hoped it was Stone on the other side of the door and not a delivery person dropping off a box.

I walked over to the door and pulled it open. A rush of relief raced through me when I saw Stone standing there with one hand resting on the doorframe, his head tipped forward and his other hand poised to knock again. He must not have expected me to answer because he quickly pulled back, his expression contorted into a look of confusion.

"Hey, Stone," I said, just loud enough so Brett would know that Stone was there.

"Emerson," Stone whispered. His gaze was dark and tortured as he studied me. "Can we talk?"

"I'm kind of busy," I said, nodding toward Brett.

He glanced into my apartment before looking back at me. I forced a smile for Brett, but inside, I was begging Stone to read my gaze. I needed his help.

"I'm sorry," he said as he started to turn away. But then he paused and studied me.

I motioned toward Brett with my eyes as I furrowed my brows, and I saw red flash in Stone's eyes. He stepped forward and dropped his head slightly as he whispered, "Go in your room and lock the door. I'll take care of him."

"Hey, Brett. Long time no see, buddy," Stone said, changing his voice as he walked into the living room.

I hurried past them and into my room, locking the door. I could hear Brett call out my name, but suddenly there was the sound of a scuffle followed by the shutting of my front door. Once my apartment fell silent, I pulled open my bedroom door and peeked out.

They were gone, so I hurried over to my front door and locked it before collapsing to the ground. Tears ran down my cheeks as my hands shook. I'd had a few bad dates, but this was the closest any guy had ever gotten to taking advantage of me. And I didn't like it.

My face was buried in my hands when I heard a soft knock on the door. My heart started to pound as fear coursed through me. Brett was back.

"Em, it's me. Stone. Open up."

A sob escaped my lips as I pushed myself up. My hands shook as I unlocked the deadbolt and pulled the door open. I didn't have time to process what happened next. As soon as the space between the door and the frame was large enough, Stone was through it. He wrapped me in his arms and pulled me to his chest.

He cradled my head in his hand and used his other arm like a vice around my waist. He buried his face into my hair. "Did he hurt you?"

I sniffled as I shook my head. "No. I'm okay," I whispered.

"I'm so sorry, I'm so sorry." His voice was deep.

I wrapped my arms around his middle and sobbed into his shirt.

"That asshole. I swear, I should have never let you go last night." His voice dropped to a whisper. "I'm so sorry."

I pulled back to look at him. "What did you do to him?"

He stared down at me. There was a fear in his gaze, mixed with the anger I'd seen earlier. "I made it clear that if I ever saw him around you again, he would regret it." He moved to cradle my face in his hands. "He said something about you owing him money?"

I sniffled and nodded. "He was the 'generous donor.' Tilly said it was legit. He helped me get this apartment."

Stone pulled me back into his arms. "Why didn't you ask me for help?"

I scoffed. Was he serious? "Well, I didn't know where you were. I didn't know you'd be my neighbor." I sniffled. "And it's not like you're my boyfriend anymore."

Memories of what happened last night came crashing into me. He'd rejected me. He'd told me to walk away. That I should have never fallen in love with him.

I moved to wiggle away, but Stone just kept his arms around me.

"Emerson," he said. His voice was deep and filled with emotion. It sent shivers down my back.

"What?" I asked, praying this was the moment that he

would get his head out of his butt and admit that he loved me.

He pulled back slightly, so he could stare down at me. "You know what you said to me last night?"

I pursed my lips and looked up, pretending to think hard. "Um...no."

"Emerson."

I glanced over at him. "When I said I loved you?" I shook my head. "I lied."

He studied me. "I should have said I love you, too."

My whole body warmed as he stared at me. "Yeah, you should have."

"Emerson, I've loved you my whole life. You're the reason I'm the MEP. I fell in love with you that night you gave me the keychain. It killed me that my dad threw it away. I got this tattoo"—he pulled my fingertips up to press them into the soft cotton of his t-shirt—"because it helped me feel close to you." He pulled my fingers away and bought them to his lips, where he gently kissed them.

"Then why did you push me away last night?" I asked.

"Because I was scared. I know what it's like to have no family, and I knew if you were with me, your family would disown you. I felt like I'd already affected your life so badly, I didn't want you to have to choose."

I frowned at him. "That is my choice to make."

He nodded. "I know that now." Then he leaned forward, pressing his forehead to mine. "And I'm pretty sure I can't ever let you go again." He reached up a hand and brushed my hair from my shoulder. "You couldn't push me away if you wanted to."

I smiled before I rose up onto my tiptoes and brushed my lips against his. "Promise?"

He startled and looked down at me. "Promise what?"

I pressed my lips to his again. "That you'll never leave me, even if I want you to."

He wrapped his arm around my waist and yanked me to his chest. Then he dipped down and pressed his lips to mine. "I promise."

I giggled as I raised my hands and rested them on his pecks. I loved how broad his chest was and how small it made my hands look. Then I frowned when I thought about the lucky charms I'd been sent, and that Brett was probably the guy who sent them. Something that had seemed so sweet was now tainted with Brett's touch.

Stone dipped down to catch my gaze. "What is it? What's wrong."

I pouted. "I just realized all those good luck charms I was sent were from Brett." I glared at my guitar case, ready to get them out of there.

Stone cleared his throat, causing me to glance up at him. His expression confused me.

"What? What is it?"

He shrugged. "I may have been the one sending those to you." He smiled sheepishly at me.

I raised an eyebrow. "You?"

He nodded and then brought his hand up to run

through my hair. "You gave me your lucky charm. I was trying to help you find a new one." He studied me. "I hope that's okay."

I slid my hands from his chest up to his face and placed them on his cheeks. "I love you," I whispered.

He growled, and it sent a shock of electricity through my body. "I love you more."

I giggled as I slowly slid my hands down to his neck and pulled him back down to me. "Good. Now kiss me, Stone Walker."

"Yes, ma'am." His lips found mine once more.

In that moment, I knew Stone was mine and I was his. The future was an unknown place, but with Stone by my side, I didn't care. My family, our careers, our future. I could face all of it with the man I loved beside me, supporting me.

My future was brighter and more hopeful than it had ever been. And I couldn't wait to start living it.

I was one lucky girl.

EPILOGUE

The roar of the crowd had my heart pounding along with it. I lingered by the open door of the dressing room in an effort to calm my nerves, but nothing was helping. Not the cool night air. Not the guitar that I gripped in my hand. And certainly not Tilly, who was pacing back and forth in the dressing room, repeating the songs that I'd chosen to perform for my first-ever live show.

I still couldn't believe this was my life.

It had been a year since I moved into the apartment across the landing from Stone. A year since we agreed to fake a relationship to help me get discovered. And a year since we both said I love you.

After talking to Cherry Red Records, I decided to sign a contract with them. My career exploded from there. There were times I feared this was all dream, and I was going to wake up back in my small, cramped apartment, searching for a new place to live.

Instead, I woke to Stone's warm, strong arms around me as he held me close.

"The merch guys really outdid themselves," Stone's Gran, Mona, said as she pushed past me into the dressing room. She was decked to the nines.

She had a custom shirt made from a picture she took of me one afternoon while Stone and I were visiting her. I was playing the guitar, and she said it was the prettiest picture she'd ever taken. The text over the photo said, *Emerson King's Number One Fan*. She was my favorite, both here at my concerts, and in the reserved family box at Stone's games.

She called me her granddaughter and adored me. The feeling was mutual.

Mona was handing out merch she'd purchased outside the arena, like we didn't already own the shot glasses, blankets, or sweatshirts that had my face and name on them.

I stepped back into the dressing room and shut the door behind me. Tilly looked up, tapping her watch before she said, "Five more minutes, Em."

I nodded and saluted her. "Yes, ma'am."

"You look beautiful," Mona said as she hurried over to me and pulled me into a gigantic hug.

"Thanks," I whispered. I was wearing a silver-beaded rhinestone unitard. My hair was curled and flowed past my shoulders. My makeup was thick and felt unnatural, but that was what was needed for all the lights and cameras.

"Stone is so disappointed that he couldn't be here. But, you know, the—"

"The game. I know." I smiled at her. "It's the curse of loving an NFL player."

Mona pressed her hands to my cheeks. "But he made sure I knew where I was needed the most."

"Thank you," I whispered.

"Ooo! That reminds me. He wanted me to give you this." She pulled her hands back and raised a finger as she headed toward her purse.

A smile broke out as I watched her in anticipation. I was heartbroken when Stone told me he had an away game and wasn't going to be able to come to my first concert. I'd tried to hide my disappointment, but I knew Stone saw it. He'd pulled me into his arms and kissed me while whispering that he was sorry.

After that moment, I made myself swear that I wouldn't feel sorry for myself. This wasn't Stone's choice, and I wasn't going to make him feel bad about it. We both had demanding jobs, and neither was more important than the other.

So, the fact that he'd given his grandmother something for me, filled the hole that was created by his absence.

"He said you'd recognize the envelope," she said as she turned and handed me a familiar white envelope.

"Tilly," I said, holding it up.

She laughed and shook her head. "Aw, Stoney."

I slid my finger under the sealed flap and tore it open. It was the exact envelope he used to have Hayden send me before every performance. I glanced inside, and my heart skipped a beat. My jaw dropped, and Tilly and Mona both asked in unison, "What is it?"

"Oh my gosh," I whispered. "I can't believe he found one." I tipped the envelope, and a gold four-leaf clover keychain fell out into my palm. Inscribed on the front were the words, *a chuisle, a chroí*. I curled my fingers around the keychain and brought it close to my chest, tears brimming my eyelids.

"That's amazing," Tilly whispered as she wrapped her arm around my shoulders. "But you cannot cry. It took an hour to get your makeup on. Let's not have a repeat. We have to leave in a minute."

I glanced over at Tilly, and I could see the panic in her eyes. I knew she meant well, so I nodded, tipped my head up, and took in deep breaths. It wasn't easy being my manager, but she was doing so well.

"Right," I said as I slipped the keychain into my brassiere. If Stone wasn't going to be here, I was going to keep a piece of him with me. I glanced at Tilly and then Mona. "Is it time?"

Tilly nodded. "It's time."

My heart started pounding once more as I crossed the

room and picked up my guitar, which I'd left just outside the door. Mona and Tilly moved to join me. They smiled, and it helped calm my nerves.

"Are you ready?" Mona asked, wrapping her arm around my shoulders.

"No," I whispered. "But that doesn't really matter now, does it?"

She squeezed my shoulder and shook her head. "Not really, hon. But I already know you're going to be amazing. So just lean on my confidence, and you'll do great."

I smiled over at her as we followed Tilly out of the dressing room. "Thanks. I really appreciate that."

"Of course, dear. Anytime."

They lingered with me backstage as I waited for my cue. Suddenly, all the lights on the stage turned off, and darkness fell around us. I nodded to Tilly and Mona as I headed out onto the stage to take my place.

Once I was on my mark, I slipped my guitar strap over my head, readied my fingers, and waited for the lights to come back on.

I WAS EXHAUSTED when I finally crawled into the back seat of the rental car after the concert. I had the time of my life, singing and engaging the audience. All the dancing. All the practice. It all came to a head tonight.

Thankfully, I remembered the choreography, and I only messed up once. The crowd didn't seem to notice. They just cheered and sang my songs right along with me.

By the time the performance was over, I was shaking as I walked off stage. Mr. Smith joined me in the dressing room with a celebratory bottle of champagne. My nerves were already shot, so I contemplated turning down the drink but decided one glass wouldn't hurt.

I wished I hadn't, though. With the adrenaline leaving my body and the alcohol in my system, my head felt as if it were buzzing. Thankfully, Tilly hired me a driver, and Max knew where to take me once the performance was over.

He pulled up to the Nashville High-Rise Apartments, and Grant, the doorman, was there to help me out. I said a quick goodbye to Max as I followed Grant, who was carrying my guitar, into the building. He pressed the call button for the elevator and kept the conversation light, which I was grateful for.

Once the doors opened, he scanned his card and pressed the button for the twentieth floor—our apartment. I leaned against the wall, and Grant wished me a good night as the doors shut.

I closed my eyes as the elevator took me home.

As soon as the doors opened, the sound of soft music filtered in from our living room. I frowned as I picked up my guitar and stepped out. Rose petals were sprinkled on the ground leading into the dining room.

Stone came into view when I cleared the entryway and peered into the kitchen. I set my case down and ran into his arms. He wrapped one tightly around my waist and pulled me up, cradling my head with his other hand.

"Em," he murmured into my hair.

"You're home!" I exclaimed. I closed my eyes and breathed him in. Then I pulled back so I could look at him. "When did you get back? And how?"

Stone set me down and pulled his arms back so he could look at his watch. "I got in, like, one minute ago. And by plane," he said as he leaned in and pressed his lips to mine.

I giggled as I parted my lips and let him in. I wanted him to kiss me—needed him to kiss me. He obliged. His arms slipped around my waist as he pulled me against him. But just as we got started, he stopped and pulled back.

"You're distracting me," he said as he tipped his forehead and rested it on mine.

"Distracting?" I asked, and then I remembered the rose petals. And, when I glanced around, I saw candles all around us. I pulled back and took it all in. "Stone, what is this?" I whispered. Then I glanced over at him. "Hayden?"

He chuckled. "Who else?" His expression stilled as he studied me before he slowly dropped to one knee.

My breath caught in my throat. "Stone," I whispered.

He slipped his hand into his front pocket and pulled out a small ring. He held it up in front of me. "Emerson King."

"Yes," I whispered.

He met my gaze. "I have loved you my entire life. You are the reason I breathe. As much as I tried to move past you, I never could. You are my soulmate. You are the breath in my lungs." He paused like he was trying to remember. "*A chuisle, a chroí.*"

I smiled at his butchered attempt.

He cleared his throat and held the ring up once more. "What I'm trying to say is, will you marry me?"

"Yes."

He studied me. "Really?"

I held out my left hand. "Yes."

He stood before he took my hand and slipped the ring onto my finger. Tears filled my eyes as I brought my hands up to his face and guided him to kiss me. His lips met mine, and a moment later, his arms were wrapped around my waist, and he was pulling me up.

I wrapped my legs around his waist as he carried me over to the kitchen counter and set me down. He broke away from my lips so he could feather kisses across my cheek to my neck and down to my collarbone. I tipped my head back and moaned in approval.

Then he pulled back, and I could feel his gaze on me, so I focused my attention back on him.

"Are you really going to be my wife?" he asked. There was a hint of disbelief in his voice.

I held his gaze, so he knew that I was never going anywhere. "I will be your wife. And you will be my husband." Then I took his hand and rested it on my belly. "And someday, I'll be the mother to your babies."

His gaze followed his hand. He paused as if he were letting my words wash over him. Then he slowly brought his gaze up to meet mine. "You promise?"

I chewed my bottom lip. "I promise."

He grinned as he wrapped his arms around my back and pulled me toward him. "I love you."

I wrapped my legs around his waist, and my arms around his neck. I pressed my lips to his a few times before I pulled back and met his gaze. "I love you, too."

***

I hope you enjoyed Emerson and Stone's romance. I had so much fun getting to know each character (Grandma Mona is my favorite). It was fun to challenge myself with writing something that went along with an event happening in pop culture right now, but making it different enough to feel like it's its own story.

If you want more of Emerson and Stone, you can grab my free bonus scenes by joining my newsletter. One is spicy (18+ only readers) and one is sweet (closed door).

Emerson and Stone's **Spicy** Scene HERE or scan the QR code below:

Emerson and Stone's **Sweet** Scene HERE or scan the QR code below:

If you're looking for a new series to dive into, check out my Sweet Tea and a Southern Gentleman series. It starts with my two times USA Today Bestselling book, The Inn on Harmony Island.

Enjoy this sneak peek of *Chapter One*:

Shelby

I'd never noticed the way rain looked as it fell into puddles. The tiny splashes each drop made caused smaller drops to spray around it. The ripples would go for only a moment until another drop would fall, and the effect would happen all over again.

A low murmur of *amens* drew my focus away from the puddles. I wrapped my black shawl tighter around my shoulders as I turned to the pastor who was standing behind my grandmother's coffin. He was speaking, but in all honesty, I couldn't hear what he was saying. My stomach was a bundle of nerves since I drove the rental car into my small hometown, and I couldn't sort out anyone's words.

I'd left this place 10 years ago, never to return. That was, until Gran up and passed away. I couldn't very well *not* go to her funeral. So, I packed my carry-on and flew down from New York to face the past that I'd tried so hard to forget.

And here I was, staring my history straight in the face.

I sighed as I ducked my head down. Miles's body tightened next to me when our arms brushed. I glanced over at him to see his jaw muscles flex, but his gaze never wavered from the pastor's face.

Was it strange that my ex-stepbrother was more broken up about my grandmother's passing than me?

I pursed my lips and turned my attention to my lap.

Yes, that was strange. And sad. And pathetic.

Even though I wanted to console my ego and convince myself that it was okay that Miles had cried more times than I had during the funeral planning. That the funeral director handed *him* the box of tissues and never offered them to me.

Nothing I could say to myself would fix the cold, hard heart my past had left me with.

I wanted to cry. I really did. But it was as if my tears were dried up. There was nothing left. I'd cried so much in the past that it was as if my body was completely incapable of producing tears. I was broken, and this was proof that I was never going to be fixed.

My body turned numb as I watched the cemetery owner lower the coffin into the ground. Even though it was raining, the early spring heat surrounded us. Mr. Jorgenson, the town's mayor, wiped his forehead with his handkerchief before stuffing it back into his suit coat. Most of the other guests were leaving, sprinting to their cars with their hands or purses over their heads. The women were slowed by their heels digging into the soft ground.

I glanced down at the dark oak coffin in the ground, wondering for a moment if Gran would have been disappointed with what we'd chosen. Even though it had been years since we'd spoken, I still wanted to please her. To settle her into her final resting place in comfort.

Movement next to me drew my attention over. Miles was standing a few yards off, shaking hands with the pastor who then nodded and turned to hurry through the rain to his car.

We were now officially alone.

Miles hesitated; his gaze focused on something in front of him. But then, as if he could feel my gaze, he turned.

I knew I should look away. Facing Miles—facing Harmony Island—was the last thing I wanted to do. But I couldn't drop my gaze. The familiarity in his stormy blue eyes as they peered into my soul paralyzed me. Miles had been my protector when we were kids, but then our parents divorced and something in him changed in high school. Our relationship was never the same. Especially now, when he seemed closer to my grandmother than I could ever be. That stung as bad as the wasps from the nest we knocked down as kids.

I shivered and focused on the hole in front of me. I was done thinking about Miles. I was finished thinking about our past. But as soon as I saw Miles approach me from the corner of my eye, I sucked in my breath.

I cursed myself. Why had I allowed our gazes to meet? I'd spent most of my three days here giving short answers and keeping to myself in the only motel in town. The other lodging options, Harmony Island Inn and the Apple Blossom B&B, were places I swore I would never go.

Too many bad memories roamed the halls.

"You okay?" Miles's voice was low and rumbly. I wasn't sure if it was because of our history or the situation we were in.

I nodded, tightening my grip on my upper arms. "I'm just glad it's over. I'm ready to get out of here." Miles remained quiet. I peeked over at him, worried that I'd said the wrong thing. "I mean—"

"I know what you mean." Miles slipped off his suit coat, folded it in half, and rested it on the chair behind him. Then he yanked at his tie and loosened the top two buttons of his white shirt. After ruffling his gelled hair, he began to unbutton his cuffs and roll up his sleeves. "She never wanted you to stay away, but she understood why you left."

His words were like poison to my soul. It was easier to believe that my grandmother hated me than to think she'd spent her life waiting for me to return. When I was in New York, I could pretend that we had a mutual understanding. Our family was toxic. A broken mix of flawed people that fate stupidly threw together. My grandmother, my mother, and me.

We were the opposite of the three musketeers. We were a mixture of oil, water, and alcohol. Three pieces of a puzzle that would never fit together. Now, they were both gone. My senior year of high school, Mom ran away with her yoga instructor and died in a car crash.

With Gran in the ground, I was the only one alive.

I was the only one left carrying the burden of the failure that was our small, dysfunctional family.

"I doubt that," I whispered as I tucked a few strands of hair behind my ear that the cool ocean breeze had managed to free from the tight bun at the nape of my neck.

Miles finished rolling his sleeve and glanced over at me. I could see that he was fighting his response, and the truth was, I didn't want to hear it. It was easier when I didn't think anyone cared.

"So, are you leaving us for good then?"

His question caught me off guard. *Leaving us.* I hated that he'd moved into my life, my hometown, and my past like this. If I had my way, we would sell Harmony Island Inn and never look back.

"Yes," I responded, nodding my head.

"And the will? Are you going to come back for the reading?"

I took in a deep breath and tipped my head back, closing my eyes. "We both know that she didn't leave me anything."

"We do?"

I opened my eyes, looking up at the white canopy that protected us from the rain. "Despite what you say, she wrote me out of her life a long time ago. There's no point in pretending otherwise."

"Shelby—"

"Miles, I'm tired." I pulled my phone out of my purse and opened my rideshare app.

Miles stepped forward with his hand extended. For a moment, I caught what looked like desperation in his gaze before it disappeared. "Why don't I give you a ride? I mean, the church organized a dinner and everything." His half smile was weak and did little to dissuade me from what I'd already decided. "The town...misses you."

I snorted as I looked up at him. Then I shook my head and returned to filling out my information and sending in the request. "I seriously doubt that." I sighed. "I'm going to go back to my hotel room and jump in the shower. My flight is early in the morning, and I can't be late."

"Oh."

I hated that he seemed disappointed. But I needed him to move on. Returning to my one-bedroom apartment in New York where I could bury my memories until they were good and dead was the only thing holding me together.

"Listen, I know my grandmother meant a lot to you, but let's not pretend that there's anything left for me here. Our family is finished." My voice cracked at the last word, which threw me off guard.

I hoped Miles didn't hear my last sentence, but after seeing the small quirk of his eyebrow, regret filled my chest.

He'd heard.

I cleared my throat. "Thank you for taking care of my grandmother in the last moments of her life." I brushed my hands down my black dress, desperate for something to do. The mixture of my grandmother's coffin in front of me and the way Miles was studying me, tugged at the fraying strands that were barely holding my life together.

But I knew if I didn't thank him, the pressure to acknowledge that he was the better grandchild would gnaw at me until I would eventually buy another plane ticket to come down here and confess it. I wanted this to be the last trip I made to my godforsaken hometown. I needed to make sure I tied up all my loose ends with a pretty little bow.

"Of course," Miles said. "She helped me a lot." His voice

deepened as he turned to face the hole where my grandmother now lay. His shoulders slumped, and I suddenly felt sorry.

I felt sorry for him. I felt sorry for my grandmother. And I felt sorry for me.

No one had it perfect. We'd messed up so bad that, sometimes, the best thing to do was to call a foul and walk away.

And that was what I was determined to do.

My phone dinged, startling us both. I lifted it up so I could see the screen.

"My ride's here," I whispered.

Miles pushed his hands through his hair once more and nodded. "Yeah, okay." Then he paused.

I could see in his body language that he wanted to say something more, and I had a sinking suspicion as to what that was. Problem was, there was no way I was ready to hear any of it.

"It's been nice knowing you," I said. And before I could stop myself, I reached out and rested my hand on his arm. His warm skin shocked my fingertips, and I blinked and pulled my hand back, cursing myself for doing that.

What was wrong with me?

Miles's gaze dropped down to the spot I had touched before he brought his gaze up to meet mine. His dark blue eyes had turned stormy, which caused my stomach to flip-flop.

My phone chimed again, pulling me from my thoughts. I pushed my purse strap higher up onto my shoulder and then gave him a weak smile.

"Goodbye, Miles," I said as I stepped around him.

He didn't say anything as I passed by. It wasn't until I'd stepped out into the rain, raising my purse up over my head that I heard his response.

"Goodbye, Shelby."

Like a dam breaking inside of me, the tears began to flow. I was grateful for the rain now more than ever. My tears mixed with the water running down my face as I crossed the cemetery lawn and pulled open the door of the black SUV.

The man asked for my name, and I managed to get that out. He didn't say much else as he put the car into drive and took off down the small, one-lane road that led to Main Street.

Thankfully, he didn't ask me what was wrong. Being picked up at a cemetery seemed to be all he needed to know. Hiding under that excuse, I allowed the tears that had refused to fall all of this time to flow. I was hurt. I was broken. And for this moment, I was going to allow myself to be weak.

As soon as I got back to New York, I'd forget. But for now, I didn't have the strength.

To read more, head on over to my store HERE and grab the series bundle! Or you can find the book on your preferred book platform.

For a full reading order of Anne-Marie's books, you can find
them HERE.
Or scan below: